STORM SURGE

A MASON SHARPE THRILLER

LOGAN RYLES

INKUBATOR
BOOKS

Published by Inkubator Books
www.inkubatorbooks.com

ISBN (eBook): 978-1-83756-359-3
ISBN (Paperback): 978-1-83756-360-9
ISBN (Hardback): 978-1-83756-361-6

In memory of the 1,833 or more lives lost during the Hurricane Katrina disaster of August and September 2005, and in honor of the thousands of first responders, National Guardsmen, and private citizens who heroically participated in rescue efforts.

Your stories are not forgotten.

1

I hit the police roadblock at sixty miles per hour. The wooden barricade erected across the road exploded over the hood of my captured Chevy Blazer and splintered against the windshield. Tires screamed, and the back end of the SUV fishtailed. I swung instinctively right, dropping beneath the dash as handguns cracked, and a bullet slammed into my rear fender.

The Mississippi state troopers were likely aiming for my tires, but they missed. The Blazer struck the concrete at the base of the on-ramp, and with a surge of overworked horsepower, I rocketed onto the highway.

The cops didn't follow. The blue lights faded. Rain pounded the SUV's roof and streamed through the busted passenger-side window. I choked on blood and swabbed my obliterated nose with the back of one hand, piloting the Blazer down the middle of twin southbound lanes.

Both lanes lay completely empty—vacated as the intensifying wind drove the rain sideways. I had to manhandle the wheel to keep the SUV on course. I swallowed blood to keep from choking on it.

But I didn't stop driving. I spun the radio's tuner dial with dirty fingers, searching for a clear signal. Most stations were obscured by static, distorted by the storm. Finally, a computerized voice broke through with a weather alert.

"The National Weather Service has issued a tropical storm warning for the entire state of Louisiana, along with southern counties in Mississippi and Alabama. Hurricane Nadia has now strengthened into an extremely dangerous Category 5 superstorm, and is expected to make landfall fifty-six miles south of New Orleans, Louisiana, at around 5:25 a.m. this morning. Winds will exceed one hundred and sixty miles per hour. Storm surge estimated at fourteen to seventeen feet. Total destruction of homes and businesses is anticipated. Seek immediate shelter—"

I mashed the dial to shut off the radio and slammed my foot deeper onto the accelerator. The aged V6 engine was pushed to its limit, topping out at eighty miles per hour. Heartbeat thundering, knuckles white around the steering wheel, I blazed past a road sign that vibrated under the gathering winds.

The sign was green. The letters white and reflective, forming only four words.

NEW ORLEANS — 52 MILES.

2

24 HOURS PREVIOUSLY

The cathedral stretched out like a cavern around me, with columns supporting an arched ceiling constructed of alternating clover leaves and fleur-de-lis printed like a checkerboard. A dome stood over the pulpit...or maybe it was an altar. I wasn't altogether sure about the correct nomenclature, but it was beautiful, with golden wallpaper serving as a backdrop behind a sculpture of Christ with his arm raised over the sanctuary.

Ecce Panis Angelorum, the inscription read. Latin for *"behold the bread of the messenger"*, according to the burner phone in my pocket. I didn't know what that meant.

I eased my way into a pew halfway down the length of the expansive room, bracing for the gunshot-like groaning of old wood straining under my bodyweight. Beneath the high ceiling, those groans echoed and reverberated, taking me off guard the first time I visited the cathedral. Now I settled down with barely a sound, faded Walmart jeans smooth under my palms as I stared at the altar.

More marble. More Latin inscriptions that I didn't

understand. They were printed on the floor, also. The windows were stained glass, the air-conditioning turned down low to defy the sticky midsummer heat blanketing the city outside.

And the room...it was perfectly quiet. I wasn't the only one seated in the sanctuary, but the nearest visitor was several pews away, and nobody bothered me as I fixated on the altar and waited. I wasn't sure what for. Maybe the still small voice my recently deceased fiancée used to talk about. Maybe a vision, or an *angelorum*...a divine messenger.

Or maybe nothing so glamorous. Just a feeling of confidence. Of some kind of understanding or gravitas. At least, some kind of peace.

I dropped my gaze and closed my eyes, breathing slowly. Enjoying the sensation of rapidly drying sweat and relaxing muscles. I didn't hear a thing as a body mass descended next to me on the same pew, but I felt the boards flex beneath my thighs. My eyes flicked open, and I turned to find an older man dressed in all black with a white collar seated alongside me, worn hands folded into his lap, white hair combed neatly above kind, gray eyes. He smiled, and I realized I had tensed into a default defensive pose.

"The Lord be with you, brother."

His voice carried the same syrupy drawl I'd become so accustomed to during my slow tour through the Deep South, now joined by a warble that marked my entrance into Cajun country. It was an unpretentious tone. Very genuine. I ducked my head, turning back to the altar. For a while we sat in silence. Then the old man spoke again.

"I've seen you here every day for a week. You seem burdened. Would you like a confession?"

The question would have felt like an intrusion not long

ago. A violation of privacy. But I was well beyond any insecurity about the state of my spirit...or soul...or whatever church people called it. When you live with your own company long enough, you come to terms with things like that.

"I don't know what that is," I said simply.

The old man smiled. "We should all be so lucky."

We lapsed into silence again, and my gaze drifted above the crucifix, back to the inscription. I never remembered Mia reading in Latin. Her Bible was printed in modern English. Maybe Latin was a Catholic thing. Mia had been a Protestant. Not that I understood the difference.

"What does it mean?" I asked.

"The inscription?"

"Yes."

He took his time responding, gazing in reverent silence. Then: "It means that God sends His word to us in time of need. If we have ears to hear it."

I was sure his explanation made sense to the average parishioner, but to me it was just more Latin. I grunted as if I understood, and the old man turned in the pew.

"Are you in need of a word, my son?"

I ran a slow hand over my face, palm grinding against five or six days of razor stubble. I had slept well the night before, but I still felt low on energy. Or maybe I was just very relaxed. The cathedral had a strange way of bringing calm to my confused mind. Maybe that was why I'd wandered inside so many times since first discovering it.

Just another stop on a long road headed nowhere. A waypoint of the rambling that had become my life. The pressure I felt to make sense of the meaninglessness was less a desperation, and more a sort of...thirst. Like I was deficient on a vitamin. An engine burning fuel, but not running well.

"I..." I started. Then stopped.

The old man sat next to me, hands folded, head cocked. Perfectly calm. Not the least bit distracted. It was such an unusual feeling, capturing somebody's full and undivided attention, that I felt a pang of guilt. Like I was wasting his time.

"I don't know who I am," I finished at last. It wasn't what I expected myself to say, or what I even wanted to say. It was just what spilled out. "I'm a road with no end. No destination. It was nice for a while, just...being free. But now I don't understand the point. It's like..." I trailed off again, gaze dropping to the marble floor.

"Like you need a direction?" His voice was so soft, I barely heard it. But the words landed with the force of artillery shells.

I looked up. "Yes, Pastor. I need direction."

A slow smile crept across his old face. Not condescending, but a little amused. I wasn't sure why.

"You aren't Catholic," he said.

"No."

"Do you believe in God?"

I hesitated. "I have no idea."

He settled back into the pew with a gentle sigh. Taking his time again, as though time itself were a nonfactor. As though neither of us had anywhere else to be.

Maybe he understood me better than I first assumed.

"Have you ever heard the story of Balaam's donkey, my son?"

"No."

"It's a good story. A very old one. It speaks of a man named Balaam, who was a servant of God. A powerful king requested for Balaam to visit him at his palace. He wanted a favor. But the favor did not honor God, so God sent an angel to block Balaam's path. Balaam couldn't see the angel, but his donkey could, and the donkey refused to proceed."

"Sounds like a smart ass," I said. It was a lame joke, but the old man indulged me with a gentle laugh anyway.

"Indeed. Balaam, not so much. He beat the donkey, but still it would go no further. The donkey injured his foot. Balaam beat it again. And then...the donkey spoke."

It wasn't the plot twist I had expected. I cocked an eyebrow. "Spoke?"

"Yes. God opened the donkey's mouth, and the donkey confronted Balaam for his abuse. They argued, in fact, which is the funniest part of the story. Then God revealed the angel to Balaam...and he finally understood."

I was at a disadvantage to Balaam. I knew the preacher— or priest, or whatever he was called—had a point. I didn't have the first clue how to unravel it.

"I'm not great with riddles," I said.

The old man's smile softened. "It's no riddle, my son. God is always with us, even when we refuse to see Him. When you need His voice, you will hear it. Even if He has to use a smart ass."

A gentle hand closed over my shoulder, and the old man squeezed. He stood with a suppressed grunt.

"God be with you. Stay as long as you like. Our doors are always open."

3

The peace of the sanctuary evaporated like mist in the morning as I stepped back onto the sidewalk outside. The Basilica of Immaculate Conception sat directly across from Cathedral Square, with the business towers of downtown Mobile, Alabama, rising from half a dozen blocks away. The square was something of a park, with tall oak trees surrounding an open green space. Or, at least, it was *usually* an open green space. Just then it was clogged by tables and cardboard boxes, both loaded with medical supplies, dry foods, and enough bottled water to flood the church behind me. Federal Emergency Management workers dressed in dark blue vests distributed the goods to a long line of cars moving slowly through a drive-up service lane running right in front of the cathedral.

All the license plates read Mississippi or Louisiana. Many of the cars were loaded with household belongings—small furniture, books, photo albums. Kids and dogs packed into back seats. Harried mothers and exhausted fathers negotiating with FEMA workers to pack as much food and water into their already overloaded minivans and SUVs as possible before grinding along through the downtown slog. The implication was clear—disaster at hand or, in this case, disaster approaching. But the wrath of the hurricane beating its way toward the gulf coast was defied by the clear blue skies and baking hot late afternoon sun, adding a twinge of irony to the entire picture. As though, if you squinted, you could imagine it was all just some elaborate prank. Maybe the set of a movie being filmed.

Slipping my hands into worn jean pockets, I turned west for my hotel, a four-block walk through the heart of historic downtown. I'd arrived in Mobile only two weeks prior after a lazy few months of exploring Florida's emerald coast. It turned out that there was a specialist living here who knew something about restoring water-damaged paper.

Thanks to a pair of thugs who offloaded my pickup truck into a Florida lagoon earlier that year, I had some water-damaged paper in need of restoration—a Bible full of it. The specialist was old, and he was neither cheap nor fast. He advised me to wait for a call, and I had no place to be, so I booked a motel and settled in to explore the local scenery and sample the local cuisine. Mobile was a very sleepy place, with quiet streets that often stood empty even during a business day. There were great seafood restaurants and museums—enough to keep my wandering thoughts at bay for a while.

Most of them, anyway. I'd found the church on the fifth day and visited it every day since. Something about the reverence of the old building spoke to me, and I was usually the only one there. At least until tropical storm Nadia rotated eastward and developed into a hurricane, crashing first for Lake Charles but moving steadily east-

ward toward a much bigger, even more vulnerable target—
New Orleans.

Mobile would take a beating, but it was far enough
outside the projected landing zone to serve as a refuge for a
growing caravan of evacuees. Hotels were booked. Traffic
clogged the streets and overwhelmed the highways. Grocery
store shelves were swept clean.

FEMA had their hands full.

I tuned out the chaos as I strolled along streets shaded by
oak trees that were older than the city. Many of the homes
dated back to the mid nineteenth century, with wrought-iron
fixtures and narrow windows. Traffic had congested considerably, and a fast-food restaurant I passed was flooded with
hungry travelers. I was hungry myself but wasn't interested
in braving the crowd. I stopped at a convenience store
instead, picking up jerky, a bottle of water, and a king-sized
Baby Ruth candy bar. Then I was back on the street, chewing
jerky as I walked.

The motel I'd called home for the past two weeks
consisted of a seedy little strip of twenty rooms built into an
L shape, ten on top and ten on the bottom, with an office
constructed into the end of the L's foot. It was ironically
named the Azalea Lodge, perhaps an homage to Mobile's
nickname of the Azalea City. Any grandeur in the reference
was long exhausted by the expired neon lights that spelled
out the letters *A* and *G*, to say nothing of the trash drifting
across the parking lot or the busted swimming pool now
clogged by weeds. It was the sort of place that rented rooms
by the hour, usually, but living the life of an unemployed
drifter meant compromising on accommodation. At least the
roof didn't leak.

The parking lot of Azalea Lodge was packed as I crossed

off the sidewalk and headed for the office. My 1967 GMC pickup had sat almost alone in the lot only four days prior, but was now joined by additional Louisiana and Mississippi license plates. A Yorkshire terrier barked from the second-floor walkway while a woman in a night-robe smoked a cigarette. Kids kicked a ball around the perimeter of the abandoned pool, and a couple of shirtless fat guys drank beer while relaxing in lawn chairs. The place had become a little metropolis almost overnight, and the serenity I had savored in Mobile had vanished just as quickly.

Not that I could blame anyone. They were probably all standing on the brink of homelessness. As I approached the glass window of the office, I noted the faded television standing on a filing cabinet in the background, a storm chart depicting Nadia's progress toward the coast. The hurricane had attained Category 3 status the previous night and was still growing. As her projected path shifted ever eastward, whispers of an unspeakable name were uttered as if by accident by the weather forecasters.

Katrina.

My gaze switched from the TV to the office chair, where a hairy guy in his late forties sat kicked back with one foot on the counter. A tablet computer rested in his lap, a half-empty bottle of soda clutched in one hand. I didn't notice at first over the shouts of the kids playing behind me, but as I drew near to the window, the telltale murmurs of ecstasy reached me from the tablet. Moaning, blended with the occasional expletive.

It was porn, and the guy was zeroed in on it.

I rapped my knuckles against the glass partition, hard enough to rattle the pane in its frame. The clerk didn't jump, taking his time to look up from the screen. His eyes were hooded, and I smelled marijuana, just as I had every time I'd paid my rent.

Setting the tablet on the desk—face up and still playing —he dragged the window open.

"Whatcha want?"

"Rent's due," I said, tugging a quintet of twenty-dollar bills out of my pocket and laying them on the counter. Enough for two additional nights.

The clerk ran a finger behind his gum and pried something slimy and orange out. He ate it, then shook his head.

"Two-fifty."

"What?"

"The rate is two-fifty. Per night."

"Are you kidding me?"

"Hurricane prices, bub. Supply and demand, that's capitalism."

I glanced across the parking lot to the crowds of harried evacuees, many of them displaced in a matter of hours. Judging from the age and condition of their vehicles, none of them were rich. None of them needed to be paying the price of a nice hotel for this rattrap.

"That's not capitalism," I said. "That's greed."

The clerk grinned, exposing yellow teeth caked with the same orange slime. "You're right. Three hundred."

I gritted my teeth and peeled off another five bills. "Two hundred," I said. "Not a dime more."

"You can't do that," he barked, taking the money anyway.

"So kick me out."

The kids' soccer ball rocketed my way as I returned to the parking lot, and I toed it back toward them with a quick kick, earning a rowdy cheer. My room sat right at the corner of the L on the lower floor, and the occupants two doors down were not new. Jessica Waverly and her ten-year-old daughter, Autumn, were residents of the Azalea Lodge when I arrived, and had been for a week or two. They lived out of an aged Chrysler station wagon with one window covered over by cardboard. There were a lot of boxes in the back, and the car bore Mississippi plates before Mississippi plates became in vogue around Mobile.

I'd befriended Autumn during my comings and goings around the motel, often finding her seated in her wheelchair just outside the open door of her room, a thick textbook spread across her lap like some kind of exotic artifact. She was paralyzed from the waist down, the result of a car accident involving a drunk driver. But while the disability had inhibited her mobility, it in no way had inhibited her mind.

Autumn was *brilliant*. More than brilliant, she could aptly be called a genius, with a special bend toward mathematics. Autumn consumed books by the stack, practiced mathematical equations for entertainment, and knew more about the world around her than most college graduates.

But best of all, Autumn was fun. She liked talking to adults. We'd become buddies.

"What's new?" I asked, spotting Autumn in her usual spot with her favorite teddy bear—a worn little brown thing that I never saw her without—tucked into her wheelchair next to her. Bright blonde hair fell over skinny shoulders as she scratched across a notepad with a blunt pencil.

More equations. More "entertainment".

"The Bailey-Borwein-Plouffe formula!" Autumn's chipper voice rose with excitement as crystal blue eyes met mine. I leaned against the wall and poked more jerky into my mouth, ignoring the stench of dog urine from not far away. I blamed the Yorkshire terrier.

"Explain," I said.

"It's a tool to find any given number in pi without having to know any other number."

"Pi is three-point-one-four," I quipped. "There, solved."

Autumn rolled her eyes. "That's just the first three digits, you doltz. Pi is an infinite number. It's irrational."

"Kinda like this conversation."

She threw the pencil at me. I caught it and laughed.

"Okay. So show it to me."

I squatted next to the wheelchair, and Autumn took the pencil back. She circled a formula about two inches long, featuring a series of numbers and letters trapped inside brackets with a summation and infinite symbol on the left-hand side.

"The nth digit—that's the digit you want to find—is represented here, by the letter K." Autumn underlined a portion of the formula with the pencil. "To find that number, you split the infinite sum of its value using hexadecimal."

"A what?"

"Hexadecimal. A number system with a base value equal to sixteen."

"Oh. Right."

"So you substitute K for the digit of pi you want to find, then work the formula. The answer presents in hexadecimal."

"Which is...?"

"A number system with a base value equal to sixteen!" Autumn's voice rose into a girlish shriek, cheeks flushing. "Gosh, Mason. Don't you listen?"

Flashing eyes locked with mine, and she caught my smirk. That earned me a punch to the arm stout enough to send me stumbling against the wall. I laughed.

"You're such a jerk!" Autumn shook her head. "I don't know why I bother with you."

"Here's why," I said, producing the king-sized Baby Ruth from my pocket. Autumn's eyes lit up like fireworks, the notebook instantly forgotten as she accepted the candy bar with a happy squeal. The foil wrapping tore, and she took a giant bite, looking suddenly so much more like a kid than she had only moments prior.

It made me smile. My gaze drifted back down to the notebook, and I scanned repeated expressions of the BBP formula used over and over to identify different random digits of pi. There was no calculator. Autumn didn't need one. Her brain was like a computer, wrapping its super-charged synapses around advanced concepts that turned my own mental state into instant mush. It was remarkable, but when I looked up from the equations, Autumn was no longer fixated on her notebook or even the candy bar. Her gaze had drifted, beyond the cars and across the lot, to where the other kids were still busy kicking their soccer ball.

My stomach descended into a leaden weight, and the grin faded from my face. Autumn chewed slowly, her gaze suddenly lost in whimsy.

"Where's your mom?" I asked.

"Laundromat," Autumn said. "She'll be right back."

As if on cue, I recognized the squeal of an old serpentine belt, and the banged-up Chrysler with the cardboard window appeared in the parking lot with Jessica Waverly seated behind the wheel. Blonde-headed and slender, like her daughter, I could never tell if Jessica had already reached her early thirties or if the first twenty-something years of her life had simply left their mark. She smoked cigarettes when Autumn wasn't around, and swore like a sailor.

But she was a good mom—a really good mom. The circumstances that had driven the two of them out of their Mississippi home all orbited around Autumn, and Jessica didn't resent that for a moment.

Clambering out of the car with a laundry basket under one arm, Jessica lifted her hand in a wave toward the two of us before she turned for the motel office. I caught the clerk ogling her over the top of his tablet computer, one finger jammed behind his gums again. The two held a confrontation, and Jessica's body language became animated. I guessed that he was grifting her for the rent money the same way he'd grifted me. Well...maybe not the *same* way. He leaned forward and whispered something. Jessica flushed. She slammed money down on the counter and extended a hand. The clerk passed her a stack of mail with a sly wink. Jessica marched off.

"Mom doesn't like him," Autumn said.

"Your mom's a smart woman," I grunted.

Jessica stopped halfway across the parking lot, shifting through the pile of letters. An advertising circular slipped from her hands, and she allowed it to flutter to the concrete. She fixated on a single white envelope and grew suddenly very still.

Fingers found an opening beneath the seal. Paper tore. I straightened instinctively off the wall as Jessica ripped a sheet of paper out and unfolded it. Her eyes scanned quickly. Her hand trembled.

Then she dropped the laundry and burst into a sprint across the parking lot, sobbing before she even reached us. She hit her knees and wrapped Autumn in a hug, clutching her close and kissing her on the forehead, heedless of anyone and everyone watching from around the hotel.

"Mom!" Autumn scoffed. "Stop it. You're messing up my hair!"

Jessica pulled away, cheeks streaked with mascara. She swallowed hard...and grinned.

"Is it over?" Autumn whispered.

Jessica nodded. Then she looked at me.

"It's over, sweetie. The judge says we're free to go."

Jessica wrapped Autumn in another big hug, defying her attempts to resist as some of the other residents of Azalea Lodge rushed in to hear the gossip. Jessica's personal business was no great secret—those of us who'd been around for a few weeks all knew about the lawsuit. The custody battle. The deadbeat dad and the school for gifted children waiting in San Francisco.

If only a judge would allow Jessica to move that far.

"It's a final ruling," Jessica mumbled, breaking away from Autumn to recover a little of her composure. "We're free to move anywhere in the country. Randy has no further claim."

I returned her smile. Jessica blushed and scrubbed her tears away as Irene from two doors down brought her toothless grin to join in the celebration.

Pushing away from the wall, I dug my phone out and ran a Google search. Then I called through the gathering crowd to Autumn, "Ham and pineapple?"

A beaming face turned my way. "Huh?"

"Pie, kid. The Italian kind. This calls for pizza."

4

I ordered half a dozen large pizzas for delivery. Then I trailed a rolling cooler to the local convenience store, where I bypassed the beer fridge in favor of canned soda. Somehow, it didn't feel respectful to drink alcohol in front of Autumn.

Back at Azalea Lodge, I dropped the tailgate on my GMC and spread the food out for anybody who wanted to stop by to partake. In short order a party kicked off, and additional pizzas were required. I didn't mind, happy to sit in the motel breezeway and sip Dr. Pepper while refugees and locals mingled together to learn the details of Jessica and Autumn's celebration.

By late evening I could smell a salt breeze laden with menace blowing in from the coast as the sun vanished behind a bank of darkening clouds. Updates from somebody's bedroom TV indicated that hurricane Nadia had gained additional strength and was now projected to reach Category 4 status before making landfall. The closer she churned toward the coast, the tighter her landfall projections became.

One thing was certain—Louisiana was about to get wrecked.

"Hey."

Jessica's heavy south Mississippi drawl rang from over my shoulder, and I looked up to see her cradling a Coke, tired eyes reflecting the closest thing to joy I'd seen in anybody's face for a good while. She offered me a gentle smile and swished the soda can.

"May I?"

"Sure." I scooted over a few inches, allowing room for Jessica to settle in next to me. Autumn had retreated to their hotel room to watch cartoons. Most of the Azalea Lodge residents who remained outside had descended into lawn chairs, swapping jokes and sweating off the pizza. Country music played from a car stereo. The traces of cigarette smoke drifted down from the second-floor walkway.

It was a strangely comforting smell. Not because I smoked, but because it smelled like calm.

Jessica must have thought the same because she dug through her neckline to retrieve a flattened pack of Marlboros.

"Want one?"

I shook my head, and Jessica lit up. She inhaled deeply and closed her eyes, shoulders drooping a little in apparent relaxation. Even from four blocks away, I could still hear a soft clamor of voices from the disaster-relief station in front of the cathedral, but darkness had brought a respite to most of the chaos.

The calm before the storm.

"Wow." Jessica sighed. "Not a moment too soon."

I knew she was referencing the court order. It had been pending for weeks while Randy Mercer, Autumn's biological father, launched petition after petition to prevent Jessica from relocating to the west coast. He didn't have any custody over Autumn—only occasional visitation—but an old clause in the divorce agreement prevented Jessica from moving beyond a certain radius without Randy's consent.

And Randy wouldn't consent. Not under any conditions. When news of Autumn's opportunity at a school for gifted children first reached him, Randy Mercer had gone ballistic. He'd harassed Jessica so violently that she'd been forced to flee her Mississippi home, finding shelter for Autumn at Azalea Lodge while the court ground slowly through the proceedings of her own petition.

It was a story she had shared with me not long after we met. A brutal, exhausting tale. But it was finally ending.

"When do you leave?" I asked.

"Tomorrow. Just gotta scoot over to the bank and get some running money. They don't have my bank out west."

"When does Autumn start school?"

"Soon as we get there. They've got an apartment for us and everything. I even get a living stipend. It's all a part of her scholarship." Jessica shook her head, flicking the cigarette. There were tears in her eyes again, but this time they weren't the tears of joy I'd witnessed when she first ripped open the court order.

This time those moist eyes reflected sadness and anguish and the sort of deep pain that takes years to build. One grinding, miserable, heart-breaker day after another. A story as old as time, yet completely unique to Jessica.

I didn't know the details of Randy's abuse, but I could guess. I'd been a cop once, responding to domestic abuse calls all over south Phoenix. Before that, I was in the army, surrounded by screwed-up kids who ran away from abusive homes to exorcise their demons against terrorists.

And before that...I was one of those kids. Drifting from one foster home to the next. Witnessing the abuse. The dysfunction. The brokenness of love betrayed and trust demolished—usually under the swollen knuckles of a deadbeat.

Yes. I could guess what kind of man Randy Mercer was. I didn't need the details. The evidence was all there, reflected in the premature aging of Jessica's forced smile.

I rocked my soda can back and gave her time, well aware that some pain is best managed in silent companionship. We'd done this before on a few occasions. Seated out on the breezeway while Autumn slept, usually sharing a six-pack, and almost never speaking.

Trauma recognizes its equal. But this time was different. This time Jessica spoke.

"It was Randy who done it."

I looked her way, a question on my face. Jessica dragged on the smoke, fingers trembling.

"The car wreck. Autumn's injury. Randy was drunk as a skunk, but..." Her voice broke. The eyes flooded. "I let him drive."

Ashes exploded over the concrete, mixing with the tears, and I remained quiet. The revelation wasn't really a revelation—I'd already guessed. But the story still hurt.

"I shoulda put a bullet in his face," Jessica whispered. "Years ago. The first time he hit me. The first bone he broke. But...I just...I didn't, you know. And Autumn was born. And that night he was deep in the whiskey, and I didn't want to argue..."

She looked up slowly. "You ever carry a pain like that, Mason? Something you can't take back. Something you'd give the world to do differently."

My shoulders slumped under an avalanche of invisible pressure, and I looked away.

Oh yes, I knew all about that kind of pain. That kind of regret. All the questions it dumped into your soul in the late hours of the night when you beg for sleep to envelop you.

Questions like: *What if I'd driven a little harder? Shot a little faster? Somehow thrown myself down that school hallway and stopped that shotgun blast from blowing my fiancée to the ground...*

But those questions were pointless, just like Jessica's questions were pointless. There was no going back, not ever. Only pressing forward, hoping to do better.

"You're almost there," I said. "Light at the end of the tunnel, right?"

I forced a smile. Jessica forced one back. She lit another cigarette, and the tears dried slowly. I saw anger instead, and a little smug satisfaction.

"Randy's gonna freak. Ever since he stopped being able to control me, he's absolutely obsessed with Autumn. Wants her under his thumb. I wish I could see his face when he opens the court order."

"You don't think he'll turn up in San Francisco, do you?"

She looked sideways at me. Blew smoke through her teeth. "He'd better not."

I lifted my can in salute and took a long drink. Jessica inhaled a lungful of clean air and closed her eyes. She seemed to let something go. Her body relaxed a little.

Maybe she was just that tired.

"I really appreciate how you've treated Autumn all these

weeks," Jessica said. "Being her friend. She don't know what it means to have a good man around. It was good for her. I really owe you one."

"You don't owe me anything," I said. "Autumn is a special kid. The world would be a better place if we all appreciated each other."

A soft grunt of agreement. Then: "So what about you? You sticking around for the big 'un?"

Jessica didn't know about Mia's Bible. She didn't know about Mia at all. It was something I'd elected to keep to myself in the context of everything Jessica and her daughter were going through.

"I'll be headed out before long," I said. "Might stick around to volunteer for a few days. I'm sure there will be cleanup to do."

Jessica snorted. "Volunteer? You're really something, you know that?"

Green eyes lingered on mine a moment longer than usual, and sudden discomfort tensed my body. It wasn't resistance, and it certainly wasn't distaste. It was just the thought of Autumn and the friendship we'd developed.

I could only imagine how many of her "friends" had bought her candy bars only to take advantage of her mother. Another story as old as time.

"I think I'm gonna get some shut-eye," I said, standing and stretching. "You should too. It's a long drive to California."

Jessica turned away quickly and dragged on the cigarette. Smoke billowed around her face, and she grinned.

"Best drive of my life."

5

"Mason! Mason!"

Fists beat on the door of my motel room, and I sat up shirtless in bed. The room was dark, the window blinds pulled closed. I blinked back the fog of sleep and turned quickly to the clock. It was nine a.m. on the dot. I'd slept much longer than usual, and as my brain awakened, I detected a howling sound from the breezeway outside.

Wind and rain. The precursor of Nadia, closing on the coast.

And fists, still beating on the door.

"Mason!"

I rolled out of bed and walked barefoot over sticky carpet. Two latches held the door closed. They both rattled as I got it open.

Jessica stood immediately outside, hair streaming with rainwater, face taut with panic. Behind her, a steady shower beat down over the roof of my GMC. The sky was dark and torn by occasional lightning, but it was the storm in Jessica's eyes that caught my attention.

"What is it?" I said. "What's wrong?"

"She's gone!" Jessica gasped.

"What?"

"Autumn! I left her to sleep in while I went to the bank. She's gone, Mason. She's gone!"

My gaze snapped toward Jessica's room, and then I pushed past her into the breezeway. Jessica's door stood open. The lamps on both nightstands shone over a room messy with unpacked luggage and assorted household items. The TV was on—cartoons played. But both Autumn and her wheelchair were missing.

As was her teddy.

"Autumn!" I shouted, stepping inside without waiting for an invite. Rushing around the end of the bed, I reached the bathroom. Cosmetics and hairbrushes lay strewn across the sink. The little neon hairbands that Autumn favored were piled on the toilet lid, and the shower curtain stood open.

But Autumn wasn't there.

"Did you check the parking lot?" I asked.

"I checked everywhere. I even drove down the street. She's gone, Mason. She's—"

I lifted a hand, breaking Jessica off in mid panic. Tears gushed down her cheeks, and her hand shook. I remained calm.

"There's no sign of forced entry on the door, Jessica. She probably just went down the street for a candy bar."

"In this?" Jessica gestured to the growing thunderstorm. "She *never* leaves. I told her not to. I told her—"

"Jessica." I put a hand on her shoulder. I squeezed once.

"Take a breath. Okay? Let's get in the car and drive around the block. She can't have gone far."

Jessica looked to the parking lot. She hesitated. "I...I already called the police. Should I not have?"

"No. That's fine. You wait for them. I'll run the block."

I left Jessica in her room and returned to my own for my shirt. Then I fired up the GMC with some effort—it had sat for nearly two weeks—and gave it thirty seconds to warm before I rumbled out of the parking lot. My left windshield wiper was the only one that worked, something I should have fixed months prior. As I reached the street, I could barely see in either direction, and I decided to roll my window down and turn left. I would orbit the block facing the sidewalk that Autumn would most likely have used. I couldn't imagine her crossing the street in her wheelchair.

Actually, I couldn't imagine her leaving the motel room at all. Jessica had left her there on occasion to run errands, and I'd witnessed her aggressive admonitions for Autumn to stay put. I'd never seen her break those rules, not once. But like I told Jessica, there was no sign of forced entry. The most obvious answer was likely the correct one. Autumn had broken the rules and gone for a Baby Ruth.

The corner convenience store stood one block away, rain gusting beneath the awning to soak the lone fuel pump. Lights were visible behind the bar-covered windows, but I didn't see a wheelchair. I barged in anyway.

"Hey, you see a kid in here?"

The clerk was watching weather updates on a washed-out TV screen. He wrinkled his nose.

"Huh?"

"A *kid*," I said. "Ten years old, blonde hair, in a wheelchair."

"Nah, man."

I returned to the truck and completed an orbit of two additional blocks before returning to the hotel, starting to question my original hypothesis. I'd seen Autumn traverse the parking lot in the wheelchair before. She was strong, but the asphalt was busted and riddled with potholes. Jessica frequently had to assist by pushing the chair. How would Autumn have managed it on her own? And why would she bother? If she needed something, she would have phoned my room. She'd done so before.

A single police cruiser waited in the parking lot, headlights blazing through the rain. A pair of Mobile city cops stood in the breezeway, one taking notes, the other working to calm an increasingly frantic mother. I cut the GMC off and joined them.

"Did you find her?" Jessica's voice cracked. I shook my head.

"I checked the convenience store. The clerk never saw her."

Jessica wrung her hands, damp and tangled hair blowing across her face in a fresh gust of wind. The cop with the notepad turned to me.

"Who are you?"

"Neighbor," I said. "You guys need to get a pair of units searching the area."

"We know what to do, sir." The cop snapped his notebook closed. "Ma'am, is there any place your child would have ventured? Any local spot where she likes to play?"

"Play?" Jessica's voice turned shrill. "She's in a *wheelchair!*"

The cop remained unfazed. "What about family members? Anybody who might have picked her up?"

"No." Jessica shook her head, sweeping hair out of her eyes. "There's nobody. No one who..."

She stopped, looking back to the door. Her mouth fell open. I knew what she was thinking even before she said it. "No..."

"What?" the cop prompted.

"Her father doesn't have custody. We were going to leave. He wanted her to stay!"

Jessica's voice descended into an incoherent babble, and the cop held up a hand to calm her, further questions ready on his lips. I simply turned away, stepping off the sidewalk and back across the parking lot toward the motel's office. Because there was no sign of forced entry on Jessica and Autumn's room, and only one person other than Jessica had a key.

The clerk sat slouched in his office chair, tablet in his lap again. Pornography was audible even before I reached the window. It was locked as before, and I rapped with my knuckles. He looked up with a huff, irritation morphing instantly into disgust when he saw me. He didn't unlock the window.

"What?"

"You see the kid leave the room?" I demanded.

"What kid?"

I spoke through my teeth. "*The kid in the wheelchair.*"

He looked to the patrol car. "That what this is about? I don't know nothing."

His gaze dropped back to the tablet. Reflections of the video flashed against bloodshot eyes.

I rounded the office corner and turned for the door. It was wooden with a simple metal latch and a reinforced glass windowpane. Locked, no doubt, but the frame was weathered by decades of Alabama humidity. Maybe a little rotten. Maybe a little soft.

My right boot struck the door with the force of a battering ram, and the frame exploded. The clerk nearly fell out of his chair as I burst into the tiny room, tablet sliding from his lap and smacking the concrete. Abject panic consumed his face as his right hand dipped beneath the desk and his head pivoted toward the cops.

The cops couldn't see him, not from that angle. And he never stood a chance of reaching whatever weapon lay beneath the desk. My right hand closed around his shoulder, fingers sinking into unprotected flesh as I wrenched him toward me. His knees struck the floor, my left hand circled behind his sweaty head, and then I drove his face straight into the desk edge—hard.

Teeth crunched and the clerk screamed. I yanked him back by the hair and rammed him again. Blood exploded as nose cartilage collapsed like a house of cards. His cry descended into a choking sob and I let him collapse against the office chair, his face a waterfall of crimson. The agony in his eyes was absolute. I knelt in front of him, grabbing his jaw with one hand.

I knew something about busted-nose pain. I'd had my own nose broken earlier that year, back in Tampa. It was still healing, technically. It still hurt on occasion. This was a lesson that would stick with him.

"You wanna try again?" I said.

The clerk squirmed, a caterpillar body wriggling against the chair. I sank my fingers into his flabby cheeks and shook.

"Answer me!"

He choked. Blood sprayed my T-shirt. He nodded.

"Okay, okay! Don't hurt me, man."

I cocked a fist. Then his resolve broke like a collapsing dam.

"I sold a key! I sold a key!"

"To the kid's room?"

He looked away. I backhanded him across his busted nose, holding his jaw closed to minimize the scream.

"Yes...yes..." Chokes mixed with sobs. I wrenched his face back toward mine.

"*Who?*"

"Some guy. I don't know, man! He offered me a hundred bucks. Said there was something in the room that belonged to him."

Randy. It had to be.

"You got a camera?" I demanded.

"Huh?"

I cocked my hand. He recoiled.

"Yes! Yes! On the computer."

I threw him sideways, away from the desk and the can of pepper spray I now saw mounted beneath it. He fell, and I found the computer. It was unlocked. The security application connected to a camera over the service window was easy enough to find.

"What time?"

No answer. I kicked him in the ribs.

"An hour!"

I scanned the video backwards. I saw myself passing in and out in the GMC. A few minutes prior, Jessica returned from the bank in the Chrysler with the cardboard window.

And then there was another vehicle, during that gap when she had been gone and I had been sleeping. It was a Chevrolet Blazer, late nineties model. Not the full-sized version based on a Silverado chassis, but the little one based on an S-10 chassis. Two doors, faded red in color. Dinged up with Mississippi license plates, wipers fighting the downpour. An average-sized guy in a wifebeater tank top climbed out. He had tattoos on his left arm—a flaming eagle clutching a burning American flag. He was bald. He had a goatee. When his face was clear on the computer screen, I withdrew my phone and snapped a picture. Then I turned for the door, my boot catching on the fallen tablet.

Bending, I scooped it up and grabbed it by the edge.

"Don't!"

The plea came too late. I shattered the tablet over the edge of the desk and tossed it to the floor.

"I'm gonna call the cops on you!" The clerk choked.

"Go ahead. While you're at it, you can explain how you abetted a kidnapping."

His face washed pale, and I rushed back into the parking lot, crashing through flooded potholes on my way to Jessica's room. The cops were still there, still taking notes and asking questions. They were following procedure, like good cops do. But we didn't have time for that.

"She's not here," I said.

"What?" Jessica turned on me.

"Does your ex drive a Chevy Blazer?"

Terror flooded her panicked eyes. I raised my phone. She surveyed the snapshot, and the terror turned to resolute rage. Without a word she spun for the parking lot, abandoning the cops and charging for the Chrysler.

"Wait!" I shouted. Jessica ignored me. I cut her off at the driver's side door, ramming my hand against it.

"Move!" she screamed. I held the door.

"Jessica. *Breathe.* Where would he take her?"

"Mississippi," she snapped. "His place."

"You have the address?"

"Of course I do!"

"So we call the Mississippi cops—"

"They're his *buddies*. He lives out in the sticks! Get out of my way, or I swear—"

"Okay." I held up a hand, my mind working to solve the equation before me with the speed of Autumn locating a random digit of pi.

Except this wasn't a difficult problem to solve. If Randy Mercer had kidnapped his daughter, he was no longer playing by the rules. He didn't give a crap about the court order, and I already knew he was a violent man. He'd beat Jessica to a pulp.

"I'm going with you," I said. "Give me the keys. You should make calls on the way."

Jessica hesitated only a moment; then she passed off the Chrysler's keys and rushed to the passenger side. The cops called from the breezeway as I fired up the old engine, rain thumping against the cardboard window to my left.

We didn't call back. I powered backward out of the parking spot, then turned for the road, headed for Mississippi.

6

"He lives outside of Beaumont. It's an hour up ninety-eight."

Jessica called the turns as I piloted the Chrysler through downtown Mobile, taking I-165 to Saraland before connecting with State Highway 98 just outside of Wilmer. Despite its overall disrepair, the windshield wipers of the station wagon worked better than the lone wiper on my GMC, clearing enough water for me to comfortably drive the vehicle up to highway speeds.

"You sure he'd take her to Beaumont?" I questioned.

Jessica sat next to me, hands trembling as she knotted them around the tail of her T-shirt over and over, gaze fixated on the path ahead. We hit the Mississippi state line even as a column of dense traffic clogged the highway along the eastbound lane. More evacuees, fleeing rural Mississippi.

And this dumb POS was taking his daughter *toward* the storm.

"It's where he lives," Jessica choked. "He has a trailer. Maybe he took her somewhere else...I don't know."

Her voice wavered. I put a hand on her arm.

"Stay calm. Focused for Autumn. We'll sort this out."

Jessica nodded several times, scrubbing her eyes.

"Is he armed?" I asked.

She glanced sideways. Panic returned. "You don't think—"

"No," I said. "I don't. But he doesn't like you, and I doubt he'll like me any better."

That made sense to her. She collected herself. "He's always had guns. I don't know what kind."

"What about neighbors? Anybody nearby? Any dogs?"

They were only semi-relevant details. Ideally, whatever happened next would be nonviolent and would be mitigated by local law enforcement. I wasn't planning on breaking bones. But keeping Jessica talking helped to keep her focused, and it never hurts to know if a Rottweiler is waiting at the end of a long muddy driveway.

"No dogs. No neighbors, either. It's the middle of nowhere."

A lonely spot out of touch with society. A redneck with a few screws loose and a kid under his thumb. Not good.

"Try the cops," I said, jabbing my thumb. Jessica dialed and spoke to a local police station. Whoever picked up the phone stopped listening the moment she said the word *father*. I understood, in a way, as an ex-cop myself. Then again, I'd also been a good cop. I'd understood the difference between a petty domestic dispute and a true emergency, or at least I cared enough to investigate. The dispatcher who answered Jessica's call was caught between a crazed woman on one end and a Cat 4 hurricane on the other, with a massive evacuation effort sandwiched in between. Her response was predictable.

"She said they'll respond when they can." Panic edged Jessica's voice. I motioned back to the phone.

"Try the state police."

Jessica pulled a phone number off Google and dialed again. This time, she couldn't even get through.

"They're overwhelmed," I said. "We'll deal with it. You just focus on what you can remember. What is the house like?"

"It's a trailer. Single wide. 'Bout half a mile off the blacktop."

Her voice wavered. I snapped my fingers. "Hey! Look at me."

Jessica twisted in the seat.

"Is this how Autumn would react?"

That brought the hint of a smile. "No."

"I agree. So let's rise to her level. Hit me with some numbers. How far?"

Jessica consulted her phone. "Twenty-six miles. Thirty-seven minutes."

"Let's make it thirty."

I mashed the accelerator, and the Chrysler roared. Water streamed across the windshield, and deep gray clouds turned gradually blacker. It wasn't yet midday, but I needed my headlights to illuminate the path ahead. Traffic became sparse as the highway arced northward for Hattiesburg. I figured most evacuees in this area would be headed for Jackson or Montgomery. Someplace farther inland. Beaumont was little more than a dot on the map, and it was a dot well within Nadia's reach. Certainly it was no place to shelter inside a trailer.

"Take the next right." Jessica pointed. I slowed and turned, front tires crashing through a flooded pothole. The next road was a two-lane maintained by the county, riddled with ruts and busted asphalt. I had no choice but to slow as dense groves of mixed pines and hardwoods closed on every side. We crossed a bridge spanning a narrow creek, and I noted the waterline rising rapidly up the bank. There were no other cars. No pedestrians, no houses. What mailboxes we passed were infrequent, leaning on wooden posts, long winding driveways disappearing into the trees.

The middle of nowhere.

"Six more miles," Jessica said. "The drive is dirt. It's gonna be slick."

I pictured the security footage at the motel, remembering the battered Chevrolet Blazer pulling up next to the office. The footage was grainy, but I remembered there being mud caked to the tires. I also remembered an elevated stance, indicating that the petite SUV was a four-wheel-drive.

Jessica's Chrysler wasn't.

"How long is the drive?"

"I don't know. Few hundred yards?"

I accelerated over a low hill, the rain finally slacking off while the sky remained pitch black. We were now caught beneath Nadia's outer bands, I realized. It would rain off and on for the next few hours before the hurricane made landfall. Then all hell would break loose. I'd never experienced a hurricane before, but I'd learned the hard way to respect the forces of nature regardless of their form. As soon as Autumn was safely back in Jessica's custody, we'd all head inland.

"There!" Jessica pointed. The mailbox wasn't a mailbox at all—it was an old microwave strapped to the top of an oil drum, with a four-digit street number spray-painted to the side. Most certainly *not* postmaster approved, but it did the job. I stepped on the brakes, and Jessica reached for the door. I caught her arm.

"Wait a minute."

She tugged. I ignored her and looked down the drive. It was impossible to tell if there were any fresh tracks pressed into the clay, but there was a pair of deep ruts, and those ruts were flooded. Looking down a gentle slope, the path disappeared into the trees, winding past a pair of *No Trespassing* signs.

"Let me go." Jessica tugged again. I released her and mashed the gas. The Chrysler rumbled another fifty yards down the road to a stretch of flat shoulder. I pulled onto the grass and cut the engine.

"We'll go through the woods," I said. "I don't want this jackass popping off a shot if he sees us coming up the driveway."

Jessica nodded. Again she reached for the door.

"Jessica."

She stopped. I held her gaze.

"Whatever happens next, you do what I say. Understand? There's a way to do this so that nobody gets hurt. That's our goal."

Jessica nodded. We both piled out. I dug my Streamlight MacroStream from my sodden pocket, clicking it on as we traversed a shallow ditch and entered the pines. It was dark enough beneath their dense foliage to obscure our path, but the flashlight dumped five hundred lumens across a bed of sodden pine needles. I took the lead, moving in a zigzag between the trees almost by default, just in case somebody was watching from a deer stand. Unlikely, but then again, this guy was clearly off his rocker.

Three hundred yards passed beneath my boots. I clicked

the MacroStream off when dim gray light illuminated a clearing beyond a tangle of undergrowth. I couldn't see a house, but I thought I detected a patch of metallic red paint —the Blazer, maybe.

I slowed. Jessica slowed with me, and we crept right to the edge of the undergrowth, dropping to our knees.

The trailer was there, just as Jessica described. Single wide, set on columns of concrete blocks with sections of aluminum skirt missing like gaps in a smile. Rusted metal steps led to the door. All the windows were closed, but dim electric light glowed behind most of them.

And the S-10 Blazer sat in the yard, tires covered in orange clay.

"That's his truck," Jessica said. She rose to move through the brush. I caught her arm again and pulled her back down, taking a moment to inspect the remainder of the clearing. It wasn't large. Maybe two acres, but most of that was overgrown, leaving the potential for any number of concealed hazards between the trailer and the trees. There was a Pontiac Bonneville set on blocks with its hood removed and the engine bay clogged by weeds. A few more oil drums, a pile of garbage bags, some rusted appliances heaped near the tree line. Lawn chairs gathered around a firepit.

Nothing else worthy of note.

"I'm gonna go," Jessica said. "I'll try the door. You can back me up if he gets obstinate."

"He's already obstinate," I said. "He kidnapped his own child. If you knock on that door, he may shoot you."

"So what do we do?" The desperation returned. I held up a hand.

"You'll stay here. I'm gonna have a closer look. I want to

know how many people are inside that trailer, and where Autumn is. Then we'll make a plan."

"But—"

"She's not in danger, Jessica. Not for the moment. We play this safe, and everybody stays alive. Okay?"

A hesitation. Then she nodded. "Okay..."

"So you stay here. And I'll have a look."

I offered a confident smile. Jessica did her best to mirror it. I squeezed her shoulder, then I turned away toward the brush, and my smile faded.

Because trailers full of angry, armed rednecks are never safe.

7

I left the tree line after circling to the back left corner of the trailer. There were no windows there, and plenty of tall grass. Keeping my body low and moving in the same slithering zigzag pattern I had learned in Army Ranger School, it was easy enough to close all the way to the junked Bonneville without ever exposing myself to a view of the trailer.

Behind the rusted-out old car, I paused to examine bullet holes decorating the Bonneville's fender and passenger-side door. They ranged in size from .22 caliber on up to .45, with brass scattered across the ground only yards away.

Brass, and a lot of beer bottles. *Terrific.*

Dropping to my chest, I peered beneath the car and inspected the underside of the trailer from twenty yards out. Jessica had promised there would be no dogs, but I wanted to be sure. Dogs aren't the sorts of variables that allow for mistakes.

I saw nothing but scattered trash, dangling plumbing lines, and mud. A lot of mud.

Crawling to the back of the car, I gained a view of the rear of the trailer. Stacked blocks took the place of metal stairs outside a sliding glass door. Just like the windows, the door was covered by a curtain, but flashing blue lights penetrated that curtain to betray the presence of a television. That was good. It might mean that Randy was distracted.

Rising to a crouch, I scoped out the windows that faced the backyard and guessed which ones might look into bedrooms. They were smaller than the rest, but if I stretched to my toes, I might still see inside. There was only the matter of the twenty-yard gap I needed to sprint across.

One more sweep of the yard, and I broke from cover. My boots squished through damp grass on my path to the house, descending back into a crouch as I neared the faded aluminum siding of the trailer. I could hear the TV now. It blared some kind of combat sporting event. I could tell by the cadence of commentators mixed with grunts and cheers.

Wiping rain from my face, I crept along the back side of the trailer to the sliding glass door. The noise of the TV grew louder. I found a gap in the curtain near the bottom corner of the door and slowed to a near crawl.

Yellow light glowed inside. I saw a sagging yellow couch and a worn leather easy chair. The TV stood on a slouching stack of porno magazines, flashing colors displaying an MMA match. The living room was unoccupied at first, but then the bald guy I'd seen in the security footage appeared.

He was shirtless, a beer in one hand and an overstuffed bologna sandwich in the other. Thick black hair covered his back, where the snake tattoo was joined by Lady Liberty standing with a blazing torch reaching for his shoulder blades, her beautiful face replaced by a hollow-eyed skull.

Randy descended into his easy chair with a crash,

mayonnaise dripping off his sandwich and landing in his lap. He didn't even notice, rocking the beer back and guzzling. Completely transfixed by the TV.

I leaned right and twisted my head for a better view of the couch. I didn't see Autumn.

Easing back from the door, I backtracked along the wall. The next window was the smallest of the lot and also stood the highest off the ground. Likely a kitchen window. I couldn't reach it, so I proceeded to the first bedroom window, closing against the slick aluminum siding and rising to my toes. A sheer curtain obscured my view, allowing for only a partial view of the interior. I swept my gaze over stacked boxes and bags of trash.

A storage room. No sign of Autumn.

From the living room Randy burst into an inebriated shout. The TV blared a combined cacophony of boos and cheers. I hurried to the next window and again rose onto my toes, squinting through another sheer curtain. It was a bedroom, but it was darker than the first, the door closed and the walls painted deep blue. With the cloud cover overhead, there wasn't enough ambient light for me to see very far into the room. I drew the MacroStream again and angled my head.

I saw a closet door. A banged-up dresser with one drawer hanging open.

And then a pair of shoes, abandoned on the floor. *Child's shoes.*

I craned my neck again, but I couldn't see beyond the corner of a bed. There was a blanket there, and I thought I detected a lump. Maybe a foot or a leg. Glancing back toward the living room, I listened for another drunken cheer. Randy didn't keep me waiting, and I dug into my pocket for the Victorinox Locksmith I carry—a Swiss made multi-tool with a bottle opener/flat head screwdriver included. That screwdriver slipped easily into the bottom of the corroded aluminum window frame as I held the flashlight between my teeth, then pried upward.

The window shifted. It squealed as damp metal scraped against more of the same. It rose an eighth inch, then stopped.

The window was locked. I jiggled the knife and leaned on it, but the window wouldn't budge, and the noises from the living room now sounded more like commercials.

Flicking the screwdriver closed, I switched to the three-inch, locking stainless-steel blade instead. It was razor-sharp, but I only needed it to be thin. The cutting edge slipped between the windowpane and the dry-rotted rubber gasket that held it in place. I scraped, prying rubber free. Inside the bedroom, the edge of the bedsheet fluttered, and I froze.

Then I matched the movement with the grind of an air-conditioning unit from someplace beyond the living room. The TV sounded with cheers and grunts again. I stripped the gasket away and wiggled the blade to displace the window. It slid out faster than I anticipated, and I never had the chance to catch it. The entire pane skated over my right shoulder and landed in the mud with a dull crack, shards of bright glass scattering around my boots.

The TV was instantly louder, a rush of cool air enveloping my face. I placed both hands on the bottom of the window frame and hauled my body upward, the Victorinox clutched in one fist, the flashlight held between my teeth. My head cleared the gap, feet dangling. I bent inward and peered right.

And then I saw her. Autumn lay on the bed, curled up beneath a stained blanket atop a bare mattress. Bright blonde hair clouded around her narrow face, chin tucked low, little fists wrapped near to her chest. Paralyzed legs helpless to provide an escape.

Pressing both boots against the sides of the trailer, I scraped for additional stability, but the wet aluminum provided zero traction. I could haul myself through the narrow window, but I was going to get beat up doing it.

I spoke around the flashlight instead.

"Autumn."

The child didn't so much as flinch, head still tucked low, body so perfectly still that for a moment a tinge of fear rushed through my chest. Biceps strained as I hauled myself up another inch and pushed my head all the way through the window. The TV had grown quiet—Randy must have turned the volume down. What little protection it offered now felt nearly worthless. Tearing the sheer curtain aside, I rocked my head right, directly toward the bed.

"Autumn!"

Still, the girl didn't budge, but from my improved vantage point, I detected a very slight flex of her chest as she inhaled...then exhaled. Perfectly silent, like only a child can sleep. She was out cold. Completely unconscious. My elbows locked and burning muscle barked as I risked one last hiss into the room.

"*Autumn!* Wake up!"

The girl didn't budge, but as if on cue, something else answered my call. A low growl of a heavy engine, followed by the short blast of a truck horn. My gaze snapped instinctively toward the driveway, even though my view of it was blocked by the trailer. From down the hall a toilet flushed, and Randy hollered, "I'm comin'!"

My muscles were about to give out. All two hundred pounds of my broad frame had hung on them like a dead cow suspended from a hook. I couldn't hold on any longer, and with Randy only yards away somewhere down the hall, attempting to wriggle inside wasn't an option.

I dropped instead, landing on the glass-covered mud and falling into an instant crouch. From the far side of the trailer, the engine had grown louder and was now joined by a twin. A horn blasted again, and Randy shouted a curse.

"Hang on!"

Boots thumped down the hallway. I dropped back onto my chest and peered beneath the trailer. I could see all the way through a tangle of loose insulation and dangling water pipes to the front yard. A pair of heavy trucks sat there— beefy four-door Fords with mud tires. Extended beds were loaded down with heavy plastic bins secured by straps. The trucks were painted utility white, with thick blue stripes and four bold letters printed on the sides.

FEMA—Federal Emergency Management Agency.

What?

Already, doors were popping open, and heavyset guys in boots, jeans, and wifebeater tank tops were spilling out. All muscled. All tattooed with long hair and graying beards. All looking decidedly like Randy, somehow.

And all of them *armed*. Handguns held in hip holsters or jammed into the smalls of their backs. Not like FEMA workers. Not like any kind of federal disaster relief. More like a crew of bumpkins turning out for a supremacy rally, but I didn't have time to speculate further. Footsteps thumped against the floor overhead, and Autumn's door creaked open.

I froze beneath the trailer, not daring to breathe as my fingers tightened around the knife.

I remembered the missing windowpane. The sheer curtain would cover it, but if a breeze came along...

Randy didn't speak. He stepped across the floor toward the bed, and I pulled my legs beneath the edge of the trailer. I waited. Bodyweight shifted overhead. Randy grunted, and I closed my eyes.

And then the breeze came. A gust from one of Nadia's outer bands, rushing out of the forest and ripping through the empty window frame. Randy grunted another curse. His feet thumped on the floor. He reached the window.

And then the game was up.

"What tha...hey! Y'all get over here. Somebody's here!"

8

The rednecks responded in record time, breaking into gut-jarring jogs and already drawing their sidearms. I wriggled quickly beneath a section of insulation, pocketing the flashlight and making for the front of the trailer. There was no chance of getting Autumn out now. Not by myself, and not unarmed. There were eight or ten guys outside, plus Randy, and they were all circling to the back of the trailer. Pretty soon they would reach the window and do the logical thing—look beneath the trailer.

I had to be outside by then. Beyond their trucks and beyond the tree line, where I could regroup with Jessica.

Mud fouled my shirt and coated my arms as I fought my way around a drooping air duct and beneath a row of water pipes. The rednecks had reached the back of the house and were closing on that patch of dirt with the shattered glass. Randy hadn't left Autumn's bedroom—he was shouting through the window, but despite the noise, I still hadn't detected any sign of Autumn waking from her sleep.

Maybe that was better. Unable to run on her own two

feet, there was little she could do besides complicate things. I needed to regain the initiative.

A gap in the trailer's skirt opened ahead of me, six feet wide and clogged by weeds. I scrambled toward it even as the boot falls of the rednecks reached the spot beneath the window. I could tell by the crunch of glass breaking beneath hard rubber soles. Then Randy shouted again.

"It's her momma! She come to get her. Y'all spread out and find 'er!"

I'd reached the gap in the skirt, but now I froze, peering back over one shoulder. The call from Randy wasn't what I'd expected. He'd jumped to a conclusion much quicker than I would have guessed, and already his comrades were falling into line, fanning out and tearing through the high weeds with guns brandished.

I looked back to the gap beneath Autumn's window, momentarily considering the possibility of snatching her while Randy and his pals were distracted. I could make it back to the trees, sprint for the truck—

"There! I see 'er!"

The shout ripped from someplace to my right, and my head snapped in that direction. Most of the skirting at the end of the trailer stood intact, but a jagged hole about the size of a basketball offered a view of the field I'd zigzagged through. I saw three guys turn in unison, like a formation of fighter jets rolling toward a target. One pointed toward the woods. Another shouted. A gunshot cracked.

And then Jessica screamed.

No.

I've been in a lot of nasty predicaments throughout the course of a career in the US Army's 75th Ranger Regiment, followed by a host of gnarly situations on the streets of

Phoenix, working in law enforcement. I'd learned the hard way what the moment feels like just before everything hits the fan—that calm before the storm that was so apropos to the incoming hurricane.

This was that moment, and I already knew it was rapidly grinding to a close. Variables I couldn't have predicted had descended on the muddy little property in the woods and were rapidly turning it into a battleground. As another shot cracked and the shouts closed on the tree line, I knew I was out of options.

I had to draw fire, or Jessica was about to be riddled with it.

Tearing through the gap in the front of the trailer, I spun left just in time to see Randy exploding through the trailer's front door like a charging running back. He landed on the metal steps with a pump shotgun in one hand, his shirtless beer gut jiggling, and I emerged from beneath the house. Covered in mud, nothing but the blade of my Victorinox to serve as a weapon.

Randy's face flushed crimson. He pivoted right, sweeping the muzzle of the shotgun along with him. I sprinted to close the distance, ducking beneath the barrel just as the shotgun belched thunder and hellfire. Lead pellets exploded over my shoulder, and I struck his knees with the full force of my charge.

Like a defensive end circling in to knock out the quarterback.

Randy toppled backward off the steps. I followed him, driving to the ground. The shotgun spun out of his hands, and I landed on top, blade flashing.

Randy screamed, and I hit him. Not with the knife, but with my closed fist instead, cracking right against his cheekbone, hard enough to elicit another cry, but not hard enough to knock him out. I *wanted* him screaming. His head slammed back into the mud, and I drove a knee into his groin, generating a third shriek. Then I was on my feet, knife spinning to the ground as I turned for the shotgun instead. It was short—a defensive model, twelve gauge, with perhaps a five-shell capacity. Now down to four. I pumped a fresh load into the chamber and spun the muzzle toward the tree line. The rednecks were fifty yards away—well outside the effective range of bird shot, but I wasn't trying to kill anybody. I wanted their attention, and the next belch of the shotgun earned it.

"Hey, you! Over here!"

Five of the eight faces spun toward me. Handguns followed them. Shots cracked like firecrackers, and I leapt over Randy's wriggling body and headed for the end of the trailer, planning to circle to the back and take temporary cover behind the Bonneville. I couldn't have them popping off shots at the trailer. Not while Autumn still lay inside, apparently *still* asleep.

Another pump of the shotgun brought a fresh shell into action. Handgun fire dissipated, but the shouts grew nearer. I reached the Bonneville and slid into cover, shotgun rising to my shoulder, muzzle pivoted toward the trees. I wouldn't get them all—likely, I wouldn't get any of them. But if I could draw their attention just long enough for Jessica to vanish into the forest, I would then do the same. We would regroup and return for Autumn on our own terms.

It was a reasonable plan, but dead on arrival. Even as my finger dropped over the shotgun's smooth trigger and I picked a target, I saw Jessica. She stumbled out of the trees at gunpoint, both hands up, tangled brown hair running with rainwater. Two men stood behind her, pressing ahead but pivoting away from my position behind the Bonneville. At one hundred plus yards, I could have dropped them both with headshots from a decent rifle, but they were well out of range of my scattergun. Even a lucky potshot was impossible with Jessica pressed closed between them, her face tear streaked, voice turning raw as she screamed over and over toward the trailer.

"Autumn! *Autumn!*"

Behind me, the back door of the trailer exploded open. I snatched the shotgun in that direction but held my fire as the barrel of a hunting rifle poked out at me. It was Randy, but his body was invisible behind the doorjamb. I could guess its location and fire anyway, but now I had other problems. Bumpkins circling in from both sides, handguns brandished. Eight targets, plus Randy. I had only three shots remaining.

And they had a hostage.

"Put it down, you!" Randy shouted.

I ignored him, drawing the weapon tight into my shoulder as though I were about to fire. I'd lost two of the bumpkins in my peripheral. Within seconds, I would be exposed again. Maybe I already was.

"*Drop it,*" somebody snarled. "Or both you and the woman get it."

Jessica had disappeared around the end of the trailer. She continued to shout Autumn's name—and Autumn still hadn't responded. My muscles tightened; my teeth clenched down until they hurt. My finger constricted.

But I didn't fire. There was no point. I'd get one of them, then they would get me, and Jessica and Autumn would be on their own. Warm steel reached my neck and pressed down hard. I smelled gunpowder. The bumpkin spoke in a snarl.

"*Drop. It.*"

I dropped the shotgun. Hands closed around my shirt collar and hauled me up as Randy appeared in the doorway, still shirtless, still wielding the hunting rifle. Rain beat down on my head, and another redneck stooped to retrieve the shotgun while my captor kept his handgun pressed into my neck. I pivoted toward him, gritted teeth flashing.

Then the shotgun butt landed in my stomach, and the wind vacated my lungs in a rush. I doubled over and choked. Rough hands grabbed me and dragged my booted feet across the mud. We reached the trailer's back door as I gasped for air. Then we were inside, and I was thrown down over greasy shag carpet. The TV still flashed. Jessica stumbled inside, screaming for Autumn.

A fist connected with her jaw. Her voice broke off in a gurgle, and I thrashed on the floor, fighting to regain my feet. A boot landed in my side, sending a wave of burning pain rushing through my rib cage. Then the rough hands grabbed my collar and my hair, wrenching me upright and pivoting my face toward the line of men now gathered in the living room.

Randy stood just left of center, a wicked grin spread across his ugly face as he fixated on Jessica. She was held by three separate men, arms spread apart, shirt ripped. Blood streamed from a busted lip, her right eye puffy and red. The other rednecks encircled me, guns at the ready, boots crushing down on my calves.

And standing next to Randy was the ringleader. I knew it by the way everyone else automatically made room for his approach. He was a short guy constructed of solid muscle, with a chest that bulged beneath a rain-soaked tank top, and a long gray beard that glistened with water. His teeth were yellow, his breath rancid as he leaned in close.

"*Who are you?*" he snarled, voice laden with an accent someplace near to a bayou.

I made no answer. One of my captors crushed down his boot, shooting more searing pain up my leg. I gritted my teeth and endured it.

"You know him?" Now it was Randy who spoke, barking at Jessica. She spat blood.

"Never seen him before."

"Horse biscuits!" Randy screamed. "You been screwin' him, ain't you? Dirty whore. Is this your new man?"

Randy rushed her. Yellow Teeth caught him by the arm and wrenched him back, all without breaking eye contact with me.

"That true?" he demanded. "You her boyfriend?"

I thought quickly and decided it wasn't a bad cover.

"That's right."

Yellow Teeth snorted. He shook his head, then swept his gaze slowly down Jessica's face, across her torn neckline, and down to her hips.

"Lucky man," he said. "Why are you here?"

"You know why," Jessica snarled. "Where is she, Randy? What have you done with her?"

"Shut up!" This time Randy got in a hit before anybody could stop him, right fist striking like a snake. Jessica's nose took the brunt of the blow, and I actually heard the crunch of cartilage as she stumbled back. Randy followed her up, raining another blow to her rib cage, hard enough to crack bone. Then his men were on him, hauling him back. Jeers and laughs filled the room as Jessica hit the floor, face covered in blood.

"Autumn!" She choked. *"Autumn!"*

"She can't hear you!" Randy taunted. "I drugged her up real nice. Gave her them sleeping pills you used to love so much. Still got your name on the bottle! Works good on a kid."

I tore my gaze away from Jessica and turned to Yellow Teeth. He was the only one of the crew who remained fixated on me. A smart boss.

"You're making a big mistake," I said. "Just give us the kid, and we'll be on our way. We'll forget all of this."

Yellow Teeth grinned. "Really?"

I nodded. He laughed.

"Whall...if it's that simple!" Another chorus of laughs. Yellow Teeth dug into his back pocket and liberated a can of chewing tobacco. A thick wad of it found his cheek. He chomped down, then shot a string of dark saliva between my knees. His breath turned ever ranker as he.leaned close.

"Just one little problem, wife porker. That there kid belongs to my brother Randy. And in this outfit, we looks after our brothers."

Tension in the room spiked as Yellow Teeth finished his declaration. Everyone grew quiet. His lip lifted into a snarl.

I dropped my tone to match his challenge. "Let them go —both of them—or it will be the last mistake you make."

Yellow Teeth laughed. He straightened.

"You know what, bub. If I weren't on such a tight schedule, we'd go a few rounds. See what you're made of. But being as there's a hurricane rollin' in, we'll have to take a shortcut."

His chin flicked sideways, and my body tensed. I knew

what was coming even before I saw the shotgun butt rocket toward my jawbone—there was simply nothing to be done about it. Hard wood collided with my face and knocked me sideways. Boots crashed into my exposed back and thighs while the shotgun changed hands, and Yellow Teeth circled sideways. In the background I heard Jessica screaming again, shouting Autumn's name. Randy's ugly snarl overpowered her.

"That girl's mine, and ain't nobody taking her from me! Imma give her a better life than you ever could, you broke slut. Imma be *rich*, and where we're going, they'll *never* find us."

I rolled right, face pivoting toward the floor, hands digging into the carpet as the boots continued to rain down. My whole body was on fire. I could barely breathe. My vision wavered. I saw Jessica curled on the floor, Randy beating her like a dead animal, blood spraying against the wall. I reached out one hand, desperate to return to my knees.

Then the boot crashed against my spine, driving me into the floor, and a split second later the shotgun slammed into the back of my head. My face rammed into the carpet, my fragile nose so recently broken in Florida collapsing in on itself. I choked for air.

Then the shotgun rose again. The butt fell a second time.

And everything went black.

9

I t was the wind that woke me. Beating hard against the flimsy walls of the trailer, windows rattling in their frames. My eyes blinked open, and blinding pain erupted through my skull, worse than any headache I'd ever experienced. It felt as though my brain was imploding, so much pressure crushing down from every angle that I was screaming before I could even clear my vision.

My mouth tasted metallic, as though I were choking on pennies. Everything around me was dark, but as I dug my fingers into the ground, I felt the same greasy carpet that I had thrashed on just before being knocked into oblivion. It slipped from beneath my palms as I struggled to push myself upright, fresh agony ripping through my rib cage and building into an inferno.

I fell again, colliding with the carpet and tasting more metal. It was blood—my mouth was full of it, dry on my lips and damp on my tongue. I rolled over with a Herculean effort and stared up at a blank ceiling.

The lights were out. The room was empty. As another

blast of wind slammed into the trailer, the floor beneath me shuddered. Under what dim gray light seeped through the windows, I saw torn carpet soiled by mud, chairs overturned, and the TV lying on its side next to a heap of collapsed porno mags. I fought my way into a seated position, and my head swam. Each breath came in a ragged gasp, my vision blurring in and out of focus as I swept the room around me.

All the rednecks were gone. All the guns were gone. The door stood open, and rain beat down outside in torrents, but the sky was black. I couldn't see beyond the block steps. Fumbling with the pocket of my jeans, I struggled to liberate the MacroStream from its place amongst loose coins and lint. None of my things had been taken by my abusers. Maybe they thought I was dead.

Mashing the tail cap, I was rewarded by a flood of bright blue light that cut across the room and blazed against a vibrating wall. I rolled onto my knees. The trailer floor vibrated.

The wind was picking up. The rain had increased substantially. Nadia was closing on the gulf coast.

I made it onto my feet and caught myself on Randy's easy chair. Then I panned the light across the kitchen, over the blood- and mud-stained floor...

And to the wall. Cold fear closed around my stomach like an icy claw as the MacroStream illuminated Jessica. She lay on her face against the far wall, a wide pool of blood spilling from gashes in her temple. One arm was twisted behind her back, clearly broken. A foot was mashed sideways, and lacerations joined the welts running up her arms and over her neck. The shirt was nearly torn off, and even as I fixated on her rib cage, I detected no movement.

No.

"Jessica!"

I called over another clap of thunder, then stumbled across the carpet to land beside her. She was all wadded up, neck twisted, and one arm trapped beneath her body. I went to work automatically, MARCH training from the Army clicking into gear just as it had so many times before.

Massive hemorrhage. Airways. Respiratory. Circulatory. Hypothermia, and head trauma.

The hypothermia was the only problem on the list I could definitely rule out. The hemorrhaging wasn't massive, but Jessica had lost half a pint of blood at the least. Her airways might be clogged. Circulation compromised. Head trauma almost certain.

But when I felt her wrist, I found a pulse. Weak but steady, joined by just the hint of breath against my palm as I placed it beneath her nose. I still couldn't see her chest move. Her skin was cold to the touch.

But she was alive. For the moment.

Hauling myself back to my feet, I fought waves of dizziness as I stumbled across the room to the kitchen. Water ran from the tap, and I used it to splash my face and erase some of the dryness in my throat. Then I was headed down the hall, still staggering, still marking my path with the Macro-Stream. I already knew that I would find the final bedroom empty, wheelchair marks in the carpet.

But I had to check, and I did. Autumn's bare mattress was vacant, the blanket tangled on the floor. Instead of wheelchair marks in the carpet, I found the wheelchair itself abandoned in one corner. Autumn was gone.

Gritting my teeth against the pain, I swept my hands over my body to inspect for injuries. Tender spots across my rib cage and down my back were abundant. The blood I'd tasted ran freely from a busted lip and an obliterated nose. My eyes burned, and the headache pounded on in a relentless, miserable tempo.

But I could stand. I could balance. With effort, I could walk.

Back in the living room, I found a dirty baseball cap abandoned in a corner and wrenched it down low over my head. The bidirectional pocket clip affixed to the Macro-Stream allowed me to slide it onto the hat's bill with the face of the light pointed out ahead of me, like a headlamp.

Then I returned to Jessica, descending to my knees and inspecting her body again. I had a choice to make. I could leave her here, avoiding any risk of inflicting permanent damage or even death by shifting her body. If her back or neck was broken, lifting her now could sever her spinal cord.

Lights out.

But she'd be dead anyway if I didn't get her to a hospital soon, and a quick inspection of my cell phone confirmed what I already knew—I had no signal. There was no chance of calling an ambulance. Even if one could be reached, how long would that take?

I made a judgment call, and I slid my arms beneath her body. As gently as I could, I hauled her limp body off the floor, every fiber of my being erupting in fiery protest as I reached my feet. I bit back a scream, and the light trembled from the end of the hat as I rolled her closer to my chest, improving my own balance. Then I was headed for the door, stepping into the pounding rain without hesitation. Down the shaky block steps and into the mud. My boots squished as I staggered toward the driveway, noting the absence of the pair of Ford pickups marked with FEMA logos. Wallowed tire tracks marked their path to the driveway and back to town.

But the two-door Chevy Blazer remained, faded paint streaming with water, tires still caked in mud. I weighed the advantages of four-wheel drive against the multi-hundred-yard slog back to Jessica's Chrysler, and the decision was easy.

I tugged the door latch with one finger, but it was locked. Easing Jessica down into the mud, I hustled to the last place I remembered using my Victorinox—the mucky corner of the trailer where I'd beaten Randy and taken his shotgun. Sure enough, the red plastic scales of the tool were visible under the beam of the MacroStream, and I snatched it up, along with the broken half of a brick.

The brick went through the Blazer's side window. Jessica went into the passenger seat. The Victorinox went to work beneath the dash, slashing ignition wires and peeling insulation back. I found the right combination on the third try, and the starter turned over with a whine. Amid the pound of the rain, the motor coughed to life, and I piled in.

Jessica's head rolled against her shoulder next to me, neck completely limp, lips parted. I put a hand on her arm to brace her as I locked the Blazer into four-wheel mode, ratcheted the transmission into drive, and turned for the muddy trail between the trees.

"Hang on, Jess! I'm getting you to a hospital."

I rammed the accelerator to the floor, and the little engine howled as we raced toward the blacktop. I didn't see any signs of Randy Mercer, his chums, or either of the lifted Ford pickups they had arrived in, but that didn't surprise me. Even before we exited the trees and turned right along the county road, I had already guessed their logic behind abandoning us, unconscious, inside that flimsy trailer.

A few hours from now, there wouldn't *be* a trailer. It would be blown into a million pieces, our bodies thrown into the trees. The bruises, lacerations, and broken bones they had left us with would no longer be judged as the damage of heavy fists, but of heavy winds and hard obstacles. When the cops found us, we would simply be storm victims.

Smart—and effective, even without Nadia. Because the broken body buckled into the seat next to me didn't need any heavy winds or hard obstacles to drag Jessica Waverly across the threshold into the great unknown. She was hanging on by a thread as it was, beaten much worse than I. With every flooded pothole and collapsed rut we crashed through, her body moved as though it were lifeless.

Just a bag of busted bones.

"Hold on," I said, flooring the accelerator. "Just hold on!"

10

My cell phone was without signal as I hurtled along the busted county road, but I remembered from previous inspections of my GPS app on the way to Randy's place that his little town—Beaumont, Mississippi—sat just southeast of Hattiesburg, the nearest city of any size. I'd never been to Hattiesburg before and had no idea where to find a hospital, but I knew Jessica's chances would be better there than back in Mobile. It was a much shorter drive.

I retreated to Highway 98 by memory, rain blowing through the shattered passenger window of the Blazer and pooling in the floorboards. The temperature had actually risen post nightfall, and sweat streamed down my face to join the rain. I turned right along the highway and pointed the little SUV northwest. The first green sign I passed was obscured by rain, but I still made out the white reflective letters.

HATTIESBURG — 30 MILES.

"Hang in there, Jess."

The Blazer topped out at just under eighty miles per hour, engine howling as it raced along. Only a few other cars braved the weather to join us on the highway, and all of them were headed inland. Long before I reached the city, I was already searching for the familiar white-on-blue of a hospital sign, but I didn't see one until I was well inside the city limits of Hattiesburg. The first I found was Forrest General, located on the west side of town. I blew through a red light on my way to the emergency center pavilion, where a trio of paramedics stood smoking alongside a parked ambulance.

"Over here!" I shouted through the busted window as I squealed to a stop. "Help me with her!"

Cigarettes fell to the pavement, and the paramedics rushed to the passenger door. A flashlight clicked on as one guy leaned in.

"She was beaten," I said. "Broken bones and possible head trauma. She's barely breathing."

Nobody asked questions. One guy snapped an order for a stretcher. The other two rushed for the ambulance and returned with a gurney.

"Easy now!" one paramedic said. "Don't let her rock."

Jessica's limp body exited the pickup slowly, resting on the gurney in a disjointed heap. Head rolling, one arm hanging off. Then the paramedics jogged toward the emergency entrance, and I followed.

A blast of cold, sterilized air flooded my lungs as we burst through automatic doors. The paramedics orbited directly for triage, calling to the nurses' station as they passed.

"Female, mid-thirties. Unconscious with possible head trauma."

Phones lifted from cradles. Nurses spoke quickly, and I ground to a stop as Jessica disappeared between double doors, her bloodied face pointed toward the ceiling.

Maybe dead...or dying.

Sudden dizziness overwhelmed me as the doors closed. I caught myself on the wall and choked. Bile exploded out of my throat, carrying chunks of the previous night's pizza party with it. My head pounded, and I almost fell. My fingers curled around a fire extinguisher cabinet just in time.

"Sir?" One of the nurses spoke from behind the desk. I barely heard.

"Are you all right?"

Footsteps tapped. I scrubbed my mouth, looking up just as a round brunette with spiked hair reached me.

"Oh my heavens," she chirped. "Miranda! Get over here. He's all banged up."

I blinked hard, my brain suddenly confused by her statement. Who was Miranda?

Then the hospital floor swayed beneath me like the deck of a Navy ship. Déjà vu of those hellish weeks I had been deployed on the USS *Bataan* rushed my mind, and my knees buckled.

And then, for the second time that day, everything went black.

I AWOKE to the murmur of detached voices punctuated by the slow beep of a heart monitor. Dry eyes fluttered open, and my throat tightened behind a wooden tongue.

I felt no pain—not like I had before. The swimminess was still there, but my head didn't pound. I only felt stiff as I squinted against fluorescent light. The voices I'd heard clarified a little, and I recognized a man and a woman speaking. Both voices deadly serious.

"We've just received word that Governor Hart of Mississippi has joined Louisiana Governor Long in issuing mandatory evacuations for additional counties well inland of the coast. With only hours remaining until hurricane Nadia's landfall, this superstorm has strengthened to just shy of a Category 5 behemoth, with sustained winds reaching one hundred fifty miles per hour. For reference, Hurricane Katrina made landfall in 2005 as a Cat 3, with winds of one hundred forty miles per hour. At that time Katrina was already weakening, but even as Nadia closes on the shallower waters just south of Louisiana, wind speeds and storm surges are only increasing. We can't overstate how serious this storm is."

"We really can't, Doug." Now the woman joined in. I flexed my neck and earned a flash of dull pain along the entire right side of my rib cage. Dulled by drugs, I guessed. I could feel the IV rammed into my left elbow.

"What's most shocking are all the parallels," the woman continued. "Katrina made landfall in the early morning hours of Monday, August 29, just south of Buras, Louisiana. Now Nadia is set to make landfall only twenty-eight miles west along Grand Isle, also in the early morning hours of a Monday. We can only pray that the results will be different this time. With better levees in place, the Army Corps of Engineers is confident that New Orleans will stand strong... but she's about to take a beating."

A beating.

My eyes flickered open again, and I rammed one hand along a groaning hospital mattress to force myself upright. Thoughts of Jessica returned in a tidal wave. Her lying on the floor. Her screaming as heavy leather boots rained kicks over her helpless body.

"Sir?"

I twisted toward the voice. It was the spiky-haired nurse standing beyond the curtain of an emergency room triage bay. The IV that I'd felt in my elbow fed fluids while wires connected to my fingers served to monitor my heartbeat. I reached up to tear them away, and Spiky's face flicked from concern to outrage.

"Hey! Don't do that."

"How is she?" I said, tossing the heart monitor to the floor and moving to the IV. Spiky cut me off, smacking my hand with the force of a medical veteran.

"Sit back, sir. The doctor will be in shortly to review your condition. You're banged up bad."

No joke.

I rotated to lift my legs out of the bed. I still wore my muddy jeans, but my boots were gone.

"Where are my boots?" I demanded.

Spiky bit back a curse. "Miranda! Get in here. I got a problem child."

Miranda appeared at the opening of the curtain like a bowling ball—twice as large as Spiky and not nearly as pleasant. Flushed red cheeks garnished a scowl as she tore the curtain out of the way and placed a powerful hand against my shoulder.

"Sir, you better lie down." Her accent spoke of bayous and crawfish. I had no choice but to capitulate, crashing back against the pillows as Miranda grabbed my hand and forced the monitor back over my finger.

"You got yersef up the crick, didn't you?" she asked. "Bar fight? Forget to pay your tab?"

I blinked hard. Memories of the trailer returned. I shook my head to clear it.

"No. Nothing like that. Where is the woman? Is she okay?"

Miranda exchanged a look with Spiky. Spiky folded her arms; then both women turned hard eyes on me. I knew what they were thinking.

"I didn't touch her," I said.

"Uh-huh."

"I *didn't*," I snapped. "Where's the doctor? I need to—"

"Right here."

The curtain moved again. A petite woman—or maybe she was average in size and her nurses simply dwarfed her— appeared next to my head. Black hair, narrow glasses. Mid-forties. Tired, but focused. She addressed a clipboard.

"Mr. Sharpe?"

I blinked again. My hand fell to my hip pocket. No wallet.

"That's right."

"Wanna tell me what happened?" The question was all business, no sympathy. Miranda and Spiky stood in the background, bulging shoulders tensed and ready to make me sorry if I attempted to leave the bed.

"Is she alive?" I demanded.

The doctor lowered the clipboard. "Barely. She's in a coma. She has a brain bleed, a half dozen broken ribs, a busted wrist, and a busted fibula. One punctured lung and some savage lacerations. Kinda looks like she was run through a woodchipper."

The doctor's eyes drifted to my knuckles. The right one was bruised—results of my collision with Randy. I didn't have time to explain.

"Is she being treated?" I demanded.

The doctor looked genuinely offended. "Of course she is. Do you have her name?"

"Jessica Waverly."

"Relationship?"

"What?"

"*How do you know her?*"

"Oh." I stopped. Hesitated. "I'm a friend."

"Sure you are." Miranda spoke through tight lips. I ignored her.

"What happened, Mr. Sharpe?" That was the doctor again, but I was barely listening. My gaze had blurred out as my mind clicked into gear. I wasn't thinking of Jessica anymore—there was nothing more I could do for her. Now I was thinking about Autumn and what had become of her. Kidnapped by Randy and his brotherhood of third-rate thugs...where would he have taken her?

I closed my eyes, ignoring the doctor's repeat of the question. I thought about the trailer. Randy's snarled words as he beat Jessica. He'd said where he was going, hadn't he? He'd bragged about it. But where...

My mind worked in slow motion, like a tank struggling through a bog. I wound the event back like a movie.

"*Where we're going, they'll never find us.*"

My eyes opened, and I stared at the floor. The two nurses and the doctor were holding a conference. There was some mention of a sheriff's department. I tuned it all out.

I couldn't tune out the TV still playing on the wall.

"...paranoid by what happened in 2005, authorities are

taking extreme measures to prevent a repeat of Katrina. National Guardsmen are already deployed to New Orleans to establish security and assist in search and rescue, and FEMA has deployed hundreds of trucks and thousands of workers to the gulf coast, ready to step in the moment the storm clears."

FEMA.

My gaze snapped toward the TV. I watched the replay of helicopter footage overlooking a highway from earlier that day. Evacuees lined up in the northbound lanes, backed up for miles. And in the southbound lanes?

FEMA trucks. Large and small, with buses sprinkled in. Not exactly like the pickups Randy's gang had pulled up in, but the logos were the same.

"Imma give her a better life than you ever could, you broke slut." Another portion of Randy's tirade echoed in my mind. *"Imma be rich."*

No way.

My gaze snapped back to the TV. The helicopter footage of the highway was gone, replaced now by replays of helicopter footage from years prior. A coastal city swamped by floodwaters. A football stadium with holes torn in the roof, survivors crowded around goal posts. Emergency boats gliding down streets, houses caved in.

And looters. Hundreds of them, armed and turning violent. Sacking drugstores and jewelry shops without discrimination.

"Imma be rich."

A dump of adrenaline surged into my bloodstream, mixing with whatever cocktail of painkillers they'd administered to block out the thunder in my head. I tore the heart monitor off and threw it to the floor. Miranda braced to charge me, and I stiff-armed her right in the sternum, ripping the IV out and landing on the floor. My boots rested in a chair alongside my shirt. My knife, flashlight, truck keys, and wallet were there also. The hospital gown came off, and my feet slid in. Spiky put a hand on my arm, and the doctor called for security.

None of it mattered. I tore free and broke into a sprint down the hallway, boot laces slapping the floor, mind numb with disbelief and semi-panic.

I thought of Autumn, paralyzed from the waist down and without her wheelchair. In the hands of a mob of idiots in fake FEMA trucks.

Headed south.

Headed into the storm.

11

I didn't have to wonder what route Randy and his thugs would have taken—it was clearly marked by temporary blue signs with two words joined by a single white arrow pointed ahead into the heart of the storm.

DISASTER RELIEF.

I hit the first police barricade at the on-ramp of I-59 south. Two Mississippi state trooper Tahoes stood on either side of a pair of wooden sawhorses, the cops sheltering inside their vehicles while blue lights blinked to mark their location. I steered the Blazer straight for the gap between them, ignoring the chirp of a siren and the bark of a loudspeaker as I closed on the sawhorses.

Wood exploded over the nose of the SUV, erupting to either side and slamming into the Tahoes. The ramp ahead lay empty, leading up onto the highway with yellow lights swaying at the top of high wooden poles. I slammed on the accelerator, and all four tires dug into the concrete, launching me toward the freeway.

The cops did not follow. I hit a pair of empty southbound lanes and swung automatically to the left into the fast lane. With the majority of daily traffic traveling along the right-hand side, the left lane ruts would be shallower and carry less water. I could push the Blazer to full speed with a reduced chance of hydroplaning.

Or so I hoped.

With the speedometer locked in at seventy-nine and the V6 engine thundering, I fought with the radio to narrow in on a weather channel. Static streamed through the speakers, and distorted country music blended with coastal jazz. Then I recognized the same male voice I'd heard in the hospital room. The guy on the TV.

"In a sinister parallel to Katrina, New Orleans officials have gathered what residents have been unable to evacuate the city into Caesar's Superdome, home of the New Orleans Saints. Correspondents on the ground inform us that as many as twenty thousand such refugees are now taking shelter under the same roof that gave way during Katrina's calmer winds. But of course, the real threat with Hurricane Nadia is the storm surge. Nadia's eye is now passing to within one hundred miles of its projected landing at Grand Isle and has officially reached Category 5 status, with winds reaching one hundred sixty miles per hour, and storm surge expected to exceed seventeen feet. Even with the redesigned and reinforced levees, overtopping is almost certain, with the possibility of mass flooding for the streets of the Big Easy. Landfall is expected at 5:25 a.m."

I rolled my wrist and inspected my watch. It was 2:30 a.m., and I was still ninety miles north of New Orleans. With four, maybe five hours of lead time, Randy could be anywhere. He could have headed west into upstate Louisiana, there to target an inland city. He might have turned north to shelter from the hurricane altogether before penetrating south.

But no. There was nothing about this crew of wife-beating thugs that spoke of smaller targets or timid strategies. Those trucks were painted with FEMA logos because it was the best way to evade police blockades and run under cover. New Orleans was the target because New Orleans would be the most vulnerable.

Randy was dragging his disabled daughter straight into the heart of the biggest natural disaster in a lifetime.

I rammed the pedal harder into the floor and forced out another three miles per hour. The gusts of wind and rain had slackened some, indicating that an outer band of the storm had passed. Another would be coming in the near future, and then one after that, always quicker than the last until there was nothing save brutal winds and endless, pounding rain.

Seventeen feet. Nearly three times my own height, a wash of water that could consume entire buildings. I couldn't picture it. I had no frame of reference other than the fleeting images of Katrina's floodwaters that I remembered from the TV set in one of my foster parents' homes.

But that memory was enough. This was going to be cataclysmic. I needed to get Autumn out first.

I crossed the Pearl River and blazed into Louisiana just past three a.m., the state line marked by a giant blue sign that flexed in a blast of wind. A mile ahead, the highway was obscured by sideways rain, but I made out the line of state troopers parked bumper to bumper across the freeway, lights blinking, completely blocking the path south. Randy might have circumvented them with a fake FEMA ID and a truckload of water bottles, but there was no room for my captured Blazer to fit between their brush guards and the concrete barriers that ran along either edge of the highway.

I opted for the exit instead, blazing past a stack of water barrels painted in reflective tape and rushing toward a county road. Additional Louisiana cops waited at the bottom of the ramp—two of them, parked at an angle across the two-lane. I picked the gap in between and floored the accelerator as the radio crackled on about mandatory evacuations. A horn blew, and headlights flashed. The Blazer exploded through the gap and slammed into a river of runoff as I reached the bottom of the ramp. Water washed over the windshield, temporarily obscuring my view. I wrestled for control, and then I was headed for the next blockade.

Three SUVs. Blue emergency lights. A cop hurtling out of his vehicle, hand on his gun. The Blazer's radio barking on.

My foot rammed against the floor, and four tires grabbed asphalt.

I clipped the fender of one trooper as the back end of the SUV fishtailed through the gap. I thought I heard a handgun pop, but if he was aiming for my tires, he missed. The Blazer scraped through and reached a stop sign at the intersection of a two-lane parish road. I followed the arrow pointing south toward the Crescent City and hauled the wheel in that direction. Tires slid. The engine raced.

Then I was pointed southward again, blowing past another green sign:

NEW ORLEANS — 44 MILES.

Think, Mason. Where would he go?

Tangled trees lined the parish road as I continued southward, water erupting at random from flooded potholes and ruts, much of it exploding through the shattered passenger's window. I retraced the mental math that had led me out of Hattiesburg and along this hell ride into uncertainty, double-checking each assumption and frantically fighting to solve for X—where would Randy go?

If I was right about his scheme, right about the looting, right about the reason for the fake FEMA trucks, then the answer was obvious. Randy would want to get as close to the heart of the disaster as possible without actually risking his own life and limb. That would open up the greatest opportunity for him and his friends to loot freely in those most lawless moments following the passage of the storm. The FEMA logos were their passport beyond the barricades.

But where would FEMA go? There would be a staging area. I heard about it on the radio. Federal emergency response had learned their lesson following Katrina. They wouldn't be caught scrambling this time. They would gather resources at a central location near the heart of the city. Someplace high enough to remain dry, but close enough to respond quickly.

Randy would go there first. Hide among the first responders. Wait out the storm.

But where?

I fumbled with my phone, zooming out on my GPS map application. A blinking blue dot marked my location moving southward along Highway 11. Slidell lay directly ahead, a small city clustered along the northern banks of Lake Pontchartrain. Then came a pair of twin bridges cutting across the narrowest portion of the lake—I-10 on the east,

Highway 11 on the left. Both striking southwest into St. Bernard Parish.

And then New Orleans.

I tossed the phone down and thought quickly. Slidell appeared directly ahead as a cluster of boarded-up buildings and swinging traffic lights. There were no cars. No cops. No pedestrians. The city was a ghost town as I rocketed through.

How far would Randy have gone? Would he wait along the north shore, sticking to the high ground?

I passed temporary signs printed on plywood, spray-painted with FEMA logos and arrows that pointed toward the staging area I had heard about on the radio. East of Slidell, on the north shore.

I stepped on the brakes and squealed to a stop, the Blazer's overworked windshield wipers grinding helplessly against the growing flood. There were no gaps between outer bands now. It was 3:13 a.m., and Nadia was only miles away. The wind howled so hard against the sides of the little SUV that the body rocked on its suspension. I clung to the wheel and faced the intersection, with a choice to make.

Dead ahead lay New Orleans, right in the path of Nadia and all the hell she had to bring. To my right lay the FEMA staging zone. Randy and his friends could have turned that way. Even now they could be hiding among the relief workers like wolves in sheep's clothing, waiting for the storm to pass before they ravaged the fold.

But my gut told me otherwise. Call it an instinct, or logic stretched to near failure. I put myself in Randy's shoes and thought about a camp full of FEMA workers. They wouldn't just be sitting around, they would be preparing for a quick response. They would be coordinating. Randy and his chums would be hard-pressed to remain invisible.

And what was more, if they waited until the storm passed, the bridges across Lake Pontchartrain might be disabled. They might need boats, or they might not be able to cross at all.

No. These guys hadn't waited on the north shore. They had driven straight into the eye of the storm, like true fools. And so would I.

My foot slid off the brake and slammed on the accelerator. Four worn tires spun, and the Blazer hurtled forward onto the bridge.

12

Wind-torn water was already slamming against the concrete crash barriers running along either side of the bridge as I raced along it. I kept the Blazer straddled over the double yellow line, headlights turned to high, wipers turned to max. I could still barely see. The sky was pitch black, and I suddenly realized that there hadn't been a single flash of lightning. Rain blasted sideways in sheets, the wind at times striking the Blazer so hard that the tires slipped over the pavement. I wrestled it back into the safety zone in the middle of the bridge, consciously choosing to ignore the surging black water on either side.

The speedometer hovered around sixty as light appeared through my windshield. Yellow and dim, the northeastern districts of New Orleans appeared as a muddy brown line speckled by streetlamps and tall transmission lines glued into marshy soil. The Blazer hurtled off the bridge and quickly rose onto an overpass, arcing over the top of I-10 before diving back toward the shoreline. I still couldn't see the core of downtown. I was too focused on keeping the Blazer on the road to mess with my phone or use the GPS. This was all foreign country to me. I'd visited New Orleans before, but that had been via plane and taxicab. I hadn't navigated, and I hadn't explored beyond the French Quarter. What I saw now meant nothing to me. Marshlands and windswept bodies of water. Low trees and scrub brush, battered by the gusts and appearing only as shadows beneath streetlamps that bent and shuddered at the tops of high poles. I slowed a little and cranked the tuner knob on the radio, searching for a station with a clear broadcast.

Only bits and pieces came through. The first semi-clear channel I found was the emergency alert system.

"...Nadia...an extremely dangerous Category 5...super-storm. Winds...one hundred-seventy miles per hour. Now expected to reach New Orleans at five thirty a.m. central standard time. Seek immediate shelter. Seek high ground. Do not venture out—"

I cut the radio off and checked my watch. It was nearly four a.m., and I didn't need a radio broadcast to know that Nadia was close. The storm would make landfall in the next ninety minutes, and from there it was a short trip across the bayous to the Big Easy.

I needed to get Autumn out before then—long before then. But first I had to find her, and even as the marshlands faded into squat little neighborhoods with lottery billboards shuddering high above them, I realized how futile this search would be.

It was worse than a needle in a haystack. It was one kid in a city full of residents who had all hidden themselves from the wrath to come. There might be a quarter million empty structures scattered across two parishes, any one of them easily occupiable by an insane kidnapper and his disabled victim. I couldn't be expected to go door to door. I didn't have the time.

I needed a break, and I needed it soon.

Slowing the Blazer to under forty miles per hour, I leaned low under the roofline and peered through the windows. Pontchartrain Drive had become Chef Menteur Highway, a divided four-lane with homes, industrial complexes, car dealerships and shopping malls scattered along either side. *Everything* was boarded up—every window, every door. Sandbags lined driveways and encircled entire properties. Vehicles were clustered together on whatever precious high ground could be found, the roads all around me completely vacant of traffic.

A haunting plywood sign leaning against a light pole was spray-painted in dripping red. The message sent a chill down my spine.

Please, God. Not again.

I drove until I reached a bridge crossing a canal. It rose in an arc, and as I neared the top, I finally saw downtown New Orleans rising from the blackness four or five miles away. Skyscrapers dotted with yellow lights defied the blast of oncoming wind, standing like soldiers braced for a barrage of artillery fire. Grungy houses and aged hotels shuddered, and a half dozen black shingles tore free of a roof and blew across the highway.

A digital billboard, set high on a metal column a

hundred yards away, displayed white letters printed beneath a golden French fleur-de-lis.

We will prevail.

I stepped on the brakes, and the Blazer slid to a stop. Wipers beat against the windshield, and I caught my breath, only then realizing that I'd been holding it. My gaze settled on the billboard...and then it blinked. The entire city blinked, a flash of yellow flicking to black, then back to yellow.

Two seconds slipped by, and then the whole of New Orleans went dark together, the yellow dots that had highlighted the skyline evaporating into the abyss. I blinked, and it was simply gone. I couldn't see beyond the underpowered high beams of the Blazer. The city had vanished, and with it any shred of hope that I could somehow pull a rabbit—or a brilliant ten-year-old prodigy—out of a hat. Panic surged into my bloodstream as a tidal wave and the headache I thought I had defeated rushed back in. I screamed and slammed my hand against the wheel, eyes blurring, chest as tight as a drum.

What now? What now, genius?

I closed my eyes, and I saw Autumn. Not seated in her wheelchair outside the motel room but cartwheeling on her stomach down an engulfed New Orleans street, filthy floodwater surging over her lifeless body as her face was forever lost in the mire. Swept away so fast it was as though she never existed.

But she had. Her mother had. They were my friends. I'd played it safe at the trailer in the woods, slipping up slowly when I should have barreled through the back door and broken Randy in half over one knee. This was *my* fault, and the situation was now beyond my ability to correct.

My fingers tightened around the wheel. I gritted my teeth and forced the panic away from my mind. Forced my body to calm.

I focused instead on the first clear picture that came to mind—the last calm and serene moment I could remember. The cathedral in Mobile. The sculpture of Christ on a cross elevated over the pulpit. The old man seated beside me, his voice soft as he recounted Balaam and his talking donkey.

The Blazer was definitely a donkey, but it wasn't talking. I opened my eyes and swept a hand over my mouth to scrub away sweat. My foot dropped off the brake, and I rolled off the bridge and back onto the streets. Trash and debris clattered against the Blazer's body panels and tore across the street, visible for only a moment before it vanished into the dark. The wind had intensified in the precious few seconds that had elapsed since I'd entered the city. I could feel it in my bones. The storm was almost there.

Give me something. Please. Give me something.

I kept the Blazer rumbling at thirty miles an hour down the vacant highway, rolling past more homes and businesses, a Baptist seminary, and a small strip mall. Palm trees lined the median, thrashing in the growing wind and littering the street with torn leaves. On my right, a power pole bent toward the ground, lines stretched, and one suddenly popped like a gunshot, snapping back toward the road. A trash bin tumbled by. The Blazer shuddered and slid a few inches sideways.

And I still saw no sign of a child prodigy kidnapped by wife-beating thugs.

Give me something! Don't let her die.

I wasn't sure if it was a thought or a prayer. It was so spontaneous and desperate a voice in my head that I didn't fully understand it until it had already exploded through my mind and then straight out of my mouth.

"Give me something!"

The trash bin came hurtling my way again, reflected off the side of a pharmacy and now spun across slick concrete. I smashed the brakes to avoid a collision, watching as the bin lifted off the ground, lid flapping, then vanished into the darkness. My gaze followed it by default, and then, out of nowhere, a flash of vibrant blue ripped in streaks across the sky, accompanied by a blast of thunder so loud the Blazer shook. For a split second, the streets on every side were as bright as day, hot blue light saturating every storm-blown house and splintered palm tree. Every tumbling trash can and warped street sign.

And every abandoned vehicle.

I saw it from a hundred yards away. Slid sideways across a sidewalk and straight into the block wall of a gas station was a minivan. Now smashed and twisted with glass gleaming on the asphalt, the vehicle had clearly spun out of control following a collision, and I didn't have to guess what the van had collided with.

The heavy-duty pickup sat ten yards away, planted right in the middle of a lane, the front left quarter panel smashed and the front left wheel missing. The truck rested against the pavement with engine fluids swept away by the rain. The windshield was shattered. The hood buckled up and the headlight obliterated. But what caught my eye was neither the nature of the wreck nor the other vehicle involved. It wasn't even the Mississippi license plate affixed to the Ford F-250's front bumper.

It was the logo painted awkwardly along the driver's side door. Royal blue on utilitarian white.

FEMA.

13

I slammed on the gas and yanked the wheel left, cutting through the median and beelining for the wrecked pickup truck. I knew it was one of the two I'd seen at Randy's property long before I slid to a stop next to it. The Blazer's door exploded open. I barreled out and ran to the mangled front end, brushing my hand against the exterior of the engine bay as I proceeded toward the cab.

The metal was cold. The wreck had sat at least long enough for the engine heat to bleed away. I braced myself on the sideview mirror as my boots slipped over spilled oil. Then I reached for the handle and tore the door open, ready for anything, but expecting nothing.

I was right. The cab was empty of passengers, with only mud and fast-food trash littering the floor. There were no rednecks in wifebeater tank tops. No disabled girl prodigy fast asleep beneath a cloud of adult-grade sleeping pills.

I spat rain from my mouth and looked up the street as a fresh gust of wind ripped past the pharmacy and hit me like a charging bull, nearly knocking me over. The rain felt like an endless shotgun blast, pelting my skin so hard that it stung. I crawled into the pickup and tore the MacroStream from my pocket, using its illumination to search the glovebox. I found nothing save empty cigarette packets and an oily pair of pliers. The center console contained napkins and more cigarette packets. Spilled toothpicks, scratched sunglasses, and a screwdriver. Nothing of use in identifying where Randy and his crew would have gone next.

But they had been there. Not all that long ago.

I slammed the console shut and bit back a curse. The blast of the wind thundered outside the pickup, rocking it on the three remaining mud tires. I resolved to take one glance into the back and rammed my head between the front seats.

And then stopped. There was something on the floor, wadded up with a boot print across the face, but glossier than the empty McDonald's bags littered around it. Leaning low, I scooped it up and cleared spilled French fries away.

It was a road map of New Orleans, with marks made in red ink across several locations throughout the city. Circles and Xs, with a line traced along the snaking trail of the Mississippi River, leading south of the city and out to the sea.

I bit down on the MacroStream and squinted at the map, focusing on the marks. One circle, situated near the heart of town about three blocks northeast of the Superdome. Two Xs, each with a circle surrounding them. The first was scrawled half a dozen blocks due east of the Superdome, halfway to the river. The second lay north of downtown amid the Gentilly neighborhood.

What?

My focus was shattered by a sudden shudder from the pickup, harsh enough to slam my face into the seat and send the MacroStream ramming into the roof of my mouth. I choked and tore the flashlight out, looking up just in time to see a mailbox hurtling toward the pickup's back glass like a ballistic missile. Throwing both hands over my head, I bent into the seat just as the mailbox struck. Glass exploded in a thousand little cubes that mixed instantly with the beating rain and pelted my back. The mailbox reached the front seat and slammed into the dash while the truck rocked again. Outside, the wind pounded like the fist of a giant against a tin wall, so loud I couldn't hear myself think. It had doubled in strength in the time I had been inside the truck, unleashing a new terror through my mind that was more immediate than the riddle of the marked-up map. More pressing than the question of where to find Autumn.

I had to find shelter. *Immediately.* Or else I might not be alive to rescue Autumn. The clock had run out.

Nadia had arrived.

Fighting my way through the back door, I fell face-first to the asphalt as the wind struck me broadside. The map was wadded up in my right hand, but long before I could ram it into my pocket, the next blast tore it right out of my grasp and swept it into the darkness. I lay on my hands and knees next to the truck and looked back to the Blazer. It was rocking on its tires, shuddering under the fury of the growing storm. Not an ideal getaway vehicle, given the circumstances, but I was out of options. I'd waited too long.

I needed brick and mortar, *fast.*

Pocketing the MacroStream, I used the bed of the truck to haul myself back to my feet. Then I stumbled to the Blazer, nearly falling again before I got the door open. The engine was still running, and I shoved it into gear. The fuel light clicked on as I mashed the gas, ripping the wheel to the left down the first street I found. I wanted to get away from the divided four-lane—away from open ground with nothing around me to break the wrath of the wind. My new path led between boarded-up houses, but they were all one-story structures built of wood, not brick. I kept my foot on the gas, crashing through three-inch puddles as storm drains overflowed into the street. My heart pounded as I passed a stop sign just as it bent in half, folding like a plastic straw. Shingles broke free of roofs on every side and fluttered down the street, smacking the side of the Blazer. I blinked, and I was back in Afghanistan. The vehicle wasn't a Chevy, it was a Humvee. The debris peppering my doors wasn't shingles, but gunfire. The roar of wind was the fog of war. The adrenaline surging through my system replayed one thought over and over in my head in the voice of my lieutenant barking through the radio: "*Don't stop! Don't stop! Don't stop!*"

I rammed my boot onto the accelerator. Houses became a blur as the compass built into the Blazer's rearview mirror read *south*. I crossed another four-lane as the back tires slid sideways across wet pavement, the entire vehicle rocking so hard that the right-hand wheels might have left the ground. I leaned against the roll and hurtled down the next street, narrower than the first, with tall and skinny homes on either side.

Downtown, I thought. *I need to get downtown.*

There would be plenty of tall buildings there. Built of robust concrete and steel, with glass windows I could break to gain entry. In the event of a flood, I could simply ascend to a higher floor. A hotel or an office tower would suffice, but I didn't have a clue in which direction the business district lay, or how far I would need to travel. Checking my watch, I found the time at four thirty. Nadia would make official landfall in the next hour. I didn't know how fast the storm was traveling, but I knew it was headed my way, and I could only assume the devastation would get worse.

Much worse. I might not have time to make it to downtown. I might—

My thoughts were cut short by an earsplitting crackling sound ripping down the street from directly ahead. I instinctively put my foot on the brake pedal, and not a moment too soon. Just as the Blazer slowed, half of a giant oak tree split away from itself and crashed toward the ground, slamming into the blacktop only yards ahead of my front bumper. The Blazer slid, and I turned automatically to my left. It was the only direction open to me. I rocketed down another residential street, wider than the one I'd left. The wind was striking me from behind now, still so strong that the Blazer shuddered. I passed a house just as an entire section of its roof ripped free of its rafters and exploded into the air.

I couldn't see more than twenty yards. I couldn't see behind me. It was like being lost inside the core of a tornado, only this tornado was large enough to engulf an entire city.

By the time I saw the bridge, it was almost too late to yank the wheel left and avoid impaling myself on the business end of a guardrail. Industrial metal mesh vibrated beneath my tires as I zipped over a canal. The water beneath was torn and muddy, already crashing against the protective sides of levees built on either bank. I blinked, and it was gone. I was back on a city street, still headed east. My headlights bounced along with the Blazer, and when they flicked upward, I saw a refrigerator lying directly ahead, squarely in the middle of my path.

I turned the Blazer, swerving hard right. The wind caught my rear bumper again as brakes locked, tires screamed, and I hurtled onward toward the fridge. I might have rolled even without the help of one-hundred-plus-mile-per-hour winds barreling against me from the side, but with them, there was no avoiding it. I turned, the Blazer's tires snagged, the wind swept beneath me, and then I was rolling.

I hadn't buckled my seat belt when I climbed back in after investigating the truck. I left the seat now, bending over and striking the ceiling with the back of my head. The Blazer crashed sideways into the pavement, and glass exploded. Then it tumbled again, landing on its roof and sliding. The windshield shattered, and I also landed on the roof, slamming my hip into torn headliner and striking the door with my back. Cubes of glass pressed into my jeans, and the SUV continued to slide, not stopping until it struck the fridge.

That was enough to halt forward progress. I choked and groaned, shaking my head to clear it while Nadia's incessant howl persisted from just outside. I fought to find the latch on the door, but couldn't reach it beneath my hip. The Blazer shuddered again and started to rotate around the end of the fridge.

I imagined what would happen if the next blast of hurricane wind was sufficient to move both items. I might not stop until I was in the river.

"You alive?"

The voice barked at me from someplace beyond the gale, so distant I thought I had imagined it. I rolled onto my knees, spitting blood that had run from my aggravated nose. Glass crunched beneath my knees, and again I looked for the door latch.

It didn't matter. The roof had bent downward, folding against the top of the doorframe. That door wasn't opening. I rotated toward the windshield instead, squinting as a sudden blast of light ripped through the darkness and landed on my face.

"Hey!" somebody shouted. "Can you move?"

I held up a hand to block the glare and nodded. Arms reached through the windshield. Hands wrapped around my elbows and tugged. I followed without objection, sliding through the shattered windshield and tearing my stomach on a shard of glass. I bit back a cry as I landed in a two-inch river surging along the street and erupting over sidewalks.

The firm hands returned to my shoulders.

"On your feet! This way!"

I fought to get up. The next wind gust was so strong that I danced sideways, catching myself against the upturned bumper of the Blazer. I turned my head away from a hail of bullet rain and found a short, stocky old-timer standing next to me. Maybe seventy years old, with wispy white hair now soaked by the rain. He jerked his head toward a house, and I followed.

We made it across the sidewalk and up a sodden embankment of slick grass before reaching the porch, catching each other from time to time as we clambered up. Fragments of shingles blasted my legs, and another mailbox spun down the street like a boomerang. The old-timer ripped a screen door open and pounded with a fist. A lock slid, and the primary door swung open.

We both crashed inside, landing on hardwood. The door shut behind us with a slam. I coughed up blood and rain-water and made no effort to get up.

I was vaguely conscious of dim flashlights playing across the floor. There were other people in the room, and I smelled hot coffee.

The old-timer hauled himself up with a groan, squeezing my shoulder gently.

"You all right, big fella?"

I rocked my head, staring up his saturated pants into a soaked face. He looked weathered. Beaten.

But rock steady.

I nodded once and pushed myself into a seated position, groaning as my back settled against the wall. Blood ran from my nose, leaking out of the overwhelmed gauze now falling out of my nostrils. I used the back of my hand to wipe it away, listening to the beat of the wind.

It only grew louder.

"Where am I?" I said at last.

When I looked up, the old man stood with his arms crossed. He shook his head. "You're in the butthole of the city, son. You're in the Lower Ninth Ward."

14

The old-timer said it as though the name was one I should recognize, but I was so disoriented by my brush with hurricane death that I could barely remember my own name let alone that of a neighborhood in a city I knew almost nothing about. I slumped against the wall and gasped, finally taking a moment to survey my surroundings.

And then I froze. The living space of the house was small, with deep blue carpet and walls hung with photographs, many of which were washed out and faded by time. There was a couch, two chairs, and a bookshelf laden with hardbacks. An open doorway into a kitchen with basic white appliances set on a tiled yellow floor. Metal table, metal chairs. All very bare and simplistic, as though a man had selected them.

But what caught my attention wasn't the rudimentary styling, it was the occupants. No less than fifteen people were jammed into the living room and kitchen, all staring at me through wide and unblinking eyes. Most were black, and several sat in wheelchairs. None were younger than sixty, and most must have been knocking on eighty. One old woman on the couch gasped as she breathed through an oxygen tube. A stooped black man with an eye patch wore a Korean War Veterans hat as he sipped coffee with a trembling hand.

Nobody spoke.

I looked back to the old-timer who had hauled me out of the street, brushing my bleeding nose with the back of one hand again. It burned like hell. He produced a handkerchief from his pocket and handed it over. I used it to stem the flow.

"Name's Frank Miller," the old-timer said, his voice a swampy drawl. "Welcome to Claiborne Avenue. And you are?"

I lowered the handkerchief and swallowed blood. My throat was swollen, as though somebody had karate chopped me in the windpipe. Maybe I had Yellow Teeth to thank for that.

"Mason Sharpe," I said. "Thanks for dragging me out of the street."

Frank grunted. "I heard you crash. Something told me I should investigate. Glad that I did. You want some coffee?"

Hot coffee didn't sound like the kind of thing that would soothe my throat, but caffeine might help to clear away the brain fog I'd been fighting ever since resuming consciousness in Hattiesburg. I nodded once, and as if on cue, a thunderclap of snapping wind rammed against the sides of the house. Walls shook, and the floor trembled beneath me. One of the old women gasped. Another began to sob. I noticed the Korean vet's coffee mug trembling worse than before.

Frank extended a hand, remaining perfectly calm. "Don't

worry, everybody. This place is solid as rock. Ain't nothin' Nadia can throw at 'er."

I took his hand, and he hauled me up with surprising strength. I swayed on my feet as he led the way between parked wheelchairs, limping a little on his right leg, but taking time to pat shoulders and offer smiles along the way. We reached the kitchen, where the source of the hot coffee and what little light permeated the home sat beneath the little metal table—a giant backup battery hooked to a warming plate and a pair of lamps. Frank poured coffee into a battered mug with a New Orleans Police Department logo printed on one side. He didn't offer cream or sugar. I didn't ask for any.

We stood in silence while I sipped coffee and surveyed the room. The pictures I'd seen in the living room carried into the little dining room, arranged over floral wallpaper. I saw Frank in several of them, usually as a much younger man. He stood on a fishing boat, cradling a bull redfish with a cigar hanging out of one corner of his mouth. There was a girl with him, maybe fifteen years old. She looked a little like him and appeared in several other photographs alongside a woman, for a time. And then it was just the two of them, sometimes at a theme park, sometimes at a restaurant or a softball game. The girl was pretty. The dates on the photographs ranged from the late eighties through the mid two thousands.

All the pictures crinkled and faded, the color running from their edges. It was water damage, and it reminded me of Mia's Bible.

Frank caught me staring and approached the wall, cradling a coffee cup himself. The house trembled under another punishing surge of wind, but Frank didn't so much as blink. He gestured with the cup toward the picture of him and the girl on the boat.

"My daughter, Sylvia. She just turned forty. Lives with her husband up in Dallas. Has a couple of kids. Real smart little squirts, top of their classes."

"You must be proud," I said.

He didn't say anything, but he didn't have to. His aged face beamed, and I couldn't help but wonder: *If she's in Dallas, why are you here?*

Frank must have sensed the question. He lowered his voice. "You live in New Orleans?"

"No." I shook my head.

"Well, you picked a heck of a time to visit. This 'uns gonna be ugly."

"Has it made landfall yet?"

"She's about to. Headed for Grand Isle first, moving north at about ten miles an hour."

"That's slow."

"Real slow. Which is real bad. Luckily for you, you're in the only house in the Lower Ninth that's likely to be standing come sunrise. I learned my lesson after Katrina. This thing's built like a tank."

He patted the wall with a confident nod, and I wasn't sure if I should congratulate him on his forethought or question his insanity for being here at all during a storm. One glance around the living room full of quaking old people, and I thought I understood.

"They won't leave?" I asked.

"Nope. Some never do. They put a lot of 'em in the Superdome, but it got ugly in there last time around. Scared the old folks. I built this place up pretty good. We'll make it."

As if Nadia had interpreted his statement as a challenge,

the next burst of hurricane wrath slammed broadside into the old home, so hard and sudden that the glass in the windows rattled even behind the thick sheets of plywood that covered them. A shrieking, ripping sound tore through the air like a goat being gutted. Something harder than wind struck the house and ripped across the front porch, screeching on down the street.

More gasps from the living room were joined by a "Dear Lawd" from one of the older women. Frank simply sucked his teeth.

"Roofing metal," he said. "There'll be a lot of that."

My eyes drifted toward the ceiling, where sheetrock trembled, little bits of it flaking off and raining across the floor. Picture frames on the wall shifted, and Frank set his coffee down, slowly removing the frames and stacking them on the floor. I helped, moving past more photos of the daughter who had moved away, and the wife whom I assumed to have died, until I stopped over a photograph of four men standing in front of a scene of absolute carnage— tangled power lines, flattened homes. Splintered two-by-fours and shredded trees.

And water. A lot of water. Reaching up to their thighs as the men stood in waders with gold emblems embroidered on their chests. I recognized the symbol—it was the same logo as was printed on my coffee cup. The New Orleans Police Department. One of the men was Frank.

"You're a cop?" I asked.

"Was. Forty-two years in the NOPD. Retired now."

I nodded. "Me too. Phoenix. Homicide."

A glint of respect reached his tired eyes. I squinted at the picture. Something about the backdrop was familiar despite the carnage. There was a brick porch painted in dull green.

The house behind it was heavily damaged, with a dirty brown line left near the eaves, where the floodwaters had topped out. Street numbers on the wall were crooked. Two feet of water still flooded the yard.

But I'd seen the house before. No—I hadn't just seen it. I was *standing* in it. It was Frank's place. The street was Claiborne Avenue, in the Lower Ninth Ward. And then I remembered why the neighborhood sounded so familiar. Why I thought I should recognize the place when Frank called it the butthole of the city.

"This place flooded," I said, my gaze snapping toward him. "The entire neighborhood was submerged. I remember hearing about it after Katrina. This was the worst part of the city."

Frank didn't so much as blink. He simply stood with a pair of photographs held under one arm as Nadia's next gust sent another earthquake shiver through the home. When the noise finally subsided, he nodded once. "That's right."

I looked to the old people huddled in the living room. Many of them infirm, none of them very strong or healthy looking. None capable of looking after themselves.

The house was a one story. The geography of the place hadn't changed. I wasn't standing in a refuge, I was standing in a deathtrap.

"What if it floods again?" I said.

"The Corps of Engineers rebuilt the levees. They'll hold."

"And overtopping?" I asked. "The storm surge is seventeen feet."

Long pause. I met his gaze. Frank still hadn't blinked.

"They'll hold."

Hurricane Nadia reached the Crescent City just before six a.m., and I didn't need Frank's battery-powered weather radio to tell me so. The ravage of roof-ripping winds from an hour previously now felt like exploratory jabs as the knockout punches arrived.

It was unlike anything I'd experienced anywhere in the world. The noise was so loud and so constant that it was impossible to speak in anything less than a shout. Frank's house vibrated in a perpetual creaking hum as shrieks of ripping roof metal and the splintering crack of house timbers echoed down the street. Rain pounded against the plywood-covered windows, and glass rattled so hard that some of it cracked. Water blew in beneath the rubber seal of the front door, and Frank and I wadded up towels to block it.

The refugees gathered in the living room made no sound. No screams. No cries. They simply sat in trembling silence, some with heads bowed, others fixating on spots on the walls or floor, breathing like winded horses, clutching blankets and pillows despite the heat. All the hallmarks of

PTSD were there. It felt like a treatment ward in the psych wing of a VA hospital, sending pangs of empathy ripping through my gut.

I knew what it was like to be blanketed by emotions you couldn't control. To be swarmed by grief. Fear. Uncertainty. They are the rawest and most unrelenting of all human emotions, and I'd made close friends with each of them over the past eighteen months. Standing there in Frank's battered home, thoughts of Autumn only added to my mental strain, leaving me to desperately hope that Randy had enough rudimentary intelligence to find suitable shelter for his daughter, even if he'd been the idiot who dragged her here in the first place.

Her security was completely out of my hands now. The only thing I could do was what I'd always done in a time of crisis—drown the anxiety in a deluge of action, and there was no shortage of action needed on Claiborne Avenue. Even as Frank's rebuilt and reinforced house withstood minute after agonizing minute of Nadia's one-hundred-sixty-plus-mile-per-hour gusts, I braced myself against the kitchen counter and listened to the weather reports, waiting for the inevitable.

Updates on the storm surge.

"Hurricane Nadia's eyewall is expected to pass four miles west of downtown New Orleans within the next twenty-five minutes," the robotic voice croaked. "The storm is currently proceeding north-northwest at a speed of eleven miles per hour, with wind gusts exceeding one hundred and sixty-five miles per hour. Storm surge of fourteen to seventeen feet is now landing along Lafourche, Jefferson, Plaquemines, Saint Bernard, and Orleans Parishes. Levees are holding strong, but overtopping is expected in low-lying regions along the

Mississippi River and the Intercoastal Waterway. As the storm passes, do not leave your shelter until granted permission to do so by authorities. Do not venture into flooded areas. Live power lines may be down, presenting risk of electrocution. Do not drink from standard water supply lines. Do not—"

The voice faded out as I directed my attention back to the front door. Something heavy and hard had just slammed into the porch, sending an earthquake shiver through the entire house. Frank ran that way and pressed his eye against the peephole. I knew he couldn't see anything in the dark. He grunted in reassurance anyway.

"Just a stove. Looks like somebody's getting a replacement!"

It might have been a joke, but nobody laughed. I walked to the door, knowing that the slam was far too hefty to have come from a kitchen appliance. More likely it had been a vehicle, but the nature of the sudden shudder was indicative of a sliding, spinning trajectory. The winds might be strong enough for that.

Or...

I pressed my ear against the door, and I thought I heard a sloshing sound beyond the heavy wood. I looked down and stepped on the towel we had wadded up at the bottom of the doorjamb. It squished, and muddy water streamed out. I looked to Frank.

He shook his head once. I remembered the height of the front porch in the photo. It had been eighteen inches, maybe two feet. Had that much water already surged onto Claiborne Avenue? Was there *that* much overtopping of the levees? Nadia's eyewall was still south of the city.

Adrenaline raced through my veins. Frank tilted his

head, and I followed him into the kitchen. He produced a city map from a drawer and spread it across the table beneath the light of the battery-powered lamps. I could tell by the creases and stains that the map was old. It was stamped with the same NOPD logo I'd seen on the coffee cup.

Frank tapped a portion of the city east of downtown, with the Mississippi River running beneath it, a wide canal to its left, and marshlands to the north. It was marked *Lower Ninth Ward.*

"The levees are likely overtopping here, along the Inner Harbor Navigation Channel. That's where it happened before."

"And they failed?" I asked. I didn't bother to hide the tension in my voice. The concern I felt wasn't for my sake so much as for those of the elders behind me. I could break through a window or climb into the attic. I could saw through the roof with the toothy blade of my Victorinox if need be.

But I was young and strong. My fellow refugees were not.

Frank nodded once in answer to my question. "The levee was breached just south of Florida Avenue. The storm surge moves north and west due to the counterclockwise rotation of the hurricane. Water moves across Lake Borgne, up the Intercoastal Waterway, and into the canals."

Frank traced the path with one finger, his voice matter of fact, the calm tone of a veteran police officer who had weathered all kinds of storms. But I could also detect a growing edge. An undercurrent of doubt.

He could build his house to withstand the winds, but if the levees failed a second time...

"You have a way into the attic?" I asked.

Frank's gaze flicked toward a hallway with bedroom doors lining each side.

"It's a ladder. Most of them can't climb."

I looked into the living room, mentally gauging each person's body mass. There was nobody I couldn't lift, even in my battered condition.

"What about the roof?"

"I put an ax in the attic. Just in case."

So he has thought ahead.

"We need eyeballs on the floodwaters," I said. "If they overtop the levees and reach your doors, you won't have minutes. You'll have seconds."

Frank grunted. "I've been through this before, remember?"

"So what's the plan?"

Frank's dark eyes swept the room full of sheltering elders, some of the women beginning to sob as they fixated on a growing pool of water seeping from beneath the front door. Between gusts of wind, I could hear the sloshing all the way from the kitchen. Levees or no levees, the bathtub that was the Lower Ninth Ward was about to flood.

"You got a death wish, Sharpe?" Frank asked.

"Most days."

He jabbed a thumb at the hallway. "Follow me."

16

F rank hauled the attic door down with a groan of popping springs. The moment he did, I could hear Nadia beating on the roof like a coked-up drummer. Small objects pelted it while the incessant wrath of the wind sent creaking shivers shooting down the rafters. Fishing for my MacroStream, I shot five hundred lumens of white-hot light into the attic, only to expose streams of water running from cracks in the roofing plywood where the shingles had been ripped away.

Nadia was coming inside—one way or the other.

"There's an attic vent just over the front porch," Frank said. "I boarded it up from the inside. Hammer is on the floor. You should be able to see the street from there."

I reached for the ladder. Frank put a hand on my arm.

"Mason."

"What?"

"Be careful."

The gravity in his gaze spoke to experiences past—a

dance with a different hurricane in years gone by. I nodded once, then started up the ladder.

Frank turned back down the hall and called cheerfully into the living room, "Who wants more coffee?"

The ladder groaned under my muddy boots. Every part of me hurt as I hauled myself through the gap and landed on a ceiling joist, shining light across the interior of the attic. There was a small platform stacked with cardboard boxes, surrounded by a field of insulation. Water ran from multiple gaps in the damaged roof, seeping into the insulation and pooling on the platform. The joist beneath my butt vibrated, and I swung my legs into the attic. Walking one foot in front of the other, I used the overhead rafters for bracing as I swept the light toward the front of the house.

The roof vent wasn't difficult to find. It was a decorative thing, octagonal in shape and not more than twelve inches across. Frank had covered the interior with three-quarter-inch plywood, held in place by framing nails. The hammer lay atop the insulation beneath it.

Twisting left, I nearly fell as the next gust shook the house as though it were made of twigs. Wood groaned and splintered overhead, shingles popping free like small-caliber gunshots. Gasps and cries echoed from the living room below. Frank calmed them with a soft laugh and a reassuring word. I steadied myself and moved to the vent.

The nails were pounded in deep. I placed the claw of the hammer beneath the edge of the plywood and shifted my bodyweight against it, pain lancing through my bruised rib cage. The headache was back in earnest, thundering in my skull. I forced thoughts of the pain away and closed my eyes, wrenching until a nail pulled gradually free. A one-inch gap opened behind the plywood, and damp wind howled inside with a roar. The little wooden slats of the vent were long since shattered, and rain sprayed across my face. I moved the hammer to the top of the plywood and pried again.

Once the top was free, I dropped the hammer and used my fingers, converting the plywood into its own lever. The nails tore free, and I fell backward as a punching blast of hurricane wrath finished the job. The attic erupted with a thunderous roar, and I scrambled to pull myself out of the insulation. Beneath me, the drywall ceiling sagged and threatened to give way. I shifted my weight back to the ceiling joists and fought my way to the window vent. Jagged shards of the wooden slats stuck out from the edges of the octagonal hole, the abyss beyond nothing but a pit of blackness. The flashlight clicked on, and I swept it toward the street. The beam cut through the darkness, spilling into Frank's front yard.

Or what had *been* a front yard. Now it was a lake. Claiborne Avenue was gone. The upturned Chevy Blazer was gone. Sidewalks and front porches were immersed in water now three or more feet deep. I couldn't see Frank's front door due to the roof over his porch, but I knew the waterline would have exceeded the bottom of the doorframe and could even now be rising toward the knob. The door would hold...for now.

But there were windows in the living room. Boarded up or otherwise, they could easily be a point of failure. If any part of the house ruptured, every room would flood within seconds.

And the water was *still* rising.

I retreated from the roof vent and scrambled back toward the ladder, knees banging against the rafters. Frank stood waiting for me on ground level, a single question on his face.

"We gotta move," I said. "*Now.*"

Frank turned calmly to the crowd of shaken refugees as I reached the end of the hallway. He kept his voice casual amid the continued howl of the storm.

"Looks like we're headed upstairs! Let's everybody remain calm. Mr. Sharpe and I will assist you, one at a time. If you can walk, go ahead and line up in the hallway."

The wash of panic was instantaneous, but Frank's practiced sense of calm and control paid off. Nobody freaked. A few of those who could stand on their own hobbled up and began to shuffle toward the hall.

Frank pushed a wheelchair, limping a little on his right leg again. He spoke under his breath as he passed me. "Can you work the ladder? I'm not the man I used to be."

I hurried back to the base of the attic ladder. Above me, the sound of the wind had intensified into a perfect squall of constant, relentless pounding. Almost all the shingles were gone, and rain streamed from multiple gaps in the roof.

But Frank's rebuilt home stood strong, defying Nadia for a little longer.

"One at a time," I said, stopping halfway up the ladder and offering my hand. "If you can't climb, I'll carry you up."

A little old lady in a faded floral dress was the first to take my hand. Her eyes were rich brown, her smile filled with gaps and a little forced. But still brave.

"Thank you, son."

I hauled upward. She struggled with each step. It took the better part of two minutes to get her to the top, where I lifted her little body and set it on the plywood platform. Then I was shuffling down again, fourteen to go.

As I reached the midpoint of the steps, the house convulsed with a frame-shaking shudder, and somebody in the living room screamed. A gurgling, sloshing sound joined the voice, and the water puddle that had been building slowly in front of the door suddenly surged into view at the end of the hallway.

"Frank?" I called.

"We got a breach!" Frank said. "It's coming in through the letter box."

I remembered the brass letter box built into the door. It was at doorknob height, fully two feet off the porch. And the porch itself was nearly two feet off the street.

"Up you go," I said, mimicking Frank's calm as I assisted the next old woman in line. She was heavier than the first and not as strong. I needed to hoist her with one arm beneath her hips, hauling myself up the ladder with my other. I passed a little orange sticker that warned of a two-hundred-fifty-pound weight limit, and my stomach tightened.

No point in worrying about that.

We reached the attic, and the woman I'd left on the platform was waiting to help her friend up.

"If you let me up the ladder, I can help them climb." It was the Korean vet with the eye patch. I moved aside, and the old man shimmied up with forced alacrity, gritting his teeth to bite back grunts. He slid through the door, and I twisted on the carpet for the next in line.

My boots squished as I moved. The sound of surging water from the living room was constant, like a bucket being emptied over the hardwood, except the bucket never ran dry. The next in line sat in a wheelchair, a frail woman with skinny arms that trembled as she reached for me. Abject fear flooded her ebony face. I smiled and lifted her up as gently as I could.

"Easy does it, ma'am. We're all gonna be okay."

The Korean vet hoisted her the rest of the way. I was already turning for the next person as Frank pushed the last wheelchair into the hallway. The crowd smelled of body odor and sweat, a murmur of fear escaping somebody's lips as she prayed.

"Lawd, have mercy on us!"

"Let's move, Sharpe!" Frank called.

He didn't have to tell me. Three inches of water had gathered in the hallway. I sloshed by up the ladder, heaving one person after the other onto my shoulders and lifting them until they could climb into the attic. I wasn't trying to be gentle any longer. I couldn't afford to be. Overhead, the Korean vet heaved and gasped, and heavy thuds shook the ceiling every time somebody landed. The thunder of the wind had reached a fever pitch, and dark spots covered the ceiling where streams of water from the compromised roof had saturated the insulation and was now dripping into the flooded floor below.

And still six more refugees remained, plus myself and Frank. When I dropped off the ladder for my next trip, the water reached halfway up my shins. I was out of breath, head spinning as I caught myself against the wall. I turned for the next in line, the trembling woman with the little oxygen bottle held close to her chest in a sling bag.

"Come along, ma'am. I got you."

I reached for her. She stumbled forward. Black water surged around our legs and nearly swept her over. I caught her arm and twisted for the ladder.

Then I heard it. A creaking, groaning sound. Splintering wood. A pop of a deadbolt bursting free of the doorframe.

And a shout from Frank, panic finally breaching his forced calm.

"Sharpe! *Move!*"

17

The deluge was instant. As the front door gave way under the crush of gathering water, a tidal wave of black immersed the living room and crashed down the hallway. Frank threw himself around the corner just in time to avoid being swept under, but one of the older men remaining in line wasn't so lucky. He lost his footing and flipped backward as the wave hit him. I caught his arm as he passed the ladder, hauling him upright with a jerk that might have dislocated his shoulder. I couldn't afford to worry. The Korean vet reached down, and I placed my shoulder beneath the old lady's hip, powering upward. Her oxygen bottle collided with the edge of the attic opening, and she grunted. Then the Korean vet caught her, and she disappeared above.

The waterline in the hallway had reached chest level now. The four remaining refugees, including the fellow who was nearly swept away, now all clung madly to the ladder as the water crashed against drywall and rammed against their bodies.

Frank braced himself against the wall behind them, resuming his calm as he called toward me, "Keep it moving, now."

Once more, I didn't need to be told. The open door had paved a highway for Nadia's storm surge to occupy the house. Whether the levee had failed or this was simply a matter of overtopping, it didn't even matter. Within minutes the house would be flooded up to the ceiling.

I could only hope the flooding would stop there.

"Up you go, now!" I forced another smile as I powered the next refugee up the ladder. There was no need to descend to the carpet anymore. The two women and one man who remained in line all clung to the ladder, floating halfway up it as the water level reached to within two feet of the ceiling. I look back to see Frank clinging to the top of a bedroom doorframe, kicking his feet to bolster his stability. His gray hair was soaked and plastered to his head, his mouth hanging open as he gasped for air.

"Hold on, Frank! I'm coming."

The next woman went up. She had been in a wheelchair before, now abandoned someplace beneath the surface. Her legs were helpless. I placed her on my shoulders and heaved. The exhausted Korean vet at the top of the stairs fought to grab her, leaning low over the opening. His knees slipped off the rafter and plummeted into the sodden ceiling. Drywall burst, and he sank right through, up to his hip, as an agonized cry erupted from his mouth. I gritted my teeth and shoved the woman up, my own head and shoulders penetrating the attic opening even as the water rose to within a foot of the ceiling.

"You gotta move!" I called.

He trembled, his lone good eye flooding with agonized

tears as I wrapped my arms around his stomach and heaved. His knee broke free of the ceiling, revealing the sloshing surface of murky water below. He fell backward, and I turned immediately for the last two.

As I dragged the first through the attic door, the worn and overworked ladder step beneath my left boot finally gave way. I crashed downward and caught myself on a ceiling joist. The water engulfing my lower body was now only six or fewer inches from the ceiling. I couldn't see Frank. I couldn't hear anything other than the beat of the wind and the crash of the water.

The last refugee choked with his face pressed close to the ceiling, two feeble hands clutching the ladder. I caught him just as he let go, descending into the depths. His body was limp as it passed into the attic, mouth hanging open. Maybe he was already dead. I left him in the care of the others and turned back toward the hallway.

The water sloshed all the way to the ceiling, a black abyss that flooded the entire lower story of the house. Frank was nowhere in sight.

"Frank!" I shouted.

No answer.

"Get away from the opening," I called. "I'll be back!"

Then I sucked down a chest full of damp air and plunged into the black. Oily water closed over my head, and I dove into the hallway, kicking away from the ladder. I turned for the living room first, fighting upstream of a surge so putrid that I couldn't see my hand in front of my face. It was pitch black and swarming with debris. My leg brushed sodden drywall, and my hand touched something furry and limp. A dead animal, spinning down the hallway next to my arm.

I was out of breath. My heart thundered, and my brain

screamed for me to inhale. I fought back the urge and reached the living room. The ceiling was no higher here, and I knew that if I ventured much farther into the open spaces of the house, I would quickly lose my way back to the attic. The narrow walls were my only guide.

I thought quickly, estimating the pressure of the crushing water against a weakening body, and remembered Frank clinging to the doorframe of a bedroom. He wouldn't have swum upstream back into the living room. No, he'd been crushed into that bedroom. I'd already passed him.

I spun in the water and launched out, kicking with both legs and scraping along the wall. My head thundered, my chest so tight it felt ready to explode. My fingers reached the molding of a doorframe, and I lunged through it, fully aware that if I'd picked the wrong room, I'd run out of air long before I could search for another.

The space was completely engulfed. I rose instinctively toward the ceiling and touched saturated drywall. My throat constricted and my chest convulsed as my body demanded a breath. There was nothing to breathe. The room was totally flooded, and as I thrashed in the emptiness, my arms collided with drifting pieces of clothing, small furniture floating aimlessly against the walls, and personal items caught in the deluge.

I was done. I couldn't hold on any longer. Each beat of my heart felt a little slower than the last. Even though my eyes were pinched closed, it felt as though my vision was tunneling. I was almost finished.

And then I touched an arm. Encased in saturated fabric, but too firm to be empty clothing, and too soft to be furniture. I wrapped one hand around it and the other around the top of the doorframe. I yanked backwards, kicking through the door and back into the hallway. My body began to shut down as I turned for the ladder. Muscles weakened, and thoughts grew fuzzy. I tugged on the arm, and Frank followed me. My foot found a wooden step and slipped off. I flailed.

And then I dug deep, way down into the basement of a battered and bruised soul that always felt empty but had never failed to give a little more. I sank my fingers into Frank's arm and found the ladder again. I shoved down with my boot and powered upward.

I broke into the attic like a submarine conducting an emergency surface maneuver, sucking down air even before I knew I was free of the depths. I choked and spluttered and flailed. Another step gave way beneath my boot, and I began to fall.

Then hands closed around my arms and shoulders—not strong hands, but a lot of them. Aged muscles tensed and dragged me upward. I found another step and launched up, dragging Frank with me. His shoulder caught on the attic entrance, and the refugees hurried to pull him free. We spilled onto ceiling joists that were already swimming beneath three inches of water. I gasped and shook, my body alive with the convulsions of near death. I blinked away the grit and landed on my back, staring up at a ceiling running with *more* water.

Frank's body lay motionless next to me, a murmur of panicked voices rising above Nadia's incessant roar. I dug back into that bottomless soul and forced myself up. Already the storage platform we rested on swam under several inches of water. Frank's ghostly pale face hovered just above the surface as he rested on the plywood.

"Stand back!" I choked. The refugees gave me room. I hit

my knees. Hands crossed over Frank's stomach, I counted and pressed. Counted and pressed. His body jerked, and a little water dripped from his lips. I pinched his nose and forced air into his lungs. Counted and pressed. Forced air again.

The murmur around me grew perfectly silent as rain sprayed over my back and the physical panic I'd experienced only moments prior was replaced by a somehow more horrible mental anguish.

"Come on, you old swamp dog! *Breathe!*"

Frank might have heard me. He might have been insulted. Or maybe the last press of my hands against his chest was just the magical number required to restart his dying heart. His eyes flickered opened, and he choked, water exploding from his mouth. I kept pumping, and his hands smacked the water. The Korean vet lifted his head out of the water, and I collapsed against the platform, heaving like an overworked mule.

Frank sat up, still choking. Still gasping for air. He puked up more sordid water and sank his fingers into any hand that would support him. A joyous cheer rang through the tired crowd, and one of the old women turned her face toward the roof, tears in her eyes.

"Thank you, Jesus!"

Frank's gaze met mine, and a dull smile crossed his filthy face. I returned it. Then Frank's smile melted, his attention passing over my shoulder. I followed his line of sight to the attic opening, and my blood ran cold.

Water was surging in. Already a foot of it had filled the attic, and I could actually see the current pumping upward through the attic opening to fill our refuge of last resort.

"Give me the ax," I said, clawing my way to my feet. The

Korean vet scrambled for the tool. I caught the handle and turned immediately for the octagonal hole of the roof vent. My exhausted muscles sagged as I sloshed along the rafters. My head went light, and my knees locked.

I spat water. Nadia bellowed.

And I swung.

18

Frank hadn't exaggerated about the reinforcements he'd made to his home. The shingles were almost all stripped away, but he'd bolstered the sub-roofing with thick, heavy-duty plywood. Screwed in, not nailed. Years of baking beneath the Louisiana sun had steamed out any moisture and left that plywood bone-dry and rock hard.

To make matters worse, the angle of the roof prevented me from swinging overhand. I had to swing sideways, cutting my leverage in half and forcing me to use muscle instead of momentum. The blade chipped quickly through the frame of the roof vent, but as soon as I hit the plywood, progress slowed to a crawl.

And it wasn't just the plywood. I would need to cut through at least one rafter to create a gap wide enough for a human to slip through. Those thick two-by-six boards were every bit as dry and hard as the plywood, and just as difficult to strike directly. There was nothing for me to do save ignore the pain racing through my body and keep swinging long after my brain told me I was finished. With each blow, I heard my old Army drill sergeant chanting a push-up cadence in my head.

"*One for the Army!*"

"One for the Army!" I repeated the chant as I swung. Heavy steel bit into pine, raining chips and splinters over the water washing against my legs. Sergeant Patrick Smiles called the next cadence in his booming Georgian drawl as I readied the ax for the next swing.

"*One for the nation!*"

"One for the nation!"

A chunk of plywood broke free. Empty blackness opened beyond, streaming with rain.

"*One cuz you're a fat slob!*"

"One cuz I'm a fat slob!"

"*One cuz you're too skinny!*"

"One cuz I'm too skinny!"

I was in a rhythm now, moving like a machine. I didn't feel the pain anymore. I didn't recognize the exhaustion or the pressure building in my skull to explosive levels. Just like it had all those years ago back at Fort Benning, the pain receded into a cage of sheer willpower, and the strength of a hundred voices chanting alongside me powered me into the next blow...and the next and the next.

Those voices were all in my mind. The men who had lined up alongside me on the parade ground at Benning were just ghosts. But they were there, and the roof was no match for the grit Sergeant Smiles had ingrained in me. Wood shattered, and plywood evaporated. The rafter was gone. The hole was three feet across inside of ten minutes. I didn't lower the ax until I felt a hand on my arm and looked to see Frank shaking me.

"That's enough!"

The ax dropped out of my hands and plunged into the water. It was up to my waist, almost to the bottom of the hole. Outside, the perfect darkness that had enveloped the city when I first took refuge with Frank had weakened to a soft gray. My watch read seven fifteen, and the winds outside had calmed a little, still blowing hard enough to sweep shingles and small debris across an expanse of black water outside, but no longer hard enough to shake the house.

"We gotta get them outside!" Frank choked.

I nodded, and the routine we'd begun at the bottom of the ladder resumed. Frank and the Korean vet ventured out onto the gently sloping roof, both looking ready to collapse into total exhaustion, but not yet giving up. Soldiers themselves, with a cadence of their own.

I lifted the first old lady through. It was the one with the gap-toothed smile, and despite her saturated clothes and trembling body, she still smiled at me as I passed her through. One after another, the refugees lined up along the ceiling joists, using the overhead rafters for support as I helped them onto the roof. Frank and his friend guided them to the apex, where the ridgeline offered them something to cling on to, and there they lay down on their stomachs and pressed their faces into the rough plywood still studded with shingle nails.

The hole I'd bashed through the roof was already semi-submerged as I passed the last of them through, then scrambled onto the roof myself. Shingle nails bit into my chest as I collapsed, face-first along the ridgeline. Nadia's diminishing winds ripped at my shirt and tore at my hair, flooding my ears with an incessant howl as I heaved for oxygen, muscles cramping from head to toe.

I didn't care. I barely even noticed. I simply closed my eyes, ignored the rain still washing across my back, and descended into unconsciousness.

19

The heat woke me. Bearing down on my back in suffocating, scalding waves. My eyes flickered open, and I saw damp wood and torn shingles. They glared in my face, reflecting bright yellow sunlight that blazed down from someplace overhead.

My eyes burned, crusted with dried sweat and dust. I swallowed past a swollen throat and lifted my face.

A gentle hand rested on my shoulder, squeezing once. "Easy goes it, Sharpe."

I recognized Frank's voice, and I twisted my head in his direction. The retired cop leaned over me, his body blocking out the sun. His face was weathered and already cherry red with sunburn. His hair damp with sweat but no longer saturated by floodwater. His shirt stuck to his chest.

"Water?" I croaked.

Frank forced a smile. "Everywhere you look...and ain't a drop to drink."

He extended a hand. I took it, rolling over on the battered plywood. Nail heads tore into my jeans and ripped at my pockets. My boots slipped, and I caught the ridgeline of the roof with one hand. I blinked back at the glare. Scrubbed the grit out of my eyes and squinted.

And then my stomach fell, and my shoulders with it. We were still on the roof of Frank's house, right where I'd left us after hacking a hole with the ax. That hole was now almost invisible, marked only by its topmost edge as pitch-black water littered with drifting debris lapped against the roof. I swept my gaze slowly from one end of the house to the other, looking down at what had once been Claiborne Avenue, and all I saw was water. Block after muddy block of it, swallowing homes until only the tops of their roofs were visible, and extending all the way to a hazy horizon on both sides. Hurricane Nadia was gone, leaving clear blue skies blazing with summer sun in her wake, but the Lower Ninth Ward had been swallowed by her storm surge. The air smelled of oil and dirt, heavy with a post-storm humidity that left my lungs feeling starved even as I gasped down oxygen. I couldn't see the canal. I couldn't see the New Orleans skyline. I couldn't see anything save rooftops...and water.

Then I heard the cry. I hadn't noticed it at first as my brain surfaced from unconsciousness, but as the fog of exhaustion receded, the noise clarified in my mind. A sort of low, distant wail. Like wind ripping down from mountaintops, but there was neither wind nor mountains. The city was strangely very still, like a graveyard, and the voice was human—not one human, but many. Not coming from any particular place, but from every place. From the entire city.

It was a unified sound of desperation. Of defeat. Of heartbreak and disbelief and wretched despair. I couldn't pinpoint the source. It was at once all around me, rising maybe from the Lower Ninth, maybe from the entire city.

I pivoted to Frank, and I saw the truth in his eyes. He sat on the roof next to me, wiping sweat from his face. Scattered about us were all fifteen of the refugees from his living room, most clustered right at the ridgeline, using hands and shoes to shelter themselves from the blast of the gulf sun while their clothes stuck to baking bodies.

More than a few were very still. Others were already scalded by the blaze, skin turning cherry red as it burned. Everyone was thirsty. I could see it in their swollen lips and frequent swallows, fighting back the clutches of building dehydration.

We were surrounded by water, just as Frank had said. And there wasn't a thing to drink.

"They'll hold, huh?" It wasn't a helpful comment, but it was the first thing I could think of to say. My voice rasped and croaked. Frank's sad eyes pivoted naturally to the west, toward the canal.

"Overtopping," he said.

I estimated the depth of the water based on its position along his roof and guessed it to be no less than fifteen feet. I was nothing of a flood expert, but that seemed like a great deal more water than overtopping alone should have produced. I thought about the levees the Corps of Engineers had rebuilt, and wondered if they ever actually expected a repeat of Katrina.

"So..." I trailed off, partly searching for words, partly searching simply for a clear thought. I'd seen devastation before—many times, in many places. But usually those places were far away from American shores, and never had I seen anything like this. It was so sweeping, so absolute, that my drained mind couldn't make sense of it. I couldn't really grasp that I was *there*, seated on a roof that had once over-looked a neighborhood and now overlooked a lake.

It wouldn't compute. It was too extreme.

"What happens now?" I said finally. It was the only thing *to* say. I looked to Frank, and the old cop slumped over with aged shoulders sagging, face dropping. He looked like a man who'd just been told his dog had been run over. Like a father of four who loses his job.

Like a man who'd just watched his entire life swept away...again.

"Now we wait," he said quietly. "And hope."

20

The deadliest things in life are almost never the flashiest. Bullets crack, and bombs rattle your teeth out, but I've seen more lives consumed by the slow erosion of narcotics, cancer, toxic relationships, and broken economies than by the wrath of any weapon of war. It's the insidious things that you don't expect to slither beneath your skin and tighten down on your very soul, slowly squeezing the lifeblood away until you're nothing more than a walking corpse. A zombie.

Dehydration is like that. So are heat and exposure. The wristwatch still strapped to my left arm displayed two p.m., and the plywood island we clung to felt like a cookie sheet in an oven. My throat tightened, my tongue swelled, and I pinched my dry eyes closed to avoid the direct glare as I felt the precious moisture leaving my body in trails of sweat.

There was nothing I could do to stop it. Nothing any of us could do to escape the burning blaze or even to fight the heat. If we stripped our clothes off, we'd only burn faster. If we bathed our skin in the filthy water lapping against the roof, we'd leave a sheen of oil on our skin that would magnify the scalding effect. The wrath of the wind had torn away not only the shingles, but also the black paper lining pinned beneath them. There was *nothing* to hide beneath. Nothing but other stripped and battered roofs to swim to— and most of us couldn't swim, anyway.

We were truly stranded, and it didn't take long for me to understand what Frank had meant by *hope*. Without a third-party rescue, many of the older folks gathered around me wouldn't last through the evening. Even as healthy and strong as I was, I wouldn't last more than a couple of days. Dehydration would shut down my organs and stall out my heart long before hunger or sun poisoning could touch me.

"Bet you wish you were in California," Frank croaked.

I squinted, pivoting toward him. "I never said I was from California."

"Nope. But I bet you wish you were there."

That brought the hint of a grin to my busted smile. I closed my eyes and focused on breathing slowly as the sun reached its apex and focused its malice on my head. It made me wish I were a Korean vet with a hat to wear. The old guy had mopped his cap through the water, and I thought the damp probably helped a little. The hat I'd picked up at Randy's place was likely still at the hospital in Hattiesburg.

"Where are you from?" Frank asked.

I licked my lips, fighting back papery dryness. "Phoenix... I guess."

"You guess?"

I hesitated. It wasn't a complicated question, but the answer didn't feel simple. I was born in Phoenix. I'd been raised there. I'd lived there for most of my tumultuous life, outside of the Army. But not recently. In fact, not for some time. Now I wasn't sure where I was from, or where I called home. Azalea Lodge was simply the next stop on a long and wandering path with no destination in mind.

"I kinda live on the road," I said. "I just...move around."

A soft grunt. I glanced sideways and saw Frank overlooking the flooded streets. He didn't seem interested in pressing the question, and I was grateful. It's never much fun delving into the reasons for my transient lifestyle.

"Take some advice from an old man," Frank said. "Pick another road."

I laughed. The laugh became a choke, and I coughed into one hand. Snot mixed with saliva. I scrubbed it away on my jeans, thinking back to the real reason I'd turned south. Thinking of the trailer in the Mississippi woods, no doubt obliterated by the storm. Thinking of Jessica, in the hospital. Autumn, doped up and dragged off.

And Randy.

My smile faded. I forced myself to sit up, and I checked the waterline. It hadn't receded even an inch. If anything, it might have risen.

"I came to New Orleans looking for somebody," I said.

"A woman?"

"A kid."

Frank squinted.

"She was kidnapped," I clarified. "I'm friends with her mother. It happened right before the storm hit. I think the guy who took her planned it that way so the cops wouldn't be able to follow."

"And you think he took her *here*?"

"I know he did," I said. "I found a vehicle he abandoned. He and his guys."

"What guys?"

I hesitated, unsure of how far I wanted to dive down the rabbit trail of my rationale. A lot of it was speculation. Other parts of it might later serve to incriminate me, depending on what actions were necessary to recover Autumn. Frank was an ex-cop, after all.

But then again...so was I.

"It's a long story," I said at last.

"If only we had the time..."

Fair enough.

I mopped sweat off my forehead, noting that my skin was already drier than it had been barely two hours prior. The sweat was moderating. I was running out of it.

"The kid's father is a member of some kind of gang. Not a good character. The kid is super gifted. She's a math whiz. Her mom won full custody and was going to take her to a school in San Fran. The dad didn't like that."

"So he snatched her." Frank said it as a fact, not a question. I looked his way and saw no hint of surprise or disbelief in his face. I remembered those forty years served in the NOPD and realized that I'd sold him short. Frank had seen things, the same as any veteran cop. Very little would surprise him.

"That's right."

"Happens more often than you'd think," Frank said. "Or maybe you know that."

"I was homicide, not kidnapping."

"Yeah, well. The second has a way of generating the first. Why would he bring her to New Orleans? He could have driven west, and the storm would still have sheltered him."

I hesitated, reprocessing my original assumptions about Randy's intentions. This was the part where speculation took over. Raw instinct, coupled with throwaway remarks.

But then again, I'd found the pickup truck. I'd found the map. Randy and his thugs were here, beyond doubt. I just couldn't be certain about why. I had to guess.

"I think they plan to loot the place," I said. "They drove through the roadblocks under fake FEMA credentials. We had a run-in back in Mississippi, and the father said something about being rich. About going someplace where nobody would find him. Outside the country, I guess, which he'd need money for."

I looked to Frank, waiting for the disbelief to cross his face. I saw nothing but resignation.

"Does that sound crazy?"

Frank turned to check on his houseguests. One of the old ladies had grown particularly still over the last half hour. Two of the others were gathered near her, doing their best to offer meager shade with their own bodies.

It wasn't helping much.

"I was on duty when Katrina hit," Frank said. "Most people don't realize that it wasn't the storm that caused the disaster. It wasn't even the flooding. It was the people."

"How do you mean?"

Frank snorted. "You ain't never spent time in Louisiana, have you?"

"Only as a tourist."

"Well, take it from an old hat. This is the most corrupt city in the most corrupt state you're likely to find. Dirty cops, twisted politicians, bureaucracy mired in backroom deals and straight-up organized crime. You take a place like that, and it's ripe for catastrophe when it all hits the fan. Nobody knows who's in charge. Nobody knows where to get help, or who can be trusted. That's why the evacuations failed. It's why it took them so long to get everybody out after Katrina rolled through. That's why the bodies stacked and rotted right where they lay. It was pure chaos. Complete anarchy. For *days*."

It wasn't difficult to picture what Frank described. I'd seen it before, many times. But not in the United States.

"Rule of law failed," I said.

Frank nodded. "And the result was predictable. Looting. Violence. Desperation. It wasn't until the National Guard deployed that things started to turn around, but by then the damage was done."

I considered Randy and his gang of bullish thugs. Yellow Teeth, and all the storage bins they'd packed into that pair of pickup trucks. The talk about being *rich*.

You don't get rich from looting convenience stores and Foot Lockers. There's only so many flat-screen TVs you can haul out of a Best Buy, and then you have to resell them. I was missing something, but maybe it didn't matter. The only thing that mattered was getting Autumn out, unscathed. I could assume Randy and his crew would have sheltered someplace smarter than I had selected. Someplace safe from winds and water. Autumn should still be alive, but surrounded by violent criminals in the heart of a sweeping natural disaster, the status quo could change in a heartbeat.

I had to get to her first, and to do that, I had to get off this roof and back onto dry land. I needed to find water, find a path back into the city, and find Autumn.

"We can only pray it won't be like last time," Frank muttered.

As he spoke, a slight tremor vibrated the plywood beneath my hands. I saw the same disturbance reflected across the surface of murky floodwaters, lapping against the sides of homes as a smacking drumbeat shook the air.

Whap, whap, whap, whap.

I shielded my eyes and looked into the sun, already knowing what I would see even before it burst out of the glare in a surge of rushing black, nose rising, tail dropping. Engines screaming.

It was a UH-60 Black Hawk, with *Louisiana National Guard* painted across the tail and a guardsman hanging out the open door, pointing right at us.

"It won't be like last time," I said. "This time, they're ready."

21

The Black Hawk orbited the Lower Ninth, a guardsman riding with his feet hanging out the door, pointing and speaking into a helmet mic. Sunlight reflected off the windscreen, and I couldn't see the pilots, but I already knew what they were doing. This was a reconnaissance flyby, designed to locate targets on a grid before deploying the ground troops.

Or in this case, the amphibious troops. The boats arrived half an hour later as a quartet of flat-bottomed, stainless-steel swamp craft loaded with more National Guardsmen. Motors churned up the gunky water as they raced down Claiborne Avenue and quickly split amongst the houses. We weren't the only refugees taking shelter on a rooftop. There were others clinging to busted shingles and fragmented sub-roofing. Most of the houses in Frank's neighborhood hadn't enjoyed the reinforcements he had invested in following Katrina, and they had suffered the consequences of Nadia's increased wind power.

When a flat-bottom finally roared up alongside Frank's

house, one of the women let out a tearful whoop of relief. "Praise the Lawd! Y'all got any water?"

The guardsmen did have water. They had stretchers, also. Medics and sunburn ointment. Heavy boots deployed onto the rooftop like Marines storming a beachhead, and within seconds the first twelve refugees were loaded onto the boat and whisked back across the floodwaters. Frank, the Korean vet and I all waited patiently for the next ride, forcing ourselves to sip on bottled water when all we wanted was to guzzle. My throat was so dry it seemed to absorb the fluids directly instead of allowing me to ingest them. My tongue felt like wood.

But I was alive, and I was already thinking ahead to the next phase of my own mission. The guardsmen would take us to a staging zone, where refugees would be processed. FEMA would be there, and I could get whatever I needed to refit. Fresh clothes, more water, possibly some medical supplies to keep on hand. Something for the headache that had yet again returned to haunt me.

And then I was headed back into the city. They wouldn't want me to go, but I wouldn't give them an option. This was a disaster zone. Chaos would reign supreme for days if not weeks. I knew all about slipping away in a disaster zone.

"Thank you."

It was the Korean vet who spoke. His weathered voice rasped, his single deep brown eye bloodshot, ebony face once again glistening with sweat. He extended a hand, and I was gratified by a firm grip.

"Thank *you*," I said, nodding to the hat. He smiled softly, and then the next boat was rumbling up to the roof, and the rest of our party climbed in. I thought all of Frank's refugees had survived the storm, although a couple of the older, frailer women had looked nearly unconscious when they were loaded onto the first boat. I could only hope the FEMA station would be able to rehydrate them quickly.

As our flat bottom churned westward along Claiborne, I stood next to the pilot and rested one hand on the center console, surveying the passing carnage with a feeling that still verged on disbelief. I had no idea what had become of Randy's Blazer or any of the vehicles that had been left on the street. They were swallowed, just like all of the yards and all of the street signs. Many of the roofs we passed had failed completely, rafters broken and exposed as floodwater lapped into attics. Others were occupied by a bizarre assortment of debris—appliances, barbecue grills, even a motorcycle.

And the smell...it was changing, right in my nostrils. What once was a blend of mud, heat, and salt now became sticky and sweet, tinged with something a great deal more sinister.

Death.

"You guys got plenty of help?" I addressed the pilot without breaking eye contact with the carnage.

"National Guardsmen from six states," he said. "Plus FEMA, state troopers, volunteers...if anything, we got too much help."

It wasn't a joke—I knew exactly what he meant. Logistics are everything when it comes to emergency response. Too many people and not enough centralized command can turn a bad situation into a catastrophic one, especially when rival agencies are involved. Hopefully, that wouldn't happen here.

"How bad is the rest of the city?"

A soft grunt. "Better than last time. Wind damage was much worse, but thus far the Lower Ninth levees are the only ones to fail. Still don't know why, yet. Overtopping was extreme. I'm sure the engineer weenies will figure it out after the fact."

They'll hold. I remembered the desperate conviction in Frank's voice and knew that it wouldn't much matter what conclusion the engineer weenies reached. It would be a moot point. The damage was done...again. Judging by most of the refugees I saw clustered in the boats that gathered around us on Claiborne, it seemed the blow couldn't have landed in a worse place.

These weren't wealthy people. They likely didn't have great insurance, or any insurance. This was the kind of thing that could leave a mark for decades to come.

"Don't leave the boat until we escort you! We'll have water and medical aid available. Please cooperate with security searches and remain calm. We're working as fast as we can."

The National Guard sergeant stationed in the bow called directions as the pilot swung our boat northward. On my right stretched the flooded expanse of the Lower Ninth, marked only by the broken tops of roofs and a swarm of churning, flat-bottomed boats. To my left ran a muddy slope with a metal wall standing only a couple of feet above the waterline. I recognized it as a levee, which meant we were now churning up the canal. Thus far, that barrier had held, protecting the core of the city, but its twin on my right-hand side was simply gone. No sign of any metal wall stood above the waterline between our boat and the Lower Ninth.

It was just...empty water.

"Catastrophic failure," the pilot said, catching me looking.

"Wind?" I asked.

He simply shrugged, shoulders falling into a slump. I

noted the gray in his hair and wondered if this wasn't his first time responding to catastrophe in the Big Easy. I knew from experience that catastrophe never gets easier.

We glided on for another five minutes before the pilot at last swung us west, landing at a muddy bank with Interstate 10 standing only yards above the inflated waterline. Federal Emergency Management workers were already there, hundreds of them. Four-wheel-drive trucks stood on slick streets, while travel trailers powered by generators served as command centers and medical stations. There were tents set up with rope aisles to guide incoming survivors toward processing stations, security checkpoints, and tables laden with food. Box trailers stood with their doors open, stacks of bottled water, blankets, clothes, and medical supplies being unloaded behind them.

It was like I had told Frank before. Everyone was ready this time, at least in principle. Something about the nervous energy of the emergency workers coupled with the sheer mass of survivors already gathered on the bank hinted at chaos yet to come. I thought about the twenty thousand survivors sheltering in the Superdome and wondered if they'd been rescued yet. If the city itself was secure.

"Right this way, everybody. If you need assistance, lift your hand!"

I dropped off the bow of the boat into six inches of murky water and assisted the National Guardsmen with offloading the passengers. Those who needed wheelchairs were carried one at a time in camping chairs between two burly privates. Two survivors went off on stretchers.

One of those two was covered by a sheet. That sheet dropped a hot rock into my stomach...but all I could do was look away.

"Right this way, sir. We need to clear you through security."

I submitted to the guidance without objection, sliding into a line of refugees stumbling toward a pair of horseshoe metal detectors. NOPD cops stood outside them, patting each passing person down and inspecting pocket contents before admitting them beyond a metal barrier to the assistance tent. The third person ahead of me was discovered to be carrying a snub-nosed .38 Special tucked into his waistband. The cops confiscated it without comment, tossing it into a bin before waving the man through. He didn't object.

I reached the metal detector, and the cop motioned for me to empty my pockets. A waterlogged phone, a wallet full of squishy cash and an Arizona driver's license, my Macro-Stream and my Victorinox dropped into the bin. The cop took one look at the knife and reached to confiscate it.

"Uh-uh." I shook my head.

He looked up. "We're confiscating weapons, sir. Mayor's orders."

"That's not a weapon, that's a tool. And regardless, Nadia destroyed the city, not the Bill of Rights."

The guy stiffened. I didn't so much as blink. The line backed up behind us, and I waited. At last he glanced sideways to the sergeant, who was busy unloading a 9mm into another plastic bin; then he tilted his head for me to step through the horseshoe. I passed without a sound, and he handed me the bin.

"Keep it in your pocket," he warned.

"No problem."

I emptied the bin as Frank appeared in the line next to me, shuffling along with tangled gray hair shiny with sweat. When he reached the horseshoe, he produced a wallet from his pocket and flipped it open. The sergeant barely glanced at it before tilting his head to the side of the horseshoe.

"Good to see you, Frank. Glad you made it out okay."

Frank stepped around the horseshoe, bypassing its metal-detecting function.

Interesting.

He migrated my way, poking the wallet back into his pocket, and limping on his right leg again. I cocked an eyebrow but didn't say anything.

"Let's find some water," Frank rasped.

The two of us moved slowly through the aid line to record our names on a digital tablet before we were inspected for medical needs and at last permitted to head to the crowded mess tent a hundred yards farther up the street. I wrote my name as Kurt Fitzgerald on the tablet, blending the names of two of my favorite Cardinals players, before typing "visitor" in the address box. Nobody needed to know who I was or why I was there.

In the mess tent, Frank and I stuck together as we collected bottled water and plates of food-truck grub cooked by a conglomerate of local vendors all assembled to feed the survivors. Payment wasn't requested. My meal was some kind of étouffée on rice, a little cold, but delicious none-theless. Frank and I sat across from each other at a crowded table and shoveled down our meals in silence while we both endured the aura of despair surrounding us.

The tent was baking hot, trapping in the Louisiana humidity as a tradeoff for blocking the sun. The voices were all low and defeated. Some people cried. Others only spoke in short, demanding snaps. A baby wailed. Children fought over a single precious toy saved from a flooded home.

It was gut wrenching.

I set my fork down and drained my fourth bottle of water as Frank surveyed the crowd with tears bubbling in his eyes. He caught me watching him, and he didn't look embarrassed as he rubbed his thumb across his face.

"I'm so sick of seeing these people suffer," he said.

"There's only so much you can do."

Frank snorted. "There's *nothing* you can do. Not really."

I paused. Set the bottle down. "Maybe not about the hurricane. But there might be something you can do about a kidnapped little girl."

Frank's eyes narrowed. "Why do I feel like you're about to make me an accessory to something?"

"Because you have impeccable instincts. I need your help."

22

"I need a map of the city and a pen."

Frank got up from the table, leaving me to start on a fifth water bottle while he filtered through the crowd to one of the cops standing security nearby. The guy wore a full plate carrier with an AR-15 slung across his chest. He looked about as friendly as a granite statue—at least until he recognized Frank. Then a handshake and a warm smile were exchanged. Frank made a request, and the cop directed him toward an administration tent.

Frank returned ten minutes later with a sheet of standard copier paper and a pen. The sheet was printed with a basic map of New Orleans, with stars marking various disaster-relief sites. A FEMA logo filled one corner. I ignored the stars and clicked open the pen, taking my time to examine the map before drawing an X near the heart of the city, just a few blocks east of the Superdome. I circled the X, then drew another north of downtown, on the western edge of the Gentilly neighborhood. I circled that X as well before moving back to the heart of downtown and drawing a final circle, this time without an X, just northeast of the Superdome. Finally, I traced a line along the Mississippi River, leading out to the Gulf of Mexico.

I clicked the pen closed and rotated the map, pushing it toward Frank. He set his bottle down and peered at it.

"Do these locations mean anything to you?" I asked.

A long pause. He shook his head.

"I know where they're at. They don't ring any immediate bells. What's this about?"

"When they took the kid, they drove off in a pair of pickup trucks marked with FEMA logos. That's what led me to believe they were headed to New Orleans. Just before I found myself on Claiborne Avenue, I located one of those trucks someplace north of downtown. It was wrecked. Nobody was inside. There was a map on the floor with marks on it, just like these."

"You don't have the map?"

"Nadia took it."

"Right."

He studied my marks again, more slowly this time. Squinting at each one. Then he shook his head. "There's nothing these three sites have in common. At least, nothing that I can think of. Your marks near the Superdome are just random business locations. That spot in Gentilly sits on the banks of the London Avenue Canal. No place special."

"Any place where you might weather a storm?"

Frank snorted. "You'd be a fool to weather it next to a canal. That's one of the places where the levees broke back in oh-five. Some of the worst flooding outside the Lower Ninth."

"What about the other two?" I pointed to the circle and the X in downtown New Orleans. They were imprecise marks, but I was relatively confident that they were somewhat accurate to the marks I'd seen on that map in the wrecked Ford.

Frank pondered. Then he shrugged. "Could be anything. The city is full of business towers and high-rises. Most are at least semi-occupied and under surveillance, but any one of them would be safer than a house."

"Would they be secured by now?" I asked.

"What do you mean?"

"I'd assume that business towers and high-rises would be prioritized by law enforcement. Some of the first locations to be secured."

A nod. "That's right."

"So we aren't looking for something like that. We're looking for something less obvious. More discreet, but just as secure against the storm."

Frank pursed his lips. He traced the map with his finger, pausing first over the X inside the circle and then over the circle without an X. He tapped it.

"Why no X?"

"I don't know."

"You sure this location is accurate?"

"More or less."

"So it could be off by a few blocks? Say...closer to here?"

He moved his finger north and west by two blocks, stopping at the corner of Tulane Avenue and La Salle Street. It was a large block, rectangular in shape, with I-10 running opposite to La Salle.

"That could be it," I said. "It was a quick look."

Frank's finger continued to tap slowly over the spot. Something in his face changed—a sort of grimness tugging at his features.

"What is it?" I asked.

Frank looked up. He blinked once, seeming to remember where he was. "That's...Big Charity."

"What?"

"Charity Hospital—Big Charity, we always used to call it. It's America's oldest continuously operating hospital. Or it was, anyway. Until Katrina. The hospital was occupied when the storm hit. Lots of patients couldn't be evacuated. They had generators, but those were located in the basement, and the basement flooded. So they lost AC, they lost power for ventilators, they lost lights...everything. And then they were forgotten."

"What?" I said again.

"It was chaos, Sharpe. For everybody. Nobody expected eighty percent of the city to be underwater. Balls were dropped, among them Charity Hospital. The name was literal. It was a nonprofit with a mission to serve the indigent. Poor minorities, mostly. The kind of people governments quickly forget. They left them in there for days. A lot of people died, and the hospital never reopened. It was replaced by University Medical Center. The old building was just...abandoned."

"And it's still there?"

Frank nodded. "It costs too much to tear down. They just fenced it off and parked a security guard down there to keep homeless folks and kids out of it. A million square feet of just...nothing. Abandoned hospital beds and broken glass."

"Sounds like a great place to hide a kidnapped kid," I said.

Frank grunted. "Could be. It would definitely be a great place to weather the storm. That building is solid, but it wouldn't be safe in general. Nobody's used it in nearly twenty years. I ain't been inside myself since...just after Katrina, I guess."

Frank trailed off, then shook his head with a sad little smile. "I was born in that hospital. Lots of locals were. It's a shame."

Frank's nostalgia was lost on me as I stared off into space, fixating on one thought over and over again—a million square feet. Multiple levels. Long hallways and lots of small rooms, all situated right in the heart of the city, with easy access to any number of looting targets. Assuming a thorough knowledge of New Orleans's streets, Randy and his crew of thugs could launch lightning strikes into the city, snatch what they wanted, and disappear back inside the hospital. Unless somebody actually saw them enter the old building, it might take law enforcement days to consider searching the place.

And even then, Randy could slip away. If he were smart, he'd have an exit strategy mapped out. A route planned well in advance that would help him elude an overworked police force.

Yes. The hospital made perfect sense, but there was only one way to know for sure.

"I need to get there," I said, tapping the map.

Frank snapped out of his daydream, immediately shaking his head. "No chance. They're keeping survivors here. Or didn't you see the fence?"

"I'm not planning on asking permission."

Frank studied me a moment. Something between a scowl and a smirk crossed his face—the conflict of a longtime peace officer colliding with an old man's mischief, I thought.

"You're a troublemaker, aren't you, Sharpe?"

"Only when I need to be."

"And I guess you get to decide when that is?"

"Obviously."

A soft grunt. A long pause.

"You're not BSing me about this kid?"

"Not for a second."

"And you really think they'd be in the hospital?"

"I have no idea. It all depends on how sound my detective work is. But..."

"But?"

"But I was a pretty good detective."

A soft nod. Frank glanced down the long line of tables to a steady current of survivors shuffling in to eat a late lunch. Or maybe it was an early dinner. I'd lost track of the time. National Guardsmen processed the crowd through check-ins and supply lines while New Orleans cops performed the security work. Metal detectors, and perimeter duty. They were all heavily armed, each wearing a sidearm at the least, and more than a few carrying shotguns or AR-15s. There were K-9s, also. Big, bushy German shepherds who panted while they maintained constant vigilance over the crowd.

It was starting to feel a little like a prison camp. I understood the rationale, but I wasn't going to stick around until they gave me a jumpsuit.

"You quick on your feet?" Frank asked.

"Sure."

He clicked the pen open and traced a circle around our current position, on the western bank of the canal, just outside a neighborhood called Gentilly Woods.

"You'll want to head west, then south. That will keep you away from Desire and St. Claude. High crime areas. Once you reach Mid City, you'll want to watch your back. The Seventh Ward, St. Roch, Treme' Lafitte, Tulane-Gravier...all these are rough parts of town. I have no idea what they'll look like. Central City isn't great, either. That's just south and west of Big Charity. There could be martial law, busted buildings, gunfire...you name it. Hopefully it's better than it was after Katrina."

He made a note on the map for each of the neighborhoods he mentioned, then sketched a squiggly line between the worst spots, arcing down to the block on Tulane Avenue. Charity Hospital. It was no more than five or six miles, as the crow flies, but I guessed Frank's rambling route to be at least twice as long.

A lengthy hike, on open sidewalks. Adding downed trees, downed power lines, police blockades, and who knew what sorts of civil unrest to the mix...it might take hours.

"That'll work," I said, folding the map and tucking it into my driest pocket. I took the pen also.

"Can you get me out?" I said.

Frank nodded. "Yeah. Just follow my lead."

We both stood. I jabbed my chin toward his invisible waistband, concealed beneath an untucked shirt.

"Wanna help a fellow blue liner with some protection?"

Frank feigned innocence. "Huh?"

I cocked an eyebrow. Frank shook his head and turned for the fence.

"I like you, Sharpe. I don't like you that much. Follow me."

23

I was right about Frank Miller. He was every bit the old fox I presumed him to be. We made it to the security station and were stopped by a pair of young buck beat cops who didn't recognize him. That didn't stall Frank for a minute. He was ready with a story about somebody in the food tent needing an extra-wide wheelchair. I guessed that he'd already observed a stack of such wheelchairs in the back of a box trailer just outside the security perimeter, and he'd also probably assumed that overworked cops with too many people to watch wouldn't take time away from security detail to unload a hefty chair.

He was right. The cops directed him to the trailer and asked him to close the fence when he was done. We slipped through a segmented section of galvanized crowd paneling. Frank went for the trailer. I split off to the side and circled beyond it.

And just like that, I was loose in New Orleans again.

My watch read five fifteen as I departed the FEMA station and ventured into Gentilly Woods, giving me just under three hours of daylight left. The only things I'd brought with me were a trio of water bottles, a power bar, and the usual stuff I kept in my pockets. Wallet, knife, and flashlight. I'd already ditched my phone. The floodwater had destroyed it, and even if it hadn't, there wasn't any cell reception in New Orleans.

Nadia had ensured that.

The street I found myself on was called Mirabeau Avenue, and despite the obvious age of the homes, I thought it was probably a pleasant place to live prior to the hurricane. There had been lots of trees, wide sidewalks, ample driveways. Pastel siding covered most of the houses in blue, green, and soft yellow. The streets were battered and heavily patched, but wide enough. Many of the mailboxes featured last names and artful customization, indicating homeowners, not renters. People who had invested in these properties for the long term.

At least, that was what I envisioned the neighborhood to have looked like based on what telltale clues remained, but that was all before the storm. Now, the neighborhood was completely and utterly *destroyed*.

The tall oak trees that lined the sidewalk were almost all blown over, flattened by the unprecedented wrath of Cat 5 winds, ripping up sidewalk as they fell and leaving behind huge holes flooded with rainwater. Roofs were ripped clean of shingles, with only about one out of every four homes still standing. The rest were blown to pieces as though a bomb had gone off in their living rooms, broken two-by-fours and mutilated furniture clogging the streets on every side. The customized mailboxes had been ripped straight out of the ground and hurled like javelins through the windshields of overturned cars, or straight into the sides of fallen oak trees, where metal mailbox posts impaled the aged hardwood. The pastel siding was shredded and scattered, every window obliterated, every privacy fence smashed into a pile of toothpicks. Power poles had not only been toppled but their lines ripped free and tangled amongst the debris. Streets that had survived the mass flooding of their neighbors in the Ninth Ward still ran with as much as three feet of oily black water —from rainfall and levee overtopping, I supposed.

There wasn't a clear path through the neighborhood. I couldn't make it farther than thirty yards before being forced to scramble over twisted appliances and fallen trees, all coated in mud and surrounded by water. When I fell back into the mire, my boots flooded with it, their soles crunching on unidentifiable objects trapped beneath the wreckage.

Some of those objects crushed beneath my body weight. A few felt fleshy and lifeless. I swallowed back an urge to vomit and waded ahead, steering clear of the power lines even though I knew that if they had been active, I would have already been electrocuted.

The smell almost choked me. Mud and rot. Maybe food rot, maybe something more sinister. It was subtle but persistent, and I knew it would be insufferable within another forty-eight hours. I pulled my shirt over my face and fought through it, referencing my marked-up FEMA map from time to time to measure my progress.

I was creeping, moving at much less than a walking pace, and there was no end to the carnage stretching out ahead of me. I passed people on occasion, each of them wading through the mess and sorting amid the devastation for what personal property could be salvaged. Some of the houses that stood upright were swimming with water. Others sat on slightly elevated ground, like islands in a lake of hell. I passed a shirtless black man seated on his front porch with his bare feet resting on his front steps, only inches over the waterline. He smoked cigarettes, vacant eyes staring across the street to a preschool that had been wiped off the block like a smudge of dirt. I knew it was a preschool because the concrete sign still stood. Part of a swing set was tangled amid a toppled oak tree, chains dangling into the water.

Behind the man, his house was flattened. Not one stick of wood stood atop another. Not one scrap of furniture remained. The block foundation was scraped so clean it looked ready for reconstruction.

But he didn't look at it. He just smoked.

By the time I exited Gentilly Woods and entered the greater neighborhood of Gentilly, I was so exhausted I had to find a front porch of my own to sit on and catch my breath. Already the étouffée I'd eaten at the FEMA station was gone, and I wolfed down the power bar, wishing I'd brought more. Half my water was gone, also. I had expected a relatively easy walk, likely with convenience stores along the way where I could pilfer what substance I needed to survive. I hadn't seen a convenience store yet, and I wasn't walking so much as scrambling.

Peering up at the empty blue sky, I was gratified to see the demon sun receding into the west. A steady *whap, whap, whap* of helicopters had beat paths over my head for most of the afternoon, both National Guard Black Hawks and cable news choppers with cameras mounted to their noses, flying low over the wreckage. There were Chinooks, also, those twin-rotored behemoths of Army aviation, rushing in low with giant nets full of sandbags suspended beneath their cargo hooks.

Rushing to fill voids in the levees of the Lower Ninth, I figured. They'd done this before.

I scrubbed sweat from my face and looked south as a new sound breached the sticky New Orleans stillness. A softer, yet more menacing snap.

Pop, pop, pop!

It was a sound I would recognize anywhere in the world, but still had difficulty reconciling with the streets of an American city.

Automatic gunfire.

Gritting my teeth, I hauled myself back to my feet and stepped back into the water, turning southward. Toward the sound of the guns.

24

I made it to the Seventh Ward just as the sun dropped over Texas and evening closed over Louisiana. The marks Frank had left on the map detailing rough neighborhoods that I should avoid were scattered all around me, but tough neighborhoods were now the least of my worries. The flooding had subsided the closer I drew to the core of the city, but the carnage was no less severe. Unlike Katrina, Nadia's wrath had been expressed in more dynamic ways than simple storm surge. The rage of one-hundred-sixty-plus-mile-per-hour winds had left its mark, ravaging like an F-5 tornado that just happened to be three hundred miles wide.

And the closer I neared to downtown, the more often I heard gunfire. Usually just a popping pistol shot here or the boom of a shotgun there. Distinct sounds that carried easily through a city silent of any engine noises or traffic. But on occasion, bursts of automatic gunfire joined the mix, galvanizing my mind with thoughts of Afghanistan and storming waves of Taliban fighters. I passed cops on occasion, deployed like Army Rangers to key intersections of the city, where they worked to outline a grid for future relief efforts, but none of them were the ones shooting.

I thought of my visit to Atlanta and all the gangs there. I thought of armed civilians sheltering inside semi-obliterated homes, small arms at the ready. Terrified and untrained, likely to pop off a shot at any shadow of a threat passing too close to their refuge of last resort.

This wasn't a safe place—not for me, and certainly not for a ten-year-old kid who couldn't walk. Having never had any children of my own, or even really considered being a father beyond brief talks with my late fiancée, I didn't consider myself to be any sort of authority on the issue of parenthood. But it was beyond question that Randy Mercer had fallen far, far short of the mark.

It would take more than a heartless deadbeat to drag their disabled child into a hellscape like this. It would take an idiot, and idiots are some of the more dangerous creatures on the planet. You can never really know for sure what they'll do next, because logic, reason, and intelligence don't play a part in their decision-making process. They're as likely to throw themselves into a fire as flee from it. There's no way to put yourself in their shoes and predict their movements. They're the most elusive of enemies, the most unpredictable, and my gut told me that Randy Mercer was surrounded by men of a similar ilk to himself.

All the more pressure to get Autumn *out* of their hands and away from the city.

When the sun finally vanished and the sky turned inky black, an unprecedented phenomenon overtook the city, something I'd rarely seen at all and had never seen in America. An entire metropolis was bathed in near-perfect dark—

no streetlights, no illuminated office buildings or soft yellow glow from dining room windows. After the sun faded and before the moon rose, the pitch of the sky was the same tar black as an Afghani midnight. I crouched at the corner of North Broad Avenue and St. Louis Street, forced to wait for the rise of the moon and for my eyes to adjust to the inky blackness.

Even in a situation like this, absolute darkness was denied by the soft glow of stars that gradually fed my adjusting eyes with enough light to make out shadows. The bulk of a pumping station situated across from me. The outline of what might have been a Ford Mustang turned over onto its roof, debris lying all around it. Most objects took the form of dark blobs, not distinct shapes, but after forty-five minutes the soft glow of a partial moon joined the stars, and once again I could see my path ahead. After another twenty minutes, my pupils were capturing enough soft light to clarify objects as far away as a hundred yards.

My watch read eleven p.m. To my left lay the core of the city, and it was from that direction that the most noise rose. I heard occasional sirens. Voices blaring through loudspeakers. Shouts.

And sporadic, random gunfire. It sounded like a war zone, not a major American city. But war zone or otherwise, those gunshots lay between me and my destination. There was nothing to do but press ahead.

I left the intersection rested, turning south through the heart of Tulane/Gravier, headed for the business district. Long before I reached downtown New Orleans, I knew where the authorities had concentrated the bulk of their response. It was no surprise, really. They would rescue the survivors out of the impoverished Lower Ninth Ward because they couldn't risk another Katrina debacle. But beyond the more glaring, newsworthy devastation of Frank's flooded neighborhood, the next logical step would be to secure the core of the city. The business district. The Superdome full of survivors.

The area surrounding Charity Hospital.

A din of voices grew louder as I fought my way through the last of a ravaged neighborhood and closed on an elevated Interstate 10. The highway stood on concrete pillars with trash and tangled roofing metal blasted against them. Six inches of water ran across the streets, bubbling out of flooded storm drains and running with oily filth. The carcass of a Golden retriever rested against a curb, legs still limp from a recent death.

The smell I had endured all day long intensified as I passed beneath the vacant highway and sloshed toward the business district, but I was now used to it. I blocked it out as a soft orange glow rose from beyond I-10, directly over the French Quarter. The loudspeakers barked, and I was able to make out individual words played on repeat from a prerecorded message.

"ATTENTION. Medical aid, emergency supplies, and food are available at the Superdome. Please proceed to that location for guidance on shelter and evacuation. Comply with the directions of all law enforcement and US military personnel deployed to the city. At this time the mayor has declared a temporary suspension of all weapons carried throughout the city, including those carried under concealed-carry permit. No weapons will be allowed to be carried by anyone other than law enforcement and US military personnel. Any weapons found will be confiscated. Any presentation of a weapon will be confronted with deadly force. ATTENTION. Medical aid, emergency supplies..."

The message cycled back, and I withdrew quickly into a narrow alley as bright blue lights flashed from the end of a street, instantly compromising my natural night vision. The prerecorded message barked even louder, and water rushed against tires as an armored police truck, painted full black with the New Orleans Police Department logo printed in white along the door, crashed by. I shielded my eyes as headlights blazed past—first the police truck, and then the deeper growl of far more familiar vehicles. I stole a glance once the headlights had passed me, and noted the presence of two National Guard Humvees trailing the police truck.

The tail vehicles were occupied by four guardsmen each, and everyone but the drivers sported an M4 assault rifle cradled across chest plates loaded with extra ammunition. It was heavy armament, but I could tell by the wide eyes and muddy faces that the kids wielding those guns weren't really prepared to use them. They were still in shock by the devastation around them, likely put on patrol to guide survivors toward the relief staging area at the Superdome.

But also told to be ready for anything, because this city had experienced catastrophe before. And this time, the government would be ready.

As soon as the vehicles passed, I left the alley and accelerated south. By my estimation, Charity Hospital stood less than a mile away, but between myself and my destination stood the business district's broadest and most famed boulevard—Canal Street. I recognized the name from my previous visits to the Big Easy alongside my fiancée. Those late, steamy nights spent stumbling between Bourbon Street bars and French Quarter hotel rooms. Too much liquor, an abundance of jazz, and hardly any sleep.

The memory tightened my stomach as the glare of generator-powered security lights illuminated the next intersection, further deteriorating my natural night vision. Another loudspeaker barked, this one broadcasting directions that weren't prerecorded.

"Proceed toward the Superdome!" a heavy Cajun drawl shouted. "Remain calm. Comply with the National Guard. We've got food and shelter for everybody."

I reached Canal Street, hugging close to the shadows alongside a hotel full of blown-out windows. Downed palm trees had been shoved into the median by heavy trucks, and a giant lottery billboard lay splintered into a thousand pieces right across the middle of the intersection. Power lines tangled amid traffic lights. A thick steel light pole was bent in half like a paperclip.

To my left lay all the action. Long lines of pedestrians stumbled along the sidewalks, moving east toward the heart of downtown, escorted by heavily armed cops and National Guardsmen. Military vehicles were *everywhere*. Not just the Humvees and armored trucks I'd seen before, but Army deuce-and-a-halves and fuel trucks, Corps of Engineers bulldozers and backhoes. All the light blazed down from high poles powered by generators, spotlighting the refugees as they were corralled into a tight, exhausted column.

It didn't look like the aftermath of a hurricane. It didn't look like a tangle of survivors assembling for disaster relief. It looked like a column of indigent locals being marched out of a village by US armed forces ahead of severe military action. It *looked* like a war zone.

"Hey! You by the hotel. Get in line!"

A light flashed across the street from the top of a Humvee and flooded my face. I shielded my eyes against the glare as the voice repeated its command through a bullhorn. "Step into line, sir! We need everybody on the sidewalk."

I ignored the command and sprinted across Canal Street, weaving amid the billboard debris and jumping over a fallen palm tree. The bullhorn barked louder, demanding compliance, but nobody followed me into the inky blackness of the next street. Weaving amid the wreckage of upturned cars, shattered glass, and tangled roofing metal, I jogged easily, unconcerned about the soldiers now left in my wake.

I reached Tulane Avenue and skidded to a stop, heart thumping as the moon cast dim illumination over the next block. Directly across the street, surrounded by a flattened and tangled chain-link fence, stood a twenty-story monolith of a concrete building dotted by rectangular windows with a tower reaching skyward at its core, and two wings running perpendicular to each other on either side to form the footprint of a capital letter *H*. The walls were filthy black with grime, the courtyard a mess of downed trees and chain-link fencing. Windows were blown out, and sidewalks lay littered with the resulting rainstorm of glass.

The building looked like something out of a horror film. Dark, vacant, and brooding beneath the New Orleans moon. Abandoned and forgotten, right in the heart of a metropolis. The site of the bookends of life—birth and death, for so many thousands.

It was Big Charity Hospital.

25

A chill ran down my spine despite the swampy heat. I couldn't help it. There was a haunting sadness to the wind-battered structure that spoke to my very soul. It felt like a graveyard. Like the hulk of the Roman Colosseum, or the nuclear war monument in Hiroshima, Japan. Both places I'd visited during my military tenure. Sites of unspeakable pain and loss, expressed in radically different ways, but still leaving a mark history would not forget.

I knew without even crossing the street that Big Charity had seen things. So long a shelter for those in need, now confronted with an encore performance of the worst pain the Crescent City had ever experienced. Still standing through it all, but no longer her old, bright self, populated by life-saving heroes who no doubt worked for a fraction of what their skill sets were worth.

Now Charity was a mausoleum. A place to be left in peace. Yet it hadn't been left in peace. I knew that within seconds of sweeping the glistening wet hospital wings and identifying the glimmer of a light shining from the central tower, on the sixth floor. Come and gone in an instant, but unmistakably man-made. Yellow, in contrast to blue moonlight. Flicking quickly, like the passage of a flashlight beam.

Somebody was inside.

Crouching on the darkened sidewalk, I snugged my bootlaces and took inventory of my gear. Other than my wallet, truck keys, Victorinox, and MacroStream, the only thing I had left with me was Frank's map. The water was now gone, and I was thirsty again as well as hungry.

I tuned out the physical distractions and focused on the plan ahead. There was a guardhouse situated at what once might have been the gate of the hospital. A little sedan with the bright yellow logo of a security company was blown against it, spiderweb cracks shooting across the windshield from where some debris had made contact. There was no security guard, and the fence was such an obliterated mess that it would be no problem to gain access to the property.

Randy had, after all. He and his thugs, or whoever else was inside that building. The real challenge would be navigating the interior. Elevators would be out of commission, of course, and stairwells would be tactically inferior options. There's no place to hide in a stairwell. No place to find cover, should somebody open fire from two floors up. They're easy to secure and difficult to sneak through.

But I didn't have a choice. If there was even a chance that Autumn was inside that hospital, held captive by the very person who had originated her existence and should have loved and protected her at any cost...I was going in. I was getting her out. It wasn't a question.

I crossed the street and navigated over the chain link with ease. From two blocks south I could hear the clammer of a few thousand voices gathered at the Superdome, but none of the generator-powered lights penetrated to my location. I slipped past the guardhouse, up the sidewalk, and approached the base of the core hospital tower under the light of the moon alone. It rose skyward with dozens of window frames staring down at me like empty eye sockets, a few of the bottom ones covered in plywood, but most of the rest standing completely open. The door was blockaded also, plastered with government warning signs all commanding me to stay out.

I turned right, boots sloshing through five inches of water standing in the yard as I approached a bank of tall, commercial air-conditioning units abandoned behind another tangled fence. They stood about six feet tall, and I hoisted myself to their tops with ease. From there, it was another stretch to wrap my fingers around the bottom of a second-story window, the frame covered in grit, and the windowpane long gone. My muscles tightened as I hoisted, walking up the sides of the concrete wall with my boots and reaching inside to pull myself through.

The metal window frame bit into my abdomen as I wriggled inside. Muscles stretched, and my feet dangled for a moment as I caught my breath. Then I rolled through, landing on a hard tile floor with a grunt.

It was a hospital room, but not a private one. Both large and sprawling, it was more like the open wards that were in medical vogue eighty years ago. There were still beds surrounding me, most of them stripped of mattresses and now standing as shadowy outlines amid a tangle of IV poles and other medical paraphernalia I couldn't even begin to identify.

The air was heavy with mildewy must. The floor was

slick and dirty, covered in soggy leaves. I pulled myself upright and drew two items from my pockets. The Macro-Stream rested in my left palm, thumb suspended over the tail switch for momentary use. The Victorinox rested in my right hand, my thumb pressed against the loop of the locking three-inch blade, ready for quick deployment at a moment's notice.

I'd spoken the truth with the cop back at the FEMA station. The Victorinox was a tool, not a weapon. But in the grimy dark halls of an abandoned building populated by who knew what sort of murderous scum, it could pull double duty.

I ventured into the hallway, using the MacroStream only in short bursts to illuminate my path to either side. The floor was filthy, the walls rotten. Drywall swelled with moisture and caved in at places. Light fixtures hung from the ceiling, wires dangling. Doors stood open, and a nurses' station lay littered with crinkled and abandoned paperwork, computers long ago pilfered, leaving only trailing wires behind.

It was the work posters that were creepiest. All the usual things you find in a hospital, posted by administrative staff and nurses. Procedures, directories, and OSHA declarations. Even a faded work schedule printed for the week of August 29, 2005, that sent another chill up my spine. It was as though the hospital were frozen in time—lost to a bygone age, undisturbed by the years that had ground by it.

I made my way past the nurses' station and rounded the corner, taking my time and using the light sparingly. I remembered what Frank had said about the size of the hospital—a million square feet—and tried not to be over-whelmed by the sheer magnitude of the search ahead. With so many hundreds of small rooms and a tangle of snaking hallways, I could walk in circles for hours without even real-izing it, and never find a prodigy kid doped up on sleeping pills. What was worse, Randy and his crew could be expected to have a better knowledge of the building than myself.

If I didn't watch my back, they could get the jump on me.

I slowed at the end of a hallway, scanning my light through a utility closet and a storage room once used to warehouse oxygen bottles. Both were empty save for a mess of rubber gloves spread across the floor. I lowered the light and took a long breath, forcing my mind to calm.

Think, Mason. Unpack this.

The hospital was a perfectly logical place for Randy and his thugs to hide. It was right in the heart of downtown, an easy place to run blazing looting raids from before disap-pearing back into a morass of hallways and small rooms. They might be out on a raid even now. If I put myself in their boots, where would I want to hide?

Someplace not too far up from ground level, likely. Low enough for easy access in and out, without having to lug my loot up too many stairs, but high enough to avoid discovery by passing cops. I remembered the flashlight beam I'd seen glimmering across the sixth-floor window and decided that sounded about right. By the look of this place, it wasn't like many homeless people dwelled here. The flashlight I'd seen was most likely wielded by one of Randy's gang.

Four floors up.

I needed stairs, and I found them around the next bend in the hall. A bank of elevators stood with their doors rolled open, empty elevator shafts reaching high into the tower overhead. Next to them stood a metal door with a dusty panel of reinforced glass. The sign mounted next to the door displayed both the stairwell symbol as well as a little map indicating that I should head downward for an evacuation.

I eased the door open and bumped the tail switch on the MacroStream. The landing beyond was concrete, painted dull gray. Steps led upward. I released the tail switch and listened.

Water dripped, echoing against block walls. The scuttle of a rodent's toenails slipped over concrete.

Nothing else.

I took the stairs with the light turned off, using the handrail for balance and easing my way upward. I stopped at the third- and fourth-floor landings and listened at the door. When I heard nothing, I pulled them open an inch and looked beyond.

Empty blackness greeted me, and when I flipped the MacroStream on, it revealed more dirty and abandoned hall-ways. More vacant window frames staring out over a devas-tated city.

So it was for the third floor and the fourth. But when I reached the fifth floor, I finally heard the voices. Not from the hallways beyond the fifth-floor access door, but from someplace overhead. A raucous laugh and the thump of soft music. Glass clinked, and a footstep fell. All the sounds were muffled by distance and block walls, barely loud enough to be distinct amid the continued splash of water dripping far below. I rotated my face upward toward the sounds, turning away from the fifth-floor door and back toward the steps.

Then I froze. The sixth-floor door latch clicked, and hinges groaned. A heavy boot thumped out over the landing.

And somebody entered the stairwell.

26

I pressed my back against the block wall and mashed my thumb automatically against the blade of the Victorinox, pivoting it open an inch as the first boot step was matched by another, then a lazy hiccup. The door smacked closed, and the footfalls fell silent. Whoever had entered the stairwell now stood directly above me, separated by a concrete floor framed in steel, only a few steps away from exposing his legs to me as he proceeded to ground level.

I thought quickly, evaluating my options of fleeing into the fifth-floor hallway or rushing down the steps. I hadn't tried the door yet, and I didn't know if the hinges squeaked. The third-floor hinges had. Such a shrill scream of metal on metal would give my position away, but if I set off down the steps, I might expose myself to the view of the channel that ran from the top floor of the hospital tower all the way to the basement. If he leaned out and looked over the railing, he might—

My train of thought was terminated by a new sound. Not

a footstep, but a metallic clicking, very rapid and smooth. Like a zipper. I pressed my back against the wall alongside the door and looked up. The guy overhead belched.

And then running liquid splashed over the concrete above me. I heard it as a stream blasting the blocks, and the ammonia stench reached my nostrils only a moment before hot urine streamed down the wall and ran onto my shoulders. I sprang away from the blocks and pivoted, watching as torrents of piss drained through a crack in the landing overhead and ran down the wall in a yellow cascade, foul enough to flood the small landing in a heartbeat. I choked and held my breath, scrubbing the back of my wet hand over my jeans. The hiccupping fire hydrant overhead continued to urinate for what felt like an eternity—torrents of the stuff, stinking up the stairwell and puddling around my feet. When at last he was finished, the zipper ran again, and he stumbled backward. The door opened. Voices and dull music sounded from inside.

The door clapped shut again, and I gasped for fresh air. There was none to be had, and I swung to the steps instead, turning upward. I made it to the sixth-floor landing and found another puddle of urine gathered against the base of the wall opposite the door to the hallway. Apparently, the landing had become a makeshift urinal.

The door to the sixth floor stood closed. As I neared it, I rotated the knife blade to full-open. The lock clicked into place, and three inches of edged stainless steel glimmered beneath the light leaking from under the door.

Blocking out the stench of raw sewage puddled behind me, I leaned close to the door and listened. The music was Merle Haggard, "The Fightin' Side of Me". It rumbled from a small stereo while bottles clinked and low voices laughed.

On occasion an outburst or a guffaw of laughter was punctuated by curses and accusations of deception.

It was a card game. I recognized as much by the mention
of aces and sleeves. I couldn't discern how many men were
involved, but the tempo of their discourse was impossible to
misdiagnose. They were drunk, all of them. A room full of
sloshed rednecks and drained beer bottles.

I put a hand on the knob and twisted gently. I already
knew it wouldn't squeak thanks to my urinating friend. The
door eased open, and an inch-wide beam of yellow light
spilled across the landing. I peered through the gap into an
open room paved in hard tile. Sagging ceiling tiles hung
overhead, wires drooping and lights dark. Dust was joined
by tangled and soiled hospital bedsheets on the floor, an ice
chest shoved against the face of a nurses' station, elevator
doors hanging half open to my left.

More of the chaos I'd witnessed on the second floor,
except this time the smell of mildew was joined by that of
sweat and body odor. The light glimmered from a pair of
battery-powered camping lanterns set up on the left-hand
side of the nurses' station, and bathed in that glow, I found
my target.

Randy Mercer and his pals, all gathered around a rolling
hospital bed, kicked back in nurses' chairs and displaced
waiting room furniture, guzzling beer and tossing cards over
the stained mattress. There were eight of them in total, and I
recognized Yellow Teeth at the foot of the bed, dealing the
cards and slurring on about making his money back. Only
three of the men faced my way, and all of them were lost in
the cards, elbowing one another and arguing about the bet.

I descended into a squat and eased the door open,
selecting my next point of cover as the four-foot-high nurses'

station built against the far wall. Randy's crew would see the door open if they looked, but with the next flop of Texas Hold'em in play, everyone was distracted. Outside the soft glow of their camping lanterns, the room was drenched in darkness, allowing ample concealment for me to slip into.

I stepped through the door and eased it closed behind me without a whisper of detection from the crowd. In another two seconds I crouched behind the nurses' station, knife still held at the ready as I peered carefully around the corner to inspect the poker circle.

There were guns. I saw them almost immediately, leaned against the wall and protruding from waistbands. Glock and Beretta pistols, a pair of Mossberg pump shotguns, and a deer rifle.

And an M4A1 carbine. I stopped and did a double take as I passed down the line of weaponry, squinting in the dim light. There were actually two of them. Short, black rifles fit with fourteen-inch barrels, A-frame sight posts, and standard GI mags. But it wasn't any of the usual military accoutrements that gave away the restricted nature of the rifles. It was the exposed selector switches mounted to the receivers, each of which could convert a standard semiautomatic sporting rifle into a fully automatic weapon of war with the flick of a thumb. They were Army rifles, not civilian AR-15s. I even thought I saw a DOD serial number stamped above the mag well of one of them.

Heavy firepower. What?

I backed deeper into the shelter of the nurses' station as the next flop of the cards produced a flurry of drunken cheers and curses. Behind me ran a hallway, striking out through the middle of the hospital tower, toward the east wing. There was a parallel hallway beyond the nurses' station, where the poker game was set up. If Autumn was being held hostage in this place, I expected her to be set up there, in one of the multi-bed wards I'd seen on the second floor. But there was no chance I could walk right through the middle of that den of thieves without catching a storm of gunfire to the chest. I needed to circle, stepping deeper into the inky blackness outside the glow of those camping lanterns.

Setting off down the hallway, I kept the Victorinox at the ready and stuck my head briefly into each room I passed. The core of the building consisted of storage closets and some kind of abandoned laboratory. It was almost impossible to make out details with so little available light, but I didn't want to risk flashing my MacroStream. As my eyes began to adjust again, I made out enough to know that Randy's gang hadn't penetrated these rooms. They appeared undisturbed under the disorganized chaos of years of abandonment.

The outside of the hallway was punctuated by doors, each leading to a five- or six-bed ward. These rooms were much easier to search, with moonlight leaking through empty window frames. Glass littered the floor amongst abandoned medical equipment and soiled mattresses. Rat poop was everywhere, but there were no other signs of life. I reached the end of the hallway and tasted salt on a damp breeze that blew in from outside. The open window frame stared south, directly across the bulging roof of the Superdome, two blocks away. Even from this distance, the dim moonlight was enough to reveal holes ripped out of the white sheet metal that protected the football field beneath. I heard that vague cry of desperation and despair again and turned to my left, blocking the noise out.

I couldn't help anyone in the Superdome. I might not be able to help anyone in New Orleans, but if I could help a little girl with a destiny in San Francisco, it would be enough.

I crossed the end of the tower and stopped at the corner. Leaning out and peering left, I squinted at the glow of those camping lanterns from a hundred yards away. The corner of the bed was visible, as was the right shoulder of one of Randy's chums. The rest of the poker game was obscured by another turn in the wall.

I left the back of the tower and moved more quickly than before, dodging the debris on the floor. I reached the first room on my left and found a storage closet full of rotten linens. Across from me lay the first ward, and I found it much as I had found those on the other side of the tower— an abandoned wreck, the floor puddled with rainwater from the busted windows. The second ward was the same. As I drew closer to the third, I slowed, conscious of the crunch of my footfalls over the dirt on the floor. Merle Haggard had been replaced by Conway Twitty and his "Slow Hand". It made me want to break a nose, witnessing classic music like that defiled in circumstances such as this, but I was more interested in what lay behind the door of that third ward.

The reinforced glass window was dusty, but there were smudges where somebody had recently cleaned away enough dirt to look through it. I slid quickly across the hall and slipped inside, pulling the door closed behind me and lifting the Victorinox, ready for action.

None was necessary. The room was unoccupied and mostly empty, but not in the same way as the other wards. Under dim moonlight, I surveyed a row of hospital beds pushed against the far wall. They were covered in sleeping bags. Cases of water were stacked on the floor alongside another ice chest and a giant duffel bag full of all the usual dry foods—chips, canned sausages, breakfast pastries. Muddy boot prints crossed the floor, leading from the beds to the door, and from the door across the room to...

My attention switched to the left side of the room and stopped. There was something there that immediately conflicted with my expectations for what should be found inside an abandoned hospital ward. It was a great lump of a thing, about the size of a compact sedan, and covered in a camouflage tarp that looked new. I eased toward it, listening to the voices during the pauses of Twitty's classic to ensure that nobody had left the poker game.

The lump rested at the end of the room in a cleared space. I reached it and glanced once over my shoulder, then knelt and lifted the tarp's edge. The MacroStream blinked on in low-output mode, just bright enough to reveal dark cardboard printed with thick black letters.

The chill returned to my spine. I squinted, certain that I wasn't looking at what I thought I was looking at. I lifted the tarp further and stuck the flashlight in my mouth, tugging the lid off a box and exposing the contents.

My chest turned tight, and the flashlight drooped. I shifted packing paper aside and withdrew a single item— brown and round, about ten inches long and about the diameter of a quarter. It was a stick of dynamite, and the box I had drawn it from was loaded with more of the same. A *lot* more.

I pulled the tarp over my head and scanned beneath it with the flashlight only to find box after box of the same. Hundreds upon hundreds of sticks, enough to blast that entire floor of the hospital into concrete dust. There were metal cans beyond the dynamite, each labeled with the familiar markings of US military-issued green-tipped 5.56mm ammunition, the standard diet of an Army M4A1 rifle, six more of which leaned against the wall beneath the far edge of the tarp. There were masks, also. Black ski masks stacked alongside rubber boots and black jumpsuits.

I tossed the dynamite stick back into the box and withdrew from the tarp, looking back to the door as my thoughts raced. I really wasn't sure what I expected to find when I entered the hospital. A little girl lost, hopefully. A few thugs who needed a lesson in fatherhood, and maybe a stack of pilfered Nikes and electronics. Petty, foolish nonsense.

But this? No. It didn't compute with what I knew about Randy and his gang. It made me think I had miscalculated, somehow. Maybe missed the forest for the trees...

I stopped myself, dropping the tarp as the next chorus of rowdy laughter erupted from the hallway.

It doesn't matter.

Whatever Randy had planned for a truckload of dynamite and some stolen small arms, I could deal with it by turning him over to the New Orleans police and their National Guard backup as soon as I found Autumn. What mattered now was simply getting her *out* of the building. Assuming she was here.

I flicked off the flashlight and departed the third ward, moving softly to the fourth—the final ward on that side of the tower. The poker game now stood barely thirty feet away at the end of the hall. I was still sheltered by the turn in the wall and the inky darkness beyond the lantern light, but I reduced my movement to a stealthy creep nonetheless. When the next round of betting produced a guffaw of jeers, I took the distraction as a window of opportunity and crept into the final room.

Disheveled hospital beds illuminated by soft moonlight greeted me as before, a walkway marked by dusty boot prints leading past another small heap of duffel bags and bottled water. Those footprints ran beyond an abandoned cafeteria cart with cups of chocolate pudding still heaped across the bottom. Across a bank of windows covered over by sheets.

Right to a bed at the end of the line, pushed against a rotten wall, with a small figure curled into a sleeping bag atop it. I moved silently on the balls of my feet. I identified the cloud of bright blonde locks spread across the pillow. The head beneath trembled a little, the sleeping bag tucked close to the face, the entire body wadded up into a fetal position.

I stopped next to the bed and closed the knife without a sound. Easing it into my pocket, I crouched and gently placed one hand on the girl's shoulder.

"Autumn?"

27

Autumn jumped as though she'd been electrocuted, head snapping back toward me with wide blue eyes locking onto mine. Terror and panic faltered into instantaneous confusion and deadlock, that moment when a brain identifies a familiar object far outside its typical context and subsequently descends into confusion.

But only for a split second, because Autumn Mercer was a child genius.

"Mason?"

Her voice rasped, turning shrill with excitement. I grinned but held a finger to my lips, motioning for her to lie still.

"Stay quiet," I whispered. "Are you hurt?"

Autumn winced. "My legs. I can't walk."

I hesitated a beat, caught off guard. Then a sudden grin broke across Autumn's girlish face, as bright as the sunrise.

"Gotcha." She chuckled.

I shook my head. "I hate you."

Glancing over my shoulder, I surveyed the door for any change in the pattern of light that spilled through the reinforced glass. There was none, but I thought I heard chairs scraping across the tile floor outside. Maybe one of Randy's chums, headed to piss down the stairwell.

Or maybe Randy himself, headed to check on his kidnapped child prodigy.

"Time to go," I said. "Your mama is worried sick."

My mention of Jessica brought a sudden gleam to Autumn's eyes, the grin melting into a deeper smile. I twisted on the floor, easing my hips toward the bedside and scooping my arms into cradles.

"Come on, kid. Piggyback."

Autumn pulled herself out of the sleeping bag with her arms, dragging limp legs across the bed and pushing them to either side of my sweaty torso. Then those same strong arms encircled my neck, and her skinny little body pulled close against my spine. I cradled her legs and stood, barely noticing her sixty-pound bulk on my back. She was lighter than the average Army rucksack.

"We gotta sneak, now," I said. "Whatever you do, don't make any noise, okay? Just hang on."

Autumn tucked her chin over my shoulder, arms wrapped around my neck. I started toward the door, but her voice stopped me.

"Mason?"

"Huh?"

"My...my teddy..."

I hesitated, the footfalls from outside the ward growing louder as additional rednecks scraped their chairs back. There was discussion of more beer. Questions about snacks.

Somebody was fiddling with the music, and a lot of people were moving.

But I remembered Autumn's teddy, that stuffed animal I never saw her without. It was a complete contrast to the adult-level conversations she practiced with ease—a reminder that she was still a kid.

"Where?" I asked.

"In the bed."

I turned back and leaned down, dropping one of her legs to scoop through the sleeping bag. I thought I felt the toy buried beneath a layer of goose-down camping insulation. I squatted and dug a little deeper, wrapping my fingers around the soft fabric of a well-loved companion.

And then the door opened. I didn't see it—I heard it. The stereo had switched to nineties Brooks and Dunn. They saw the light the same moment as I saw Randy Mercer appear over my shoulder, dressed in his customary torn blue jeans and sweaty wifebeater. He stopped in the doorframe, disorientation flashing across his face as he experienced the same mental deadlock that his daughter had—but longer, because unlike Autumn, Randy Mercer was as dumb as a fence post. Brooks and Dunn were almost brand-new men before he seemed to realize what—and *who*—he was looking at. And by then, it was much too late.

I cleared the gap between Autumn's bed and the doorway in two quick strides, releasing her right leg and cocking my arm like a battering ram. Randy's mouth opened for a scream a split second before I closed it for him—hard. Teeth busted, and his head snapped back, eyes rolling. Randy hit the wall and knocked over an IV pole. It clattered to the ground as loud and jarring as a gunshot—plenty loud enough to be heard by the crowd of rednecks outside. Even as I extricated myself from the tangle of Randy's legs and the fallen medical equipment, I could hear shouts in the hallway. Calls to Randy. Concerned demands for an update.

Yes, my cover was blown. And if I didn't get out of that room quickly, I'd be boxed in. The only thing left to do was make a run for it.

"Hang on, kid. Time to go!"

Autumn's bony arms clenched around my neck, and I barreled back into the hallway. I didn't have a plan. It wouldn't matter if I had. The moment Randy stepped into that room, every variable became an active variable. The only thing that remained was violence of action. Moving faster and harder than the enemy and hoping for a little luck.

My path of escape had to be the stairwell—the one route from the sixth floor to the ground floor that didn't involve a suicidal jump.

I hit the hallway outside the nurses' station like the rolling stone described by the stereo. The makeshift poker table was still there, a gunky hospital mattress covered in cards and cash. Four of Randy's wife-beating chums surrounded it, staggering to their feet even as I burst around the corner. None of them had time to rise or reach for guns before I hurtled past, spinning around the nurses' station and headed for the stairwell.

That was when I hit the fifth guy—a regular cow of a man with flabby arms and a bulging beer gut. He stood just outside an open elevator door, a box full of beer bottles upturned as he dumped them down the shaft. Glass shattered, and a wounded Randy screamed from the hallway behind me.

"Duke! *Get 'em!*"

Duke spun. The box dropped. His hand closed around the grip of a Beretta 96 tucked into his waistband, rotten brown teeth exposed by snarling lips as he drew.

I never gave him the chance to raise the weapon. I released Autumn's right leg again and flat-palmed Duke right in his sternum, driving with a twist of my shoulders. He stumbled back and dropped the gun as the force of my blow shoved him backward over a slick floor.

His foot hit the threshold of the elevator shaft. His flabby, oversized body carried him on. He shrieked once, slipped and flailed.

And then he was simply gone, vanishing into the shaft like the bottles he'd just dumped, screaming all the way to the bottom. I kept going, reaching the stairwell door and tearing it open as the first shot cracked from behind, shattering reinforced glass and zipping into a concrete wall.

"Stop, fool! You'll hit her!"

Randy called the cease-fire as we reached the stairs. I nearly wiped out over the raw sewage still coating the landing. We turned right and went down, Autumn's chest thumping against my shoulder blades as she clung on for dear life. A cacophony of shouts, curses, and pounding boots mixed with the Brooks and Dunn drawl just overhead. I could feel the hounds on my heels, maybe only yards behind, but I didn't dare look.

"Are they coming?" I shouted.

"They're seventeen steps back!" Autumn replied.

"Seventeen?"

"I count fast!"

My heart thundered as we reached the third floor. Autumn clung relentlessly on, conscious to keep her forearms clear of my windpipe as her fingers wrapped around my shirt. I thought ahead to the bottom, weighing my options. We could head all the way to the first floor, but I didn't know where to find an exit that low. Hiding would be a short-term option at best, and not a good one with all the guns bearing down on us. Randy might be afraid of shooting his daughter, but I wouldn't use her as a shield.

No. We had to get *out* of Big Charity, back onto the streets. Lose them in the chaos. Get out of New Orleans and *back* to Mississippi. Our best option was the window, the air-conditioning unit, and the tangle of chain-link fence. It would be a lot harder to navigate with a kid on my back, but I didn't have much of a choice.

"Hang on tight!" I called, exploding through the stairwell door on the second level and spinning immediately for the sick ward I had infiltrated through barely half an hour prior. I didn't bother trying to lock the stairwell door. I already knew that it wouldn't have a lock—it was against standard fire codes, and I didn't have time to improvise. I just needed to run.

The sick ward was exactly as I'd left it. I skidded over broken glass and reached the window just as the stairwell door burst open behind me.

"Seventy feet!" Autumn said. "By my calculations you've got about three seconds!"

Gee, thanks, kid.

I swung a leg through the window. Autumn pressed her face close to my shoulder, and I swung the other leg out. Then I dropped, eight feet to the top of the AC unit. Sheet metal dented as we landed with a boom. I dropped to my knees and broke my roll with my left hand.

Then the gunshots resumed. Two quick pops from overhead. The first bullet struck the AC unit, while the second zipped just past my face.

"Stop shootin'!" Randy screamed.

"He seen us, fool! He seen everything!"

I left them to argue and dropped off the AC unit, breaking into a sprint again. We crashed over the fallen chain-link fence, and I hurtled toward the guard shack. Heavy bodies struck the AC unit behind me. Redneck cursing and confused orders flooded the air. I stretched my legs out and reached the sidewalk, turning automatically left —away from I-10, toward the tangle of buildings that clogged the business district. The soft glow of security lights from the refuge station guided me forward. I stretched out my legs.

And then I ground to a halt. Two hundred feet directly ahead, rolling down Tulane Avenue, were a pair of armored NOPD trucks, fully equipped with spotlights and bullhorns, a small detachment of SWAT officers walking alongside them, dressed in full riot gear. They saw me the same moment I saw them, a spotlight dropping over my face and blazing as bright as the sun.

"Stop right there!"

28

I had only a split second to make a decision, but it was a simple decision to make. Nothing about the armored cops rumbling toward me, barking through a bull-horn, spoke to safety or security. There were half a dozen heavily armed, half-drunk rednecks on my heels, all ready to pop off a shot at the first thing that moved. If I ran toward the cops, Autumn would be caught dead in the inevitable crossfire.

I had to run the other way.

Spinning on the wet pavement, I hitched Autumn up my back. Then I burst westward, dead toward I-10. The bullhorn blared behind me, commanding me to stop. I thought I heard one of the trucks accelerating. I didn't wait to find out, commanding every last ounce of strength out of my worn muscles. I was giving out. I could feel it. A cocktail of too much physical effort combined with loads of mental strain was taking its toll. New Orleans had swallowed me whole, thrashed me around, and was ready to spit me back out.

But I couldn't stop running until we were well clear of

the hospital. Autumn called into my ear that Randy's crew was spilling out of the building. The bullhorn blared again, this time addressing the gang, but I knew they would ignore it. I rounded the corner onto South Robertson Street. Gentle moonlight illuminated a tangle of downed power lines and a street sign bent fully in half, with a sidewalk running along the right-hand side of the street and an expanse of parking lots littered by trash and battered cars standing to my left. I hopped a splintered power pole and took my chances with the downed power lines, muddy water exploding over my jeans as I hurtled along.

"They're just behind us!" Autumn said. "They got away from the cops. Can you run any faster?"

"What do you think?" I couldn't resist the sarcasm as my foot caught on a power line and I nearly fell. I knew Randy and his pals were right on our heels without needing to be told. I could still hear the bullhorn from Tulane Avenue, joined now by the growl of a motor. We were being driven from that angle, but even amid the clamor of the armored vehicle, I imagined the pound of redneck boots mixed with the heaving gasps of overweight men pushing their bodies well beyond their established limits.

South Robertson Street intersected with Cleveland Avenue dead ahead. A large office tower stood on the left-hand corner, Fire Station 14 sitting catty-cornered across from it. Both buildings cast thick shadows across a field of debris that littered the intersection. Torn pieces of two-by-fours, industrial insulation, and even chunks of a brick wall. A Mazda Miata lay on its roof, four tires pointed toward the midnight sky as the rednecks closed behind me.

And then I heard another engine—a deeper, harsher growl than that of the armored police truck. Diesel, not gas.

Chugging steadily amid the squeak of battered and abused suspension. It was a sound I'd heard before that night, and a sound I would recognize anywhere in the world—any combat veteran would.

It was the growl of a US Army Humvee.

The vehicle appeared to my right, exploding off of Cleveland Avenue with headlights blazing, and crashing over the storm-scattered building materials as though they were Legos. Tires barked as the Humvee ground to a stop, blocking my path at eighty feet. Doors burst open, and National Guardsmen rolled out, fully dressed in combat fatigues with M4 carbines held over their chests. The guy from the front passenger's seat led the group, raising a hand and shouting through the night.

"*Halt!*"

I knew what would happen next the moment I noticed the National Guardsman falling into a shooting kneel at the front bumper of the Humvee, M4 rising to his shoulder just as he'd been trained, body sheltered by the heavy steel of the truck. Muzzle pointed down Robertson Avenue. Just doing his job. Protecting his fellow guardsmen. Following protocol.

The last mistake he would ever make.

"*Don't!*" I screamed.

The handgun fire erupted behind me almost instantly, a chorus of crazed and drunken pops directed at the perceived threat of the peacekeepers ahead. I hurled myself right, off the street and toward the sidewalk as the bullets zipped over my shoulders and struck the Humvee. The guardsman at the front bumper screamed and tumbled sideways as his fellow troops scrambled for cover. I struck the concrete, air exploding from my lungs as I tumbled over gravel. Autumn screamed and fell off my shoulders. My nose hit the ground and erupted in blinding, flashing pain as blood surged out over my face. I saw stars, and I saw blacktop. The gunshots continued behind me—both the pops of a handgun and the sporadic thunder of 5.56 green tips spat from Army M4s. Bullets pinged off the armored sides of the Humvee, and for a moment I was no longer in New Orleans. I was no longer in Louisiana at all.

I was careening down an Afghani mountainside, dirt flooding my mouth and my boots, rifle spinning out of my grasp as I skidded amongst trees and hurtled over rocks, gunfire shredding the air overhead.

I rolled over with a groan, spitting blood from my mouth as my nose continued to stream. The pain was so bad I could barely see. My eyes burned, and my brain swam. I felt Autumn's hand on my arm, squeezing as her little face appeared in a blur directly overhead.

"Mason! Are you shot?"

I clawed my way to my feet, ignoring the question. I bent to wrap one arm around Autumn's middle, hauling her up against my side before I glanced quickly back toward the heart of the spontaneous firefight.

The guardsman was dead—I knew that the moment I saw him. He lay face up on the pavement, his body bathed by the glare of the Humvee's headlights, his rifle trapped under his hip. A giant pool of blood stained the asphalt around his head, further blood still dripping down his neck from the gunshot that had torn right through an artery.

He'd bled out in seconds.

My gaze locked with the NCO now dug in behind the rear bumper of the Humvee, shouting into a radio for backup. His gloved hand jerked once, motioning for me to take cover.

I didn't wait for another order. I clutched Autumn close, pinning her skinny body against my side before I turned east along Cleveland. The gunshots faded behind me, and the Humvee engine surged. Randy and his pals were splitting, I figured. The guardsmen wouldn't be able to keep up amongst the wreckage. The rednecks would likely escape.

But so would we. I ran, taking turns at random onto increasingly narrow streets, working away from the business district and the tangle of law enforcement and armed thugs it contained. Blood streamed from my nose, and my head thundered, but I didn't stop until a hotel loomed up directly ahead of me—a six-story building, boarded up on every side, a big sign pinned to the face of a locked glass entrance.

Closed For Storm.

My boot crashed three times into the glass panel before it shattered. The lock was key operated on both sides. I simply kicked a larger hole through the glass and ducked through. The lobby was dark, an empty receptionist desk on one side, an equally empty lounge and dining room to my left. Walls hung with hotel branding and directories for the gym and indoor pool.

I lowered Autumn to the tile floor, heaving and gasping for air as I spat blood from my mouth. Her T-shirt was speckled with it, but she made no complaint, simply clinging to her teddy. Behind the receptionist counter, I found a box of tissue paper and wadded several sheets into each nostril to stem the flow of crimson. It was all I could do not to scream as fresh pain burned through my face, reigniting agonies that I had *thought* were behind me.

When my vision finally cleared, I used my Victorinox to

break into a locked drawer, shuffling around for only a moment before I located a master card key. The hotel's power was out, the same as the rest of the city, but the electronic locks on hotel doors would be battery operated. They would function even in a power outage.

I offered Autumn a forced smile—maybe closer to a grimace—before scooping her up again, more gingerly this time. She rode my back up two flights of steps to the third floor, which was as far as my weary body could move. My MacroStream illuminated the hallway, and I selected a room at random a few doors down from the stairwell. The lock blinked green beneath the master key, and we pushed inside.

The room was small. Two queen beds, a useless microwave and TV, and a bathroom. The curtains were drawn, blocking out the chaos outside.

It was hot, also. Suffocatingly so, the air so stagnant I felt like I was wading into a sauna. But it was quiet, the beds looked soft, and most importantly of all, we were safely out of the path of Randy, his friends, or any of the law enforcement now chasing them. It would do.

I shut the door and flipped the latch; then I carried Autumn to the first of the two beds and squatted, allowing her to slide off my back. She landed with a little grunt, and I collapsed onto the bed across from her, blood- and sweat-coated face pointed at the ceiling.

Every part of me ached. I was so exhausted I felt as though I could pass out sitting up. My brain pounded again. My entire face burned. My eyes felt packed with grit.

But it wasn't the physical pain that tormented me. When I closed my eyes, I saw the intersection of Robertson Street and Cleveland Avenue. That familiar grind of a diesel engine, the prelude to gunfire. That kid wearing private stripes slamming to the ground under Humvee headlights. Spurting blood. Screaming for a split second before choking on his own body fluids.

He might have drowned before he bled out. His brain would have shut down either way. Was he from New Orleans? Maybe he was from some little town way up in the northern part of the state. Far from the bayous and beignets. Maybe he had joined the National Guard just to get through college, but he jumped at the chance to help innocent disaster victims.

Surely, he never expected to be shot at. He never expected to die in a domestic war zone.

"Are you okay, Mason?"

I lifted my head, blinking away the vision and suddenly remembering Autumn. She sat on the bed, the teddy clutched across her lap. One of its ears was stained crimson —likely with my own blood. But Autumn wasn't focused on the toy. She was focused on *me*, wide child eyes unblinking, and perfectly calm. She was filthy, and I noted vague bruising on her left forearm. The marks looked like thick fingers, clamped too harshly.

But she wasn't crying. She didn't even look afraid. She was perfectly calm, just as she had been during our entire frantic escape.

"I'm...I'm fine," I managed. "Are you okay?"

Autumn shrugged. "I could sleep. Haven't slept much lately."

I nodded. "Right..."

My vision wavered at the mention of sleep, and I was suddenly so exhausted I could barely hold my eyes open. The bed felt soft beneath me. Welcoming.

"Let's sleep awhile," Autumn said. "They won't find us here."

I nodded again. Then I kicked my shoes off and helped Autumn to remove her own. She snuggled down amid the pillows, and I collapsed right on top of the comforter on my bed, not even caring that I was filthy and coated in sweat.

Within seconds, I was passed out cold.

29

I didn't dream of the dying National Guardsman. I didn't even dream of Autumn or Jessica or Randy. The place I saw in my exhaustion could have been New Orleans, or it could have been any other city near the coast. Palm trees bent in the wind. Dirt and debris swirled around me like the interior of a tornado. I struggled to breathe, and I could barely see.

I shielded my head beneath one arm, desperate to find cover, but unable to move. With each grinding second, my heart rate accelerated. Adrenaline and panic surged into my bloodstream, forming a cocktail of desperation. I tried to slog forward, but every direction was cloaked in inky blackness. I fell to my knees. The pressure of the darkness was swallowing me—consuming me. I couldn't force it back.

I screamed into the night. *"Give me something!"*

It was a hoarse and desperate cry, drowned out by the wind. I didn't know why I shouted it, but even as the air vacated my lungs, I fought for another breath. I hit my hands and knees and clawed my way forward—just an inch. A foot. A yard.

And I screamed again. *"Please! Give me something!"*

Dirt clogged my eyes. My body trembled in the blast. I looked toward the sky.

And then the lightning struck. A flash of brilliant, all-consuming blue that raced across the sky in every direction, a spiderweb of illumination that was so bright and so sudden, it almost blinded me.

I blinked, and the light remained. Thunder rolled, but the streaks of blue never faded. I shielded my eyes with one hand, gasping for air. I looked through the whirlwind directly ahead...

And I saw my path.

I AWOKE WITH A START, sitting up in bed and gasping for air, sweat still streaming down my chest. Dull orange light shone through the hotel window, breaking across the floor in wavy patterns as it filtered through the curtain. My head was foggy, my mind moving slowly, but I remembered where I was. I remembered my desperate escape from Charity Hospital. I remembered Autumn riding on my back. I remember the gunshots and the dead guardsman.

I remembered the dream. Lightning blazing across a storm-torn sky and not fading. Never vanishing. If I closed my eyes, I could still see it.

Lowering my face into one hand, I breathed in deep and winced as fresh, hot pain raced through my face. It all exploded from my nose, where the twin wads of tissue paper were now stiff and crusty with dried blood. My eyes burned when I opened them, and racing pain ran up and down my spine and throughout my arms. Not the pain of injury or broken bones. Just the pain of shredded muscles, strained and overworked. The pain of weakness, my old drill instructor used to say.

What a cheerleader.

Pressing both hands against the bed, I forced myself to its edge and dropped both feet on the floor. My socks were filthy and still damp, as were my jeans. I barely noticed, flexing my toes over commercial carpet. Then I looked for Autumn.

She wasn't there. The bed next to mine was empty and neatly made. Her shoes rested on the floor next to it, but the little girl was gone. My heart thumped with sudden panic, and I bolted to my feet.

"Autumn?"

My voice boomed in the perfectly quiet room devoid of the usual electronic and HVAC hums.

"Over here," a soft voice squeaked. I spun toward the window, head suddenly light with dizziness.

Autumn sat in a chair propped directly beside it, the curtain pulled back three inches, allowing her to look out over the city. Her legs draped lifelessly over the edge of the chair, the teddy held beneath one arm. The toy's ear was clean, and a dirty wet washcloth lay on the windowsill next to her.

Autumn smiled. "Good afternoon."

I blinked. "Afternoon?"

"Seems so. The sun is in the west."

My wrist snapped toward my face, exposing the face of a filthy digital watch. It read 2:31 p.m. I breathed a curse.

"You needed to sleep," Autumn said. "I didn't want to wake you."

I sat on the end of the bed again, rubbing both eyes with my finger and thumb. Still trying to clear my mind. I blinked at my own reflection in the TV set and wished I hadn't. I looked like hell—not just dirty and worn, but kind of...well...old.

I wasn't a twenty-one-year-old Army Ranger anymore, and I was feeling it.

"You sleep okay?" I asked, forcing my mind back to Autumn.

"Yep. It's a good bed."

I nodded slowly, then squinted. "Wait...how did you get over there?"

Autumn rolled her eyes. "I have *arms*."

The first picture that popped into my mind was of Autumn walking on her hands across the little room. I knew it wasn't accurate, but it made me smile anyway. The kid seemed totally unfazed by the predicament of being kidnapped, dragged into a superstorm, and left to shelter in a hotel room with a near stranger.

It made me wonder what other trauma she had already endured—what misery had empowered her to shut her feelings down, drowning the moment in sarcasm for her own emotional survival.

"So...you're good?" I wasn't exactly sure what I was asking. I figured I would let Autumn decide.

"I'm kinda hungry," Autumn said. "I didn't drink the water. I read one time that you shouldn't drink tap water after a storm. The floodwaters can contaminate the water supply."

I nodded slowly, my own stomach growling at the

mention of food. I had only eaten the power bar since my meal with Frank at the FEMA station. I hadn't drunk much, either, but I'd certainly sweated.

"Wait here," I said.

I found a pair of vending machines down the hallway. Both were dead without power, of course, leaving the damp cash in my pocket worthless. But one of them had a glass face, allowing a full view of chips, crackers, candy bars, and a small assortment of drinks. That glass shattered beneath the butt of my Victorinox, and I used the tail of my shirt as a makeshift wheelbarrow. Loaded down with snacks and a half dozen bottles of water, I hesitated over the vending machine for a moment, a sudden flash of guilt washing over me.

I'd been smashing a lot of things lately. I knew insurance would cover it, but I still felt like a bum. Dropping three twenties into the bottom of the machine to ease my culpability, I waddled back to the room.

"Lunch first," I said, dumping the supplies onto the end of my bed. "Then dessert."

I tossed Autumn three packs of crackers, a sleeve of peanuts, and two Baby Ruth candy bars. She lit up like a kid at Christmas at the sight of the candy, but submitted to my instructions to consume the protein and carbohydrates first. We both guzzled warm water and ate in silence for a while, wrappers piling up on the floor as Autumn munched in quiet contentment.

"Are you familiar with the infinite chocolate paradox?" Autumn spoke around a mouth full of Baby Ruth, her cheeks puffed out like a chipmunk's. I sipped water.

"No," I said. "But I like the sound of it."

Autumn grinned, extending a chocolate-smeared hand. "Let me see your knife."

I cocked an eyebrow. She jabbed the hand at me. "Come on! Mom lets me use knives all the time."

I wasn't sure if I believed her, but I handed the Victorinox off to Autumn anyway. She opened the blade, flinching a little as it locked with a sharp *pop*. Then she reached for a Hershey's candy bar, pulling the foil wrapper away to reveal a five-by-five block constructed of little chocolate rectangles.

"It works like this," Autumn said, laying the candy bar on the windowsill. She cut with the knife, starting two blocks down on the right-hand side and working at an angle until the cut finished exactly at the bottom of the third block on the left-hand side. Then she cut a vertical line through the top half of the bar, two blocks in from the right. Her final cut ran across the top of the front left piece, liberating three squares of chocolate.

I watched with detached interest as my mind skipped ahead to the next problem at hand. Now rested and refueled, we would need to leave the hotel. I had evaded Randy and his thugs, but I needed to get out of the city. The longer we waited, the more difficult that would be. If we were detained by police, we would almost certainly be corralled into some disaster-relief zone near the Superdome, packed in with thousands of other survivors all clamoring for relief.

That wouldn't be a good situation, especially with Randy and his thugs still lurking around. It would be much better to simply get out of the city, then find our way back to Mississippi. I had enough cash in my wallet to float the expenses. Autumn would be safer with Jessica.

Assuming...

My mind stopped cold at the thought of Jessica in the hospital room, beaten to within an inch of her life. Maybe pushed over the edge.

No. I didn't want to think about that.

"And there you go!" Autumn clapped her hands. I blinked and refocused on the windowsill. She had rearranged the chocolate bar back into a five-by-five rectangle...except now there was an extra cube of chocolate set to one side. I frowned and scooted down the bed, squinting at the puzzle.

"What did you do?"

"I made more chocolate," Autumn said with a goofy grin.

I picked up the piece of chocolate and turned it over in my hand. Then I looked to the floor.

"I didn't open another," Autumn said. "Here, I'll show you."

She took the block back and rearranged the pieces. In a split second it was a part of the bar again, still five-by-five in size. I muttered a laugh.

"Okay. You got me. What did you do?"

Autumn shifted the blocks a few more times, adding and removing the same piece over and over, and finishing with a five-by-five chocolate bar every time.

"It's a function of the Banach-Tarski paradox," she said.

"Oh, sure. The Banach-Tarski paradox. Why didn't you say so?"

Autumn rolled her eyes. "Mason, I'm being serious! It's a mathematical theory. Basically, that one equals two. Which is, of course, patently absurd!"

Autumn laughed again. It was a pleasant little sound, like water rolling over stones in a mountain brook. It made me want to smile also.

"The idea is that any object, split into enough parts, can create two objects of the same size. It's an illusion."

"Looks pretty real to me." I gestured to the chocolate bar. Autumn shook her head, extending her thumb and forefinger into an L shape and pressing it against the outside of the chocolate bar like a framing square. She arranged the bar both ways.

"See? It's smaller without the other bar. Still five-by-five, but not as big. It's a geometrical illusion!"

Another broad grin. This time I returned it. Autumn went back to work shifting the little blocks around, and I settled onto the bed. As I watched her, I noticed the smile remained on her face, but it failed to reach her eyes. She blinked a lot as she fiddled with the chocolate, looking more like a child playing with toys than a prodigy exploring an elusive phenomenon. I thought about her father and her mother and suddenly realized she hadn't asked about either of them. She hadn't inquired about our travel plans. She hadn't asked why I had been sent to save her, or what my intentions were. When I'd found her in the hospital, she hadn't been crying or distraught. She'd been sleeping quietly.

And then she'd simply gone along with me, unfazed by the gunfire and chaos. It wasn't natural. It wasn't the way a child should behave, and I didn't think her emotional detachment had much to do with her spectacular brilliance. This felt more like trauma, like when a soldier jokes about being blown in half as a way of managing his own fear.

"Autumn?" I said.

She didn't look up. She continued to fiddle with the chocolate.

"Autumn, I need to talk to you."

She blinked hard. Suddenly her eyes filled with tears, but she still didn't look up. The chocolate was melting under the warmth of her fingertips, leaving brown trails across the windowsill.

"Is she gone?" Autumn whispered, her voice barely audible.

"What?"

Autumn looked up. "My mother."

I frowned, then shook my head. "No. No, of course not. Why would you think that?"

Autumn shrugged, looking down again. Still crying.

And then I understood. It was a logical trail of thought that any genius could traverse with ease. Jessica loved her daughter more than anything. More than life itself.

Yet Jessica hadn't come to save her.

"She got hurt," I said, deciding that frank honesty was the best approach. "She's in a hospital, but she's going to be okay. We're headed there next."

Autumn nodded slowly. She sniffed. Then she looked up.

"Did Daddy do it?"

An invisible fist hit me in the gut. I tensed, my chest suddenly tight. My mouth half open, but unable to move. Unsure what to say. Autumn just stared at me, unblinking. Waiting.

I nodded, again deciding that honesty was the only approach. This kid was nobody's fool. She deserved the truth.

Autumn looked down again, gently scrubbing her hands on the damp washcloth she'd used to clean her teddy. When she spoke again, she sounded years older than she was. Like a young adult.

"Daddy doesn't mean it. He just gets that way, sometimes.

Like when he's had too much to drink. He just gets...angry, sometimes."

More heavy blinking. The fist that struck my gut pressed harder, twisting now. Digging in deep. I thought of Randy Mercer inside Charity Hospital, and suddenly I wanted to beat him with a pipe wrench. I wanted to break every miserable bone in his body, crushing him into a million pieces.

How *dare* he do this to his own daughter? To his own wife? What kind of miserable scum...

I broke my thoughts off. The anger wouldn't help Autumn. I didn't have the first clue about how to tend to the psychological damage Randy had unleashed. I could barely deal with my own psychological problems. Autumn needed her mother.

Sliding to my knees, I grabbed her little hands in my own and offered her a smile. Autumn looked up, tangled hair framing her face. She was still crying.

"Hey," I said. "Here's a math problem for you. If I had infinite pockets, how many Baby Ruths could you steal from them?"

That brought a little grin. I winked.

"Come on, kid. You can ride piggyback again. We're getting out of here."

30

I cut strips of hotel towels and used them to fashion twin slings that draped crossways over my shoulders and down to my hips. The slings were wide and strong, offering plenty of support for Autumn's legs and allowing my hands to remain free as she clung to my shoulders, the teddy riding between us. Then I revisited the busted vending machine and loaded a laundry bag with more peanuts, crackers and bottled water.

And, of course, Baby Ruth candy bars.

We departed the hotel at three p.m., giving us an ample five hours of daylight to escape the city. I stuck to the sidewalks of quieter, narrower streets, striking east through the French Quarter before turning north for the FEMA station where I'd left Frank.

I figured that whatever connections had allowed him to sneak a firearm past the metal detectors might be enough to secure passage for Autumn and me out of New Orleans. Or at least a phone call on a borrowed emergency satellite phone to the hospital in Hattiesburg. If Jessica had surfaced from her coma, she'd want to know that Autumn was safe. And if she hadn't...well, I didn't want to think about that.

The demon sun had returned in full wrath as I slogged along narrow streets that sliced through the oldest portion of the city in a neat grid of rectangles, a little like Autumn's chocolate bar, but not as easy to manipulate. French Quarter New Orleans is the classic part of the city you always see in travel guides and postcards. Multicolored, multileveled buildings all built directly together, with scrollwork iron columns and railings. Tall, narrow windows, grimy streets, and an absolute menagerie of bars, restaurants, boutique hotels, gift shops, voodoo stores, and three-hundred-year-old apartments with iron gates held closed by deadbolts.

I chose the French Quarter as our method of egress because I remembered hearing that this part of the city was built on the highest ground in New Orleans and had sustained minimal damage during Katrina. Even though they were significantly different storms, I hoped the same would hold true for Nadia, meaning that police and recovery personnel so hell-bent on corralling citizens toward the Superdome would be occupied elsewhere.

I was right. The French Quarter was boarded up solid, with trash and debris strewn about the streets and clogging storm gutters that bubbled with muddy water. Lampposts were bent, and occasional porches dropped under the abuse of one-hundred-sixty-mile-per-hour winds. One old building had caved in altogether, dumping a two-story wall of bricks atop a parked Nissan. Portions of the street ran with as much as three inches of water, and *everything* stank. It smelled of mud and rot and spoiled food. It stank of heat and mildew and the everlasting punishment of that demon Louisiana sun.

But for all that, it was relatively easy to navigate eastward along the northern banks of the flooded Mississippi, side-stepping debris and crashing through mud puddles at times, but remaining undisturbed by cops or refugees. What law enforcement officers I did pass rumbled by astride all-terrain vehicles, nodding at me occasionally but making no effort to stop our progress.

They were looking for something else. I wondered if that *something* was a soldier-slaying gang of Mississippi rednecks.

Stopping at the corner of Saint Philip Street, I sipped bottled water and squinted into the sun as I stared down the length of New Orleans's most famous avenue of drunkenness and revelry. I had deliberately avoided Bourbon Street during our multi-mile trek away from the hotel, not only because I thought a bar-laden portion of the city might be likely to draw more looters and law enforcement, but also because...I didn't want to face the memories. Already standing surrounded by the distinct architecture of the French Quarter was unleashing long-dormant feelings of passion and heat. The burn of whiskey on my throat and the taste of my fiancée's lips on my tongue.

No matter how many decades passed, I thought I would always remember that long weekend. Our first little getaway as a couple. She hadn't wanted to go—she was a good girl and old-fashioned. She didn't believe in shacking up with boyfriends.

I was considerably less noble, if I'm being honest. I couldn't wait to get her into bed. In hindsight, I don't think she ever would have succumbed to the temptations of spicy seafood and good New Orleans jazz if she hadn't already come to terms with spending her life with me.

Mia was like that. She was one in a billion.

"You okay, Mason?" Autumn spoke quietly from my shoulder. She'd sagged a little in the sling over the past hour, arms loosening around my shoulders. The heat was getting to her. She was slender, but not in overly great shape. I imagined that exercise opportunities must be limited, living in a wheelchair.

"Terrific," I said. "We're making good progress."

I passed her the bottle and waited until she drained it, steadying myself on a bent stop sign. Then we were off again, slogging across Bourbon Street and up St. Philip. Leaving all those memories in the muck.

"What does math say about hurricanes?" I asked, just to make conversation.

"Not to get caught in one." Autumn giggled.

"I don't need a doctorate to know that. Hit me with something impressive."

"I was reading something interesting about energy. An average hurricane can produce as much as one-point-five *trillion* watts of it. That's about half the total energy generated by the world's power grid each year. Of course, Nadia was bigger. Much bigger."

"Like a nuclear bomb," I muttered, surveying a block of aged French-style buildings that had succumbed to the pressure of the winds. Their former architectural style was only recognizable by their now mangled wrought-iron railings.

"Much more than just one nuclear bomb," Autumn corrected. "Over the life cycle of a hurricane, the total energy produced can be as much as ten thousand nuclear bombs, depending on variables, of course. It's not really a very good juxtaposition. Bombs release all their energy at once, very fast. Hurricanes sustain their efforts over extended periods of time."

"Juxtaposition?"

"Comparison. Simile. Two things held in contrast."

I laughed. "I know what it means, kid. You read too much."

"I've been that way since I was little. I've always enjoyed books. There's so much you can find in them...it's a whole other world."

And your world isn't so wonderful.

I thought it, I didn't say it. Instead, my mind circled back to something else Autumn had said—that throwaway comment about Nadia producing over a trillion watts of raw energy. It reminded me of my dreams. That repeated vision of fighting through the dark, screaming for help.

The sudden flash of sustained lightning, as bright as the blast that had illuminated the wrecked Ford pickup where I'd found that abandoned map. My gateway to locating Autumn.

"Is that why the lightning is brighter?" I asked.

"What do you mean?"

"The lightning in hurricanes. Is it brighter because of all the energy hurricanes produce?"

Autumn paused. I could hear her scratching one cheek.

"Hurricanes don't really produce lightning," she said. "You need vertical winds for that. Hurricanes produce horizontal, circular winds. That's why you wouldn't have seen any lightning during the storm."

I stopped on the sidewalk, twisting my head back toward her. "But I did see lightning. A lot of it, all at once. The brightest lightning I ever saw. It lit up the whole city."

Autumn puckered her lips. I could tell she was struggling with the puzzle, fascinated by it. Trying to solve it, right there in her head. I waited.

At last, she simply shrugged. "I'd need to pursue that line of study before I could explain it. All I know is...hurricanes don't produce lightning. Not usually."

I accepted her explanation with a nod, then hefted her farther up my back as I slogged out of the French Quarter and into the heart of the Seventh Ward. It was by far the largest neighborhood I had visited yet in New Orleans, sprawling on every side in an endless field of devastation. Nadia had hit *hard* here, leveling entire blocks and obliterating anything that wasn't built of solid concrete. There was flooding, also. Not as bad as the Lower Ninth Ward, and already receding, but in places the overtopping of the levees had produced as much as three feet of runoff. I kept to the high ground the best I could, but it was inevitable that I had to wade amongst rivers of inky black floodwater, marked by street signs and shattered light poles.

The smell had worsened considerably since we migrated out of the French Quarter. The sewage, rotten food, and mildew stenches were all there, but now that ominous odor I'd first detected only hours after Nadia's passing dominated my senses. It was death, and it was much stronger than what I had smelled the previous day. Rotting flesh and decaying bodies, sweet and sticky like the perfume of hell. I choked and tried to ignore it, but I knew Autumn had noticed. She said nothing, simply lifting her little T-shirt over her nose while we powered on beneath thundering helicopters that circled overhead like flies over dog crap. For the first time since leaving downtown, I saw refugees en masse, many of them sorting through their shattered homes for what could be salvaged. New Orleans police patrolled in flat-bottom boats, but they didn't attempt to intrude. Based on simple observation, I judged the Seventh Ward to be a poorer part of town. Maybe it was low on the priority list of places to secure.

Judging by Frank's tattered FEMA map, we were nearing the outskirts of St. Roch when I first heard the scream. The street I trudged along was mired in shin-deep water, a dead cat floating slowly by amid chunks of residential insulation. Most of the houses were blown to matchsticks, with only a few standing atop muddy block foundations. The paint schemes were pastel, the roofs fragmented and sagging, cars tossed at random among the streets like abandoned toys in a sandbox.

The scream was female—shrill and not young. It tore from beyond the next block, loud with desperation and fear. As I ground to a halt and listened, the voice of panic repeated, joined now by a rowdy jeer and a burst of profane threats.

I broke into a jog down the street, shoving past the cat carcass to reach the next intersection. I looked right and located the source of the disturbance fifty yards away on the next block—three homes erased from their foundations, leaving only one standing. The surviving structure was pastel pink in color, a hundred years old at the youngest, with a sagging roof and slouching front porch.

The front door was open, and four beefy black guys stood on the steps, skin glistening with sweat as they jeered at an aged black woman. She stood with a broomstick poking at them like a spear, blocking the way to her front door and pleading for them to leave her alone.

They weren't leaving. That much was clear in a millisecond. Whatever lay inside that house, they'd come to take it.

"Come on, granny! We hungry!"

"I ain't got nothing," the old lady sobbed. "I ain't ate since yesterday!"

"Sheesh. You sure look like you been packin'. Don't she?"

A chorus of laughter. The ringleader swung onto the porch, and the old lady stumbled backward. He bypassed her broom and reached for the door.

Then I saw the kids. Two of them, maybe three or four years old, sheltering inside with wide eyes.

"Mason!" Autumn hissed. "Do something!"

I hesitated, uncertainty slowing my natural instincts. Alone, I would have already broken bones. But with Autumn on my back and—

My thought process was cut short as the woman struck one of the intruders with the broom, cracking him across the arm. Thick muscles flexed, and he tore the broom from her grasp. His three buddies reached the porch, and one shoved the old lady. She crashed backwards, slamming into a screen door. The ringleader cocked a hand and slapped her right across the face—hard.

Enough.

I slid my arms out of the makeshift sling and set Autumn down on the raised foundation of a house.

"Stay here," I said. "Don't make any noise."

"Go get 'em!" Autumn urged. "Hurry!"

31

I departed the intersection and fast-slogged down the next street, heedless of the noise I was making as I closed the gap to the pastel pink house.

"Hey, you!"

My shout was enough to draw the attention of the ring-leader. His hand was still wrapped around the old lady's blouse, hauling her up and pinning her against the door. Wide eyes and flashing teeth turned on me, joined by his three companions. I reached the sidewalk and climbed out of the floodwater, kicking debris out of my way on my path to the front porch.

"Put her down," I said.

The ringleader snorted a laugh, scanning the streets behind me. Double-checking for cops, probably. Weighing his options.

I already knew which route he would choose.

"You betta *roll*, cracka," he snarled.

I reached the steps but didn't ascend. I wanted to keep a little distance between myself and the group of four, giving me precious time to make tactical decisions. I was unarmed, relatively speaking. They might be heavily armed. This wasn't a good situation.

I had to play it smart.

"Let her go," I said. "She's got nothing you need."

Another laugh, joined by a wolfish grin. "That what you think?"

"That's what I know."

He released the old lady, allowing her to crumple against the door. His buddies parted as he approached me, bulky biceps shining beneath the blazing sunlight, a black tank top stretched over corded muscles. He'd spent some time in a weight room—a lot of time. Judging by some of the janky tattoos that adorned his bulky arms, it might have been a prison weight room. It looked like prison ink.

I wasn't intimidated. Lots of people go to prison. Not all of them belong there. Even amongst those who do, very few are half as tough as they think they are.

The guy reached the last of the steps, standing just six or eight inches above me, and dropped a hand over his crotch. He lifted the tail of the shirt, exposing the grip of a battered and abused Smith and Wesson SD9. His lip curled again.

"*Roll,*" he growled. "Befo' I ventilate yo ass."

I glanced only momentarily to the handgun. Then I looked over his shoulder to the old lady quaking against the doorframe. The two dark faces hiding in the shadows within the house.

"You gonna leave them be?" I asked.

A snort. He spat a long stream of saliva onto the sidewalk.

I sighed. "Well. You'd better ventilate me, then."

Eyes widened in disbelief. Then disgust. The hand

dropped for the pistol again, just the way I knew it would. Carried without a holster, it was difficult for him to get his hand around the grip. It took precious time.

And he was out of time.

I struck his left knee with a lightning kick of my left boot, driving every ounce of force I could muster into the joint that supported the bulk of his bodyweight. A shriek exploded from his lips as the joint shattered. Then he was going down, the gun still caught in his pants. I grabbed his arm and snatched it toward me, pulling the gun with it. As he plummeted toward the floodwater, I twisted the arm backwards, and the pistol spun from his hand. Then he face-planted into the sidewalk, still shrieking.

The other three were on me before I could even think about retrieving the weapon. It didn't matter. People think there is value in the high ground during a fistfight, and there can be. But when you throw stair steps into the mix, I'll take the low ground any time. Moving upward, my leg muscles were always tensed, my body weight always securely planted on a firm foundation.

Moving downward, none of those advantages were available to my adversaries. Their bodyweight rocked forward over empty air with each step they took.

All I had to do to take the first of the three out of the fight was to grab him by the belt as his right foot swung out to take the next step. I yanked him easily off balance, and he went tumbling past me in a flailing mass of arms and panicked cries, landing alongside his knee-shattered leader in the muck.

But then the last two were rushing in, and this time, a knife was involved. I heard the snap of a switchblade even as I engaged the left-hand man with a right hook, driving the wind out of his lungs with a blow to his ribs. He choked, and I twisted toward his partner.

Just a moment too late. The knife thrust toward me, a glistening blade reflecting the summer sun, and I was forced to lean quickly to the left to avoid it. The blade passed beneath my arm, missing my vital organs, but it didn't miss my flesh. Steel sliced straight through my T-shirt and then through flesh, tearing a long gash in my rib cage. I slammed my right arm back down against my side, pinning his knife hand in place. Then I pulled him close. Blocking out the pain with sheer adrenaline, I yanked him sideways.

He was caught off guard, still standing off balance after the knife thrust. He toppled left, and I let him go, ignoring the knife as it flailed helplessly past my knees. His head struck the steps. My boot smashed into his face. Bones crunched, and cartilage burst. He screamed in agony and dropped the knife. I bent for the fallen Smith and Wesson, scooping it up and pivoting quickly toward the last guy. The guy I had winded.

He'd backed up as his buddy fell. He saw the gun rising toward him, and he made a lifesaving decision—he turned and ran, flinging himself off the porch and landing in the floodwater lapping against the house. In a split second he was gone, thrashing around the corner, out of sight and out of my line of fire. I stood with my arm clamped against my side, fighting to stem the flow of blood seeping out of my torn rib cage.

And then I heard two things at once—both shrill, high-pitched sounds that broke through the city as loud as the gunshots I'd just fired. The first was the wail of a police vehicle, heralding the arrival of a four-wheel-drive Ford F-150 that crashed down the street toward me, blue emergency lights blinking.

The second was a child's scream. Loud and desperate, ringing from down the street where I'd left Autumn.

My gaze snapped in that direction just in time to see two guys fighting their way toward another jacked-up Ford, this one painted white with blue labels running down its sides. The labels read *FEMA*, and the guys wore wifebeater tank tops.

Between them, they dragged Autumn.

"Stop!" I leapt over the vanquished thugs still cowering on the sidewalk and hurtled toward the flooded street. Already the rednecks had reached their pickup. Doors popped open, and Autumn was thrust inside. She screamed again and reached for me. I raised the pistol.

There was no shot—not at nearly a hundred yards. The New Orleans police truck was almost on top of me, water exploding from its front tires as a loudspeaker blared down the flooded street.

"Drop the weapon! Hands up, or we shoot!"

I looked left as the truck ground to a halt. A wave of murky water surged up my thighs even as blood drained from my wounded side. Two cops deployed into the street. Both wore body armor. Both wielded pump-action shotguns.

There was no time to run, and no place to hide. I flung the pistol down and gritted my teeth, raising one arm while I used my other to maintain pressure on my wound. The first cop stopped at the nose of the still-chugging Ford, shotgun pointed at my chest. The second grabbed me by the arm and manhandled me against a grimy black brush guard.

He was sweaty and smelled of body odor. His uniform

was speckled with mud, but I could read the nametape as I looked over one shoulder. *Broussard.*

"Hands behind your back!"

"You need to listen to me." I spoke through my teeth as damp steel handcuffs ratcheted down over my wrists, tighter than necessary, binding my hands over my spine. "There's a girl who was just kidnapped. Put me in the truck, and I'll point the way—"

"Shut up," Broussard snapped, shoving me against the brush guard as he turned to overlook the house behind us. The front porch. The one thug with the busted knee, and the second with an obliterated face. Where the final man had gone, I had no idea. He had the good sense to join his fleeing buddy, apparently, but there was more than enough evidence left behind. The face-smashed guy hadn't stopped screeching yet, hands pressed against his flattened nose, writhing on the front porch steps.

"Did you do this?" Broussard demanded.

I said nothing. He shook me.

"Hey! You'd better start talking!"

I just glared, and the cop with the shotgun twitched the weapon.

"Put him in the truck. Backup's on the way."

I didn't fight as Broussard hauled me to the back seat of the pickup. A steel partition divided the back seat from the front, but it wasn't a purpose-built containment compartment like you might find in the back of a patrol car. The door handles remained on the insides of the back doors, and the windows were unprotected.

The cop shoved me in anyway, manhandling my body into the seat before slamming the door. I'd barely landed on my back before I was at work with the hidden compartment stitched into my nylon belt. There was a handcuff key hidden there, planted right at the base of my spine. This wasn't the first time I'd used it. The practice was becoming downright familiar.

As the two cops rushed to triage the bleeding street thug, my fingers found the keys. While he continued to thrash, I broke out of the handcuffs and threw them on the floor. As the cops called for backup, I dropped out of the far side of the pickup, back into the floodwater.

Then I was rushing across the street, clamping one arm against my wound, headed back the way I'd come. Back toward the last place I'd seen Autumn. I reached the intersection and looked both ways.

But the fake FEMA truck was long gone. The rednecks in wifebeater tank tops were long gone.

Autumn was long gone.

32

I staggered to a stop at the intersection and looked both ways, breath running ragged through my lungs as I searched the streets for any sign of the departing pickup. Floodwater lapped against the sides of houses and ran up to my knees, but there was no discernible trend to the current. No specific direction of the ripples that might give away the truck's direction of travel. Already, too much time had passed. The vehicle had vanished...but the streets were far from empty.

A pair of armored New Orleans police vehicles and a National Guard Humvee rumbled up the street toward me, water exploding over their front bumpers and crashing over muddy windshields. Blue lights flashed, and the scream of the face-smashed thug behind me served as a homing beacon to draw them right toward my position.

Backup had arrived in force, and I had to move.

I held my bleeding rib cage as I crashed through the collapsed side of a shotgun home, bricks and broken boards peeking out of the murky water like alligator teeth. Clambering over them, I found footing on a soggy hardwood floor just as the convoy of heavy vehicles reached my block. Descending into a crouch behind a busted wall, I grimaced through the pain racing up my side and exploding in my brain. Blood seeped between my fingers, and I looked over one shoulder.

The convoy reached the intersection, but they didn't so much as pause at a wind-bent stop sign, rumbling right through and turning for the parked police pickup in front of the pastel pink house. Through cracks in the damaged wall, I recognized the outline of a SWAT helmet behind armored glass. Then came the Humvee, occupied by another wide-eyed kid from the Louisiana National Guard, an M4 rifle held across his chest.

Terrific.

I sagged against the wall and fought to catch my breath, regarding my newfound hiding spot for the first time. It was a nursery. Or it had been a nursery before Nadia. The walls were flood stained but decorated with cartoon characters. A busted crib lay pinned beneath a fallen roof timber. Plastic toys painted in bright primary colors lay strewn across the floor.

There was no child. Thank God.

Peeling my hand back, I finally inspected the nature of the knife wound to my side. The cut was deep, I could already tell that. Four inches long and jagged near one end, but I didn't think the blade had cut beyond my rib cage. I forced myself to spread the cut and contort my body until I could gain a direct view.

No—the blade had only sliced muscle. No organs were reached, but one of my ribs was visible, scraped by razor steel. Dirty steel also, more than likely. Grit in the cut was visible. It made me think of all the billions of microbes that swarmed amid the floodwater. Rotten flesh and decaying food stuffs, all baking beneath the heat. It was an infection incubator in the truest sense of the term. If the cut wasn't cleaned, it would swell and inflame by midnight.

There was only one problem. I had nothing to clean it with. I'd left my laundry bag full of snacks and bottled water next to Autumn, one block closer to the old lady's house. The cops would see me if I attempted to recover it. I could surrender myself, of course, and receive medical care.

But I would also go to jail. I would have to answer for the blood sprayed across the old lady's front porch steps. Precious hours would be lost while I pled my case, and all the while Autumn would be held by Randy and his team of trigger-happy thugs, locked into the epicenter of prolonged violence and almost certain injury, if not death.

How did they find us?

The frustrated question thundered through my mind over and over again as I ripped my T-shirt off. The blade of my Victorinox snapped open, tearing the shirt into strips. I selected the cleanest section of cloth and wadded it into the gash, igniting fresh pain that seared into my brain.

I blocked out the agony and focused my thoughts on the problem at hand. The problem of—yet again—finding Autumn in the midst of a big city wrecked by a superstorm and swarming with now hostile cops and National Guard.

Had Randy been trailing us all the way from the French Quarter? Had I been that blind?

No way. I'd checked my six regularly. I'd taken a weaving, irregular path. He couldn't know where we were. He couldn't possibly know where we were headed. We'd lost him. I'd made sure of it.

Unless...

The teddy.

My mind locked on Autumn's beloved toy bear, and I gritted my teeth in fury. Not at Autumn, and not even at Randy, but at myself.

Stupid.

Randy knew that Autumn never went anywhere without the toy. He was also paranoid and controlling. He must have placed some kind of tracking device inside it while she was doped up with sleeping pills. The moment we slipped away at Cleveland Avenue, he would have known where we went. He would even have known that we were holed up in that hotel.

But the hotel wouldn't have been a safe place to strike. Not so close to the heart of the city, with so many cops around. Randy would have bided his time. He might even have paid those third-rate street thugs to harass the old lady, knowing that it was an injustice I couldn't ignore.

Stupid, stupid, stupid.

Peeling the T-shirt strip away from my injury, I inspected the blood flow. It had subsided a little. I replaced the makeshift bandage and used a shard of busted hardwood flooring as a makeshift windlass to tighten down another strip of T-shirt around my torso. It held the wadded-up T-shirt in place, freeing my hands.

My fingers were stained in crimson as I pulled them away. They trembled as I swallowed past a dry throat and looked to my watch.

It was nearly five p.m. The demon Cajun sun had crossed into its final stretch of torment, but hours still remained before darkness resumed. The grimy map I pulled out of my pocket still bore Frank's markings, now blurred by water damage as I spread it across my thighs. I referenced the bent street sign, still visible through the busted wall, to obtain the names of the intersecting streets.

Then I pinpointed my position on the map in the northern section of the Seventh Ward. Thinking quickly, I forced my mind to focus past the pain and stress and frustration, cutting down to what truly mattered. To what the army had trained me to zero in on: the next tactical step.

As badly as I wanted to go after Autumn directly, I knew I couldn't. I was injured, now, and without food or water. Worst of all, I still didn't know where to *find* Autumn.

Back at the hospital? Would Randy and his pals really return there?

I needed to think about it. Unpack the problem logically. And in the meantime, I needed medical care. I needed to refit and refuel. Where could I do that?

It wasn't a difficult decision. I was far closer to the FEMA aid station where I'd left Frank than I was to the core of the city, where Randy had likely retreated. I would need to sneak out of the Seventh Ward, keeping my head down as I approached the FEMA aid station. Every cop in New Orleans would be notified to be on the lookout for a tall white male with a bloody rib cage.

But they'd also be on the lookout for a few hundred other suspects by now. They'd still be engulfed in chaos, and they weren't trained like I was to slip through a war zone like a wraith, capitalizing on the chaos.

I would make it to the FEMA station. I would stitch up the wound and swallow some antibiotics. Then I was headed back into the city.

This time, I would take no prisoners.

33

The final leg of my journey back to the FEMA aid station, even minus the presence of a sixty-pound kid on my back, was the worst stage of my storm-torn trip to New Orleans by far. The sun was arcing toward the west, but the heat that had blanketed the city all day long seemed to have seeped into its very soul. Steam rose from stagnant rivers of water flooding out of storm sewers and at times consuming entire streets. The smell was worse than ever. A thick cocktail of death and despair, dragging the Seventh Ward into a new level of misery as the cries of desperate survivors rose toward National Guard helicopters beating paths back and forth across the city.

I was desperately thirsty. Hungry, aching with pain, and so tired I thought I could drop. But I wasn't the only one. I could feel the despair of thousands of displaced and devastated souls in the very air, hanging like a blanket as thick as the Louisiana humidity that sucked the energy from my muscles. Those broken thousands were gathered on front porches and spread across muddy yards, huddled around what imperfect shelter they could find, just sweating it out.

Some acknowledged me with a grunt or a dip of their heads as I staggered past, but most just stared off into empty space. Waiting. Hoping. Praying for the next chug of a heavy vehicle to promise water and aid—or at least, transportation to an aid station. But every truck that passed, both military and police, was destined for a clearly different purpose. Word of the gunfight north of Charity Hospital had spread quickly, I judged. I could see the aggression and mistrust in the face of every cop and National Guardsman as I shrank into the shadows of obliterated homes and let them roll by.

They weren't here to get people out or to deliver relief. They were here to establish security and pave a way for secondary convoys to bring the aid. With gunfire still popping from distant neighborhoods across the city, and occasional shrieks echoing down flooded streets, I couldn't say that I blamed them. Nothing about the environment I was lost in felt like the Land of the Free. If I blinked, I was back in the Middle East. The sun beating down drew sweat out of my Army ACUs.

And those guns popping from blocks away were wielded by Taliban insurgents rolling my way.

I made it through St. Roch and back to the swollen banks of the Mighty Mississippi just as my knees began to give out beneath me, the cumulative effects of exhaustion, blood loss, and dehydration building into a new kind of storm that battered the levees of my resolve. My makeshift bandage had stemmed most of the blood flow, but a trail of it still ran down my leg, and the pain had only magnified as inflammation set in.

The perimeter of the FEMA aid station was more

defined than before. The fence had been expanded, and powerful spotlights blazed down over the camp as aid workers scuttled along lengthy lines of survivors unloading from the beds of National Guard trucks. New Orleans cops provided a security perimeter, doing their best to search the newcomers for weapons or elicit material before admitting them into the camp. It was a losing battle—the ratio of survivors to law enforcement was at least fifty to one, and everybody was starving, thirsty, and desperate. I had no trouble slipping through a gap in the fence and staggering along the back side of a parked box trailer, swiping a bottle of water from an aid stack on my way toward the darkest corner of the camp. There were cots set up there under massive green tents. All military issue, all adding to my existing delusions of what continent I was standing on. As I walked, I sipped water and searched the faces I passed, looking for one of two things—Frank or a medical tent.

I found the medical tent first, managed by the Red Cross and marked as such. There were cops lined up outside it, however, each wearing a radio and surveying the crowd with earned suspicion. I thought it was unlikely that they would recognize my face based on description alone, but the knife injury would draw questions.

I pivoted away from the Red Cross tent, slipped through a long food line, and headed for the field of cots. I made it halfway through them before I finally found the face I was looking for, like a needle in a stack of dirty, beleaguered hay.

"Frank." I kept my voice down as I slipped up behind him. The retired cop sat on a cot, cleaning the soles of his boots with a stick. He startled as I laid a hand on his shoulder, and one hand dropped toward his waistline.

He never reached the gun. He recognized me first, and his eyes turned wide.

"Sharpe! Lord have mercy, what happened—"

"Quiet," I rasped. "Follow me."

I stumbled off before allowing him an opportunity to interrogate me further. Frank had the good sense to shove his feet back into the boots and follow me through the maze of cots, limping a little on that right leg again. I led him to the back corner of the furthest tent from the camp entrance. It was the least occupied, most of the survivors still gathered in the chow lines for dinner. I went straight to the darkest corner and sat down on a cot, gritting my teeth past the pain in my side as my head swam.

It was the dehydration getting to me more than the hunger, sunburn, or inflammation. Luckily, dehydration is relatively quick to reverse, but for the moment it left me foggy brained and dizzy. I almost toppled sideways. Frank got to me first, one strong hand clamping down on my shoulder. He asked no questions as I stretched out on the cot, but he found the injury quickly enough. A quick inspection of the battlefield bandage, and he breathed a curse.

"You need a medic. Stay here."

He turned. I caught his arm.

"No," I said. "No medic. No cops."

Frank hesitated. His eyes narrowed, and I knew what he was thinking. You never say "no cops" to a cop.

"Listen carefully," I rasped. "I need an anti-inflammatory, an antibiotic, and stitching supplies. Hydrogen peroxide, if you can find it. It's just a flesh wound, but it's deep, and it's dirty."

"You need a *medic*," Frank repeated.

I shook my head. "No good. I can't answer questions right

now. Get me the stuff and stitch me up. If you're too squeamish, I'll do it myself."

A flash of indignation passed across his face. Lips tightened.

"Why no cops?"

A predictable question. I probably would have asked the same in his shoes. I decided to go for the truth.

"I collided with some gangbangers in the Seventh Ward. They were mugging an old lady. I didn't kill them, but the cops aren't interested in my side of the story."

The pucker of the lips remained, just for a moment. I could see Frank weighing the sincerity in my eyes, just the way discerning old cops do. Sussing out the truth. Making a judgment.

Then he grunted. "Wait here."

34

I descended into semiconsciousness while Frank was gone, eyes closed and brain tuning out the noise of the camp. The water bottle I'd picked up on my way to the cot was already empty, but I trusted Frank to bring me another. It was a good bet—he returned twenty minutes later with a small canvas bag loaded with exactly what I'd asked for. Topical antibiotics, tablet painkillers, a stitching kit in a foil wrapper, and hydrogen peroxide in a brown bottle. He brought four bottles of water, also, and a sleeve of something pink and powdery. Upturning the powder into a water bottle, he shook it, then handed it to me.

"Electrolytes," he said. "Sip, don't chug."

I didn't need to be told. I'd learned the dangers of chugging while dehydrated in boot camp. Sergeant Smiles had been only too happy to laugh at my misery as I puked most of the fluid back up.

"On your side," Frank said, twisting the cap off the peroxide. I rolled away from him, lifting my right arm to expose the knife wound. He pulled the blood- and sweat-soaked bandage away, muttering another curse around the flashlight held in his mouth. I gritted my teeth when I heard the peroxide slosh, but I still wasn't ready for the tidal wave of burning agony that erupted across my rib cage as the cleansing agent drenched my side and continued to gush.

Frank used the entire bottle on the wound, washing out dirt and contaminants before he dabbed it dry with a clean towel, then applied the antibiotic cream. A lot of it.

At last, the foil wrapper rustled as he opened the stitching kit.

"You find the kid?" Frank held the flashlight in the corner of his mouth as though it were a cigar.

"Yeah," I grunted.

"Big Charity?"

"Yeah."

Short pause. "And Cleveland Avenue?"

I twisted my neck over one shoulder. Frank held a curved stitching needle and didn't blink as our gazes met.

"You heard?" I asked.

"Cops talk."

I looked away. "That was them. The guys who took the kid. I got her out of the hospital, and we were on the run. They came after us. They opened fire on the National Guard."

Frank said nothing. He simply placed one hand on my rib cage to pinch the flesh together; then came the first bite of the needle. A little like a bee sting, followed by the uncomfortable sensation of my skin being tugged together by the thread. I kept my teeth gritted and my eyes closed while he worked. Frank didn't say a word until the job was done. He knotted the thread and bit off the end. Then came a final splash of peroxide, followed by a large adhesive bandage.

"Okay," Frank said. "That's about as good as I know how to do. You're gonna have a scar."

I rotated with a restrained grunt, sitting up on the cot. Four painkillers washed down easily with half a bottle of electrolyte-enhanced water. Frank peeled surgical gloves off and sat down on the cot next to me, clicking the flashlight off. Outside the tent, the noise of the camp churned on, but nobody had bothered or even so much as noticed us. It was uncomfortably warm beneath the thick Army canvas.

It reminded me of deployment.

"I'm gonna ask you once, and you're gonna tell me the truth," Frank said. "No BS. One cop to another."

I met his gaze. "I didn't shoot that guardsman. I didn't shoot any cops."

"Just some gangbanger."

"I didn't shoot him either," I said. "I just stomped his face and broke his buddy's knee. Less than they deserved."

Slow consideration. Frank pursed his lips. Then he cracked open a bottle of water.

"Where's the kid?"

"They got her while I was dealing with the gangbangers. Slipped right up on us."

"They were following you?"

"Tracking us, I think. The girl had a teddy bear. I neglected to inspect it."

Frank sipped his water, swishing it a little in his mouth before swallowing. Thinking slowly and methodically, like veteran cops do. Not rushing to hasty and misguided judgments.

"What now?" he asked, at last.

I straightened with another grimace, finishing my water and reaching for a third bottle. Then I pulled the abused map out of my pocket and unfolded it over my knee. I tapped the location of Charity Hospital with one dirty index finger.

"We were wrong about the looting," I said.

"How so?"

"I found them in the hospital. Drinking, playing cards. Killing time. In the next room they had enough small arms to lay down a platoon of Marines. Not civilian stuff, this was Army issue. Likely stolen from a nearby National Guard armory during the relief deployments."

"Smart," Frank grunted. "Difficult to trace back to them."

"Especially after the big bang," I said.

Frank cocked an eyebrow. I looked up from the map.

"The second thing in that room: dynamite. A *lot* of it. Enough to blow out that entire floor of the hospital, maybe bring the building down."

Frank squinted in disbelief. "Seriously?"

"I don't know how they got it up there. They must have trucked it in using their fake FEMA vehicles. At least one of those trucks survived the storm. I'm guessing they parked it in a garage near the hospital."

"Is the dynamite rigged to blow?"

I shook my head. "No. It's stacked in boxes."

Another pause. Frank finished his bottle. Then he straightened.

"We need to report this. I'll do it if you want. Keep your name out of it. The National Guard needs to know."

I shook my head. "Not an option. Remember Cleveland Avenue. Whatever these thugs are planning, they're willing to unleash hell to make it happen. They've already killed a

National Guardsman, which likely wasn't part of the original plan, but it must have escalated their timeline. If the Guard goes charging into that hospital, they're going to have a bloodbath on their hands. Dozens of casualties, maybe hundreds if the dynamite goes off. This is a powder keg, Frank, and you know as well as anyone that these cops are amped out of their minds. So is the Guard. There's no central command. It's a disaster waiting to happen."

Frank considered, visibly bending more of his decades-long experience against the problem. Adjusting the pieces and eventually reaching the same conclusion I had, only a little more reluctantly. He was a man of law and order, after all. He disliked the vigilante method.

I was growing more comfortable with it by the day.

"What's your play?" Frank said at last.

"I've got to get the kid out. That's priority number one. If the fireworks start, she'll be caught in the crossfire."

Frank shook his head. "I don't understand that. You said her father kidnapped her?"

"Right."

"And dragged her into the middle of a room full of dynamite in the heart of the storm?"

"He isn't father of the year," I said.

"Obviously. I've seen my share of domestic violence. I was a cop, remember? Some men are dogs."

"Most men. What's your point?"

"My point is that even dogs are rational. If these guys are killing guardsmen and ready to set off a mountain of dynamite, there must be an end game in sight. They can't seriously expect to head back to wherever they're from and crack open a keg."

My gaze drifted back to the crinkled map. I'd thought the

same about Randy and his gang. Whatever they were up to, it was clearly both violent and insane, but unless they were a band of political revolutionaries willing to martyr themselves, I couldn't imagine rational men backing themselves into a corner like this, ready to gun down guardsmen and blow up the world without any sort of escape plan in mind.

"The kid is the linchpin," Frank said. "There's nothing unusual about a deadbeat, controlling father. He wants his kid under his thumb. I've seen it a thousand times. But she won't be under his thumb if he goes to jail or blows himself up. He has to know that."

"So there's a next step," I said.

Frank nodded. "And soon. That business on Cleveland Avenue kicked up the heat. The Guard may not have traced these guys back to the hospital yet, or wherever else they're hiding. But they will, and it's over when they do. You need to know why these jerkwads came to New Orleans."

I focused on the map, chewing one corner of my lip. The painkillers hadn't kicked in yet, but the rehydration was already working some magic. My brain began to clear. I thought back to the confrontation at the trailer in Mississippi—the wife beating and all the excessive bravado. Randy bragging about taking his kid back.

About taking her someplace where nobody would ever catch them. About being *rich*.

"We're thinking too small," I said. "You don't need a truckload of dynamite to loot a jewelry store, especially after a storm. They're planning something else. Something *bigger*."

I ran both hands over the map, stretching the crinkled paper over my knee. I tapped the intersection of Tulane Avenue and La Salle Street. Big Charity Hospital.

"It's a lot of dynamite, Frank. Too much to move quickly or move far. The target is close. What about this other circle? The one with the X."

I pivoted my hand east and south of the hospital, right to the heart of the Central Business district. The X was a little distorted by water damage, but still visible. Frank clicked his flashlight back on and took the map. He squinted through aged eyes, taking his time. Tracing streets with one finger, maybe imagining the layout of the city in his mind. Picturing each corner, each building. A lifetime of policing his hometown now leveraged into the mindset of a criminal.

He shook his head. "This is nothing. Just a hotel building. I think there's a sandwich shop there. It's honestly been a while since I was downtown."

"No bank?" I asked.

A dry laugh. "Kid, there might be six retail banks in the whole of downtown. It's too dangerous for bankers."

"A bank would make sense, though," I pressed. "With that much dynamite, maybe they're figuring on blowing a vault..."

I trailed off, thinking. Frank's eyebrows pinched together, and he rotated the map.

"You sure this X is in the right place?" he questioned.

"No," I said. "I told you before, I drew it from memory."

"So it could be off by a few blocks?"

"Sure. What are you thinking?"

Frank didn't answer. His finger dragged along the paper, moving farther eastward. And then stopping. He muttered a disbelieving curse.

"What?" I said. "Is it a bank?"

This time Frank croaked a laugh, still not taking his eyes

off the paper. "You could say that. More like a bankers' bank."

"Huh?"

Frank looked up, lowering the flashlight. His smile melted.

"It's the United States Federal Reserve."

35

"That's it," I said.

Frank snorted another laugh. "They'd have to be out of their minds."

"They are. One hundred percent. They're half drunk and strung out on idiocy. You can reason with dogs and you can debate children, but there's no talking to idiots, Frank. Help me up."

I extended a hand, grimacing past the fire in my rib cage. The painkillers helped, but nothing from over the counter was going to completely dull the abuse of the past few days.

Or weeks. Or months. If I thought about it, I could be accused of more than a little idiocy of my own.

Frank ignored my hand, crossing his arms instead. "What are you going to do?"

"What do you think? I gotta get the kid out before they start setting off dynamite."

Another pause. "Maybe we should notify the cops..."

I shook my head. "Not before I get the kid out. They'll roll in with guns blazing, and who could blame them? They want blood, and they'll get it. But only *after* the kid is out. We talked about this."

I made as if to stand on my own. Frank put a hand on my shoulder and pushed me back onto the cot.

"Sit down, hotshot. Wait a minute."

He rose with an exhausted sigh and limped off to his backpack. A moment later he returned with a small yellow canister plastered with a white label. He cracked the lid open and shook out two tablets. Then he extended his hand.

"What's that?" I demanded.

"Hydrocodone. Super Tylenol."

I knew what it was. I'd consumed it before, several times. Potentially addictive and even dangerous, but relentlessly effective.

I squinted at the label. It was printed with Frank's name.

"Knee replacement last year." Frank sighed. "Doc prescribed them. I never took them. Saw too many kids addicted on the streets. Now, you want them or not?"

I took the tablets and swallowed them on a dry throat. "Is that why you're limping?"

"I'm limping because I only let them replace one knee. Now the other is going bad. Take it from me, Sharpe. Growing old ain't for sissies."

Frank sat down with a gentle grunt and took the map, producing a pen from his pocket. He tapped the location of the Federal Reserve.

"This is a public spot. Lots of witnesses."

"And there's an aid center at the Superdome," I added. "Only a few blocks up Poydras Street. Twenty plus thousand people."

Frank sighed, shaking his head. "They'd have to be out of their minds," he said again.

"Maybe they didn't bet on the refugee center being located so close by. Or maybe they didn't bet on refugees at all. Given the amount of preparation at hand, it's reasonable to assume that they were plotting this long before the hurricane arrived. I guess they assumed that Nadia would help them."

A snort from Frank. "Stupid fools."

He tapped with the pen, lips puckering. He didn't comment further.

"What's the hang-up, Frank?"

"I'm trying to think of how to go about this without blowing up a whole bunch of people."

"There's one way."

He looked up. Raised both eyebrows.

"You put one of those National Guard M4s in my hands and call for a truckload of body bags."

Frank didn't blink. There was no bravado in my voice, and he didn't seem to doubt my statement. A smart man.

"I'll hazard a guess that method lands you in prison," he said.

"Not if I'm gone before sunrise."

"So then it lands *me* in prison." A dry smile.

"Free knee replacements in prison."

Frank huffed. He looked back to the map. Studied a moment, then nodded.

"The kid is the priority. You get her out. And then..."

He stood again, shuffled over to his bag, and returned with a pair of black plastic police radios. A little outdated and more than a little battered by heavy use. But they crackled straight to life when he rotated the dials.

"You call in the cavalry," he finished. "I've got some contacts on the force. People who will trust my intel without too many questions. You let me know where the targets are, and I'll point the cops that way. Then you slip out. No need for direct contact between you and the authorities."

Frank handed me a radio, and I rolled it in my hand as I considered. It was a good plan—logical and simple. Two key ingredients for any tactical ambition. But it left me with a question.

"Why are you covering for me, Frank?"

The old man folded his arms. "What if we just say I owe you a favor?"

"I'd say I appreciate it. But I don't believe you."

Another long pause. Frank looked over his shoulder toward the entrance of the tent. Nobody was there. He settled onto a cot again, voice dropping.

"Look. I don't know who you are, Sharpe, but I'm a pretty good judge of character. My gut says you're a man who colors outside the lines."

I waited. Frank's shoulders fell.

"My discharge papers say I retired from the NOPD, but... truth is, I was pushed out."

"Corruption?" I asked. It wasn't an accusation. Just a logical guess.

"No, confrontation. I spent thirty years watching the city I loved descend into an abyss of corruption and crime. Lawlessness ruling the streets. Greasy politicians setting the tempo, and sticky-fingered cops getting in line. Truth be told, I barely recognize this place. The government is so crooked they're kissing their own asses."

"And you got tired of it," I said.

A nod. "I busted a prostitution ring. Lots of young kids, most of them immigrants. It was all fireworks and champagne in city hall. At least until I wouldn't stop digging.

Turns out the mayor had a hand in it. Couple of state senators, also. I was just about to investigate our own congressman when I was offered a retirement package and an exit...or else."

Frank's gaze fell. I saw a little shame in his posture. And a lot of anger.

"My wife had just died. Cancer. Kids all out of town. Lots of my buddies already retired, a few of them already dead. My knees were going bad. I just...I was so tired..."

I put a hand on Frank's shoulder. Squeezed it once, but didn't say anything.

He didn't have to explain. I'd been a cop myself—a good one, I thought. Or at least, an effective one. I'd witnessed corruption. I'd watched colleagues go dirty and usually get away with it. I understood the impossibility of it all.

Frank met my gaze. His eyes turned hard. "You do what you have to do to get that kid out, Sharpe. Then you call me. There's still a lot of good cops on the force. They'll take it from there."

I extended my hand. Frank shook it once. Then we were both on our feet. He emptied out his backpack and loaded it for me, dropping in the bottle of hydrocodone, three bottles of water, several power bars, the police radio, and last of all the map.

He handed me the bag, and I slung it over my shoulders.

"There's a small convention center just south of the Federal Reserve. Gallier Hall. It's an auxiliary facility for the city. My guess is that they would have evacuated it and locked it down prior to the hurricane, meaning that it should still be empty. If I was going to stage a truckload of dynamite someplace just outside the Reserve building, that would be a good spot. With the electricity out, all the security systems should be down."

"And the reserve building?" I asked.

"They'll have generators. Remote security monitoring. But you can't put generators in a basement around here. We learned that lesson with Big Charity. My guess is the feds will have parked mobile generator trucks behind the bank. Enough to keep the security systems running."

"But easy to sabotage," I said.

Another nod.

I extended my hand again. We shook once. I turned for the tent door.

"Sharpe?"

I looked back. Frank sighed. Then he tugged up the tail of his shirt, exposing a small black leather holster affixed to his belt just over his appendix. Polished stainless steel glinted as he deholstered the weapon.

"Here. You might need this."

I extended my hand. Something very small and very light dropped into it, like a pocketknife. I rotated the object into the light spilling through the tent door and opened my hand.

It was a gun. Sort of. Not even five inches long and only a few ounces heavy, it had a cylinder, a hammer, and something that might have been considered a grip. Maybe for a baby. *North American Arms* was printed along the frame, the scuff marks of years spent in a holster wearing against shiny steel.

"What's this?" I said, not bothering to disguise the disappointment in my voice.

Frank appeared next to me. "It's a revolver."

"A revolver?" I laughed. "No, Frank. This is a straw with a spit wad."

My fingers found the textured end of the guide rod held just beneath the barrel, and I mashed a button on the end to draw it out. The cylinder dropped into my palm, and I exposed the butt of it to the light. Just as I suspected, five rounds of .22 Magnum ammunition lay housed within.

"I stand corrected," I said. "*Five* spit wads. This is useless."

Frank folded his arms, lips pursed. "That was my backup piece for fifteen years."

"Well, I'm glad you never had to use it. You'd be dead."

A derisive snort. Frank extended his hand. "Fine. Give it back."

I looked to the pistol, rotating the cylinder in my palm. It fit neatly back into the frame, clicking like a toy as the guide rod locked back into place. I flexed the hammer. The revolver was single-action, and the trigger didn't even look like a trigger. More like a button.

Useless. Or directly adjacent. But still better than nothing.

"I'll take it," I said, slipping it into my pocket. It vanished like a stick of gum.

Frank remained unmoved, arms folded again. I saw some uncertainty in his gaze. Not about the gun, and maybe not even about me. Maybe about what lay ahead.

"I'd go myself, but with my knee..."

"You're more use here. Stand by the radio. Make sure the cavalry is ready."

Frank nodded a couple of times. Then he extended his hand for a final shake. The grip was firm. I turned for the door. Frank caught me with a final question.

"One other thing..."

"Yeah?"

He scratched one cheek. "The circle was the hospital... and the first X might be the Reserve Bank. So what are the other marks on the map?"

It was a question I'd already considered, and I didn't have an answer. The second X in Gentilly and the squiggling mark along the Mississippi River—what did those mean?

It doesn't matter.

"I just gotta get the kid," I said.

I turned back for the door. Outside, sticky New Orleans midnight waited for me. And somewhere in the midst of it, a dozen rednecks sitting on a pile of dynamite, with a disabled girl prodigy held captive.

36

Mixing hydrocodone with whatever manner of anti-inflammatory I'd already consumed was likely ill advised, but the resulting physical relaxation was nothing short of divine. Warm and encompassing, almost as good as afterglow, it blanketed my body and loosened my muscles, numbing pain out of existence, soreness out of memory. I was lithe and awake, my head a little floaty and my stomach a touch nauseated, but none of the stiffness or aching agony that had plagued me ever since my beatdown in Mississippi remained.

I was unfettered and energized, ready to take on the city for the third day in a row, and not the least bit intimidated by it. Guided by the water-stained map, using the MacroStream only sparingly to illuminate the darkest of city streets, I kept up a fast walk out of the FEMA station and into Desire Area. Contrary to my previous incursion into downtown New Orleans, I skipped the long orbit into Gentilly and turned directly south into St. Roch.

It was theoretically the more dangerous path, but also

the shorter one. Streets pointed almost directly south, but from time to time I skipped a block westward, ensuring that when I popped out on the far side of the devastated neighborhood, I would collide with the French Quarter instead of the north bank of the Mississippi. From there I would skirt westward again, avoiding lights and avoiding cops. Swinging out and arcing ever southward, all the way to the Central Business District.

It was there that I had a choice to make. I could return to Big Charity and ascend to the sixth floor, hoping to collide with Randy's crew right where I last left them. Or I could roll the dice and head directly for the Federal Reserve. It all depended on how confident I was in my assumptions about Randy's plans. If he really was striking the Reserve Bank that night, I likely didn't have time to visit Big Charity first. My wristwatch had already crossed eleven p.m. and was now edging toward midnight. There was no logical reason for an explosive bank heist to happen much closer to sunrise.

But did I believe it? Was it too crazy to presume? Frank had been right on the money when he said that only a fool would try something this brazen. This absurd.

The only way it made sense was if I switched my brain into the tried-and-true gear that had already helped me solve so many cases during my brief career as a homicide detective. The gear of thinking like a criminal. Or, in this case, thinking like an idiot.

A city reduced to chaos, law enforcement overwhelmed, and most security systems compromised by the loss of power. A truckload of dynamite able to blast straight through brick and hardened steel. Into a vault maybe—a vault loaded with federal banknotes and possibly even gold.

Yeah. It made sense if I were an idiot. But being an idiot

didn't make Randy Mercer any less dangerous, and it gave me no more wiggle room. My best bet was to proceed straight to the bank and roll the dice. Find out if Randy was really as dumb as he looked.

The moon was a little brighter on the second night of my nocturnal activities, and my eyes adjusted more quickly. Marigny and Vieux Carre—neighborhoods northeast of the French Quarter—were every bit as devastated as the rest of the city, but by then the carnage had become a familiar landscape, losing its shock value as I hustled onward, blocking out the stench of rotting things. Ignoring the anguish of homes flattened and lives demolished. Cutting westward at the northern extremity of the French Quarter and skirting along Rampart Street.

There were no cops. No National Guard patrols. No heavy vehicles churning up streets strewn with debris. Bulldozers had been through to ram smashed cars and rubble out of the way, but authorities had now concentrated their efforts farther south. I knew by the glow of security lights reflecting off scattered clouds hanging above the Superdome. It was the primary refuge center for the heart of town, that place where cops had been working to corral survivors the night before. I could hear the hum of distressed life there, even from blocks away. Voices were distorted beyond interpretation, but were still loud even at this hour.

It was a lot of people. Tens of thousands, and they were only five or six blocks west of the Reserve Bank.

This fool.

I reached Canal Street, and at last I saw cops. Patrol cars and armored trucks clustered around a temporary command post, a buzz of law enforcement gathered beneath tents and around the open tailgates of pickup trucks. They were enjoying a midnight meal, apparently. Recharging and digging deep for some way to power through the long weeks of recovery ahead.

I stopped at the corner and leaned out from a building, surveying them from a hundred yards away and mapping out their own patterns of surveillance. Except there wasn't one, really. The cops and soldiers were invested in their meal and very likely exhausted. I watched for sixty seconds; then I simply slipped across Canal Street and made it to Tulane Avenue. Big Charity stood a few blocks to my west, but I turned east into the Central Business District, accelerating now as the instincts born of a few dozen firefights whispered to my subconscious that the moment was near.

I could feel it. I wasn't wrong about the reserve bank. I wasn't wrong about Randy and his idiocy. This thing was going down, and there was a kid stuck right in the middle of it. I thought of Autumn and her easygoing calm. Her perfect mellow that spoke more to the trauma she'd experienced than any superhuman strength that matched her super-human intelligence. And her mother, way back in Missis-sippi, maybe no longer breathing. Maybe hanging on to life by a thread.

I accelerated to a soft jog, counting the blocks and noting the street names. O'Keefe. Baron. Carondelet.

I finally turned south when I reached Saint Charles Avenue. Another few blocks of tall business towers and ordi-nary commercial banks passed on either side, glass littering the sidewalk, inky dark water bubbling from the storm drains. Not a human in sight.

The cops had done a good job of corralling everyone into the survivors' camp at the Superdome, and suddenly I wondered if Randy was a little less of a fool than I thought him to be. It was starting to make sense why the gang would have waited until the second night after the storm to make their move. Certainly, there were cops everywhere. There were National Guardsmen everywhere, also. But the bulldozers had cleared the streets, and civilians were safely isolated. Escaping, assuming the gang actually succeeded in cracking a federal vault, would be easy.

Yet there was still that army of cops on Canal Street. Had Randy and his pals forgotten about them? Or was I still missing something?

The other marks on the map. I remembered Frank's question about the final X and the squiggly line along the Mississippi, but I didn't focus on it. I didn't really need to understand Randy's full plan, so long as I could locate him.

I reached Poydras Street and slowed to a halt, breathing easily as the hydrocodone continued to work its opioid magic. Six lanes wide with broken palm trees standing in the median, Poydras ran east to west, with the glowing mass of the generator-powered Superdome planted a thousand yards to my right.

Across the street stood a tall business tower, some of its higher windows blown out by the storm. Trees encircled the block directly across from it. Old trees—hardwoods with drooping limbs that disguised the structure behind. Not a commercial place that needed to be visible, this was a federal establishment.

The Reserve Bank.

I checked my watch. It was nearly two a.m. The hike south from the FEMA station had taken almost three hours. Now sweat dripped from my swollen and busted nose, my body alive with a strange form of opioid-dulled tension. I gave myself a full minute to scope out every corner of the intersection, searching for cops. Homeless people. Pedestrian survivors.

Or Mississippi thugs in wifebeater tank tops.

The intersection was empty, but from the direction of the Superdome a steady churn of distressed voices clouded the air like tailpipe pollution. Angry. Agitated. Bottled up in too small a space for too long. NOPD squad cars formed a barrier, lights flashing slowly while cops patrolled, actively containing the survivors.

And leaving their backs turned to the Federal Reserve.

This is crazy.

I departed the shadows and sprinted across the intersection, reaching the office tower and keeping close to the building as I hurried south along Saint Charles. The Reserve Bank stood to my right, still sheltered by trees and a five-foot-tall decorative steel fence. Ahead, the business tower was cut off by a narrow street, and the block transitioned into a simple park beyond. More old trees and some ghostly tall statue. Shelter, in my mind. I hurried into it, sliding behind an oak before I rotated to look back across Saint Charles to the bank.

It stood as a black monolith, only partially visible behind the trees, but illuminated by soft yellow lights behind narrow windows. Frank had been right about the generator trucks. I could hear them churning from beyond the bank, supplying enough juice to fuel security systems and a handful of lights. Beneath the glow of decorative lamps, I saw the name of the building displayed in silver letters above the door.

Federal Reserve.

The bankers' bank. The place where the US government actually kept so much of its hard currency.

Directly to the left of the bank, a narrow alley sliced through the block, and next to that stood another building. Not hidden by trees, this structure advanced all the way to the sidewalk, tall columns supporting an arched, Greek-style roof. All white marble and granite steps, dusted with dirt and storm debris. Two giant white doors, bolted closed.

It was Gallier Hall, the auxiliary convention center that Frank had mentioned. Its windows were tall and boarded over, *KEEP OUT* signs posted to the front entrance. Closed for the storm. But as I watched from the park, a glimmer of yellow light cut from a crack between the plywood sheets covering the windows. It was there for a moment and then gone in a blink.

Somebody was inside.

37

I checked the almost useless .22 Magnum revolver before I sprinted across the street. All five rounds loaded into the little cylinder were ready for action, but I doubted whether any of them would deliver terminal velocity after penetrating the layers of beer fat that encased each member of Randy's gang.

Maybe up close. But if things got that bad, I might opt for my knife.

The alley between Gallier Hall and the Federal Reserve would be the most likely intrusion point for Randy and his gang, I decided. A quick sprint through the shadows to a wall, over the wall and up to a side entrance of the bank building. With the generators already terminated, security cameras would be blind. An application of dynamite would open the door, with a much larger application held back for the vault.

All those millions of federal dollars, churning in from banks across the region, held in literal reserve. A prime target, assuming Randy didn't bring the entire building down. I'm not an explosives expert, but the quantity of dynamite I encountered on the sixth floor of Big Charity still seemed like far too much.

He wouldn't just breach the vault, he'd level the building. More urgency for me to get Autumn out.

Moving south, I orbited the left-hand corner of Gallier Hall and advanced to the far side of the building—the side furthest from the Federal Reserve. It was lined by windows, some of them only a couple of feet off the ground, and all of them boarded over with plywood. I advanced far enough into the alley to be lost in shadow, then deployed my Victorinox.

Instead of the blade, I opted instead for the thick bottle-opener/screwdriver, an exceptional prying implement that had never let me down. The plywood sheets were affixed by framing nails, likely shot in place with an air nailer. It took me a moment to locate a groove behind the plywood to insert the screwdriver. I braced my boot against the block foundation of Gallier Hall and pried backward, leaning against the strength of the embedded nails. It was imperfect leverage. I really needed a crowbar.

But the plywood creaked a little, and the groove widened. I relocated the Victorinox closer to the corner nail and pried again, wiggling until a one-inch gap was opened. Then I abandoned the knife and used my fingers, reaching in deep and tugging.

It was easier than it should have been. The nails were relatively short, designed to hold the plywood in place against the force of direct wind, but also designed to be easy to remove. The plywood quickly became its own lever. Nails slid free of damp wood. A two-by-four-foot section peeled away, revealing pitch-black windowpanes in a forest green frame, white shutters behind.

I set the plywood aside and looked back down the street, listening. The hum of life at the Superdome continued, but nobody advanced toward my position.

Flipping the knife around, I drove the screwdriver into a windowpane just above the middle of the frame. Glass fell in a shower against the shutters beyond, leaving a grapefruit-sized hole. I leaned in and listened for a moment, intent on any indicators of disturbance inside.

Everything was graveyard quiet, musty damp air rushing out from the hall's interior.

Returning the knife to my pocket, I reached through the hole and found a window latch. The window opened with a little effort, swollen pine scraping against itself as aged paint cracked and peeled. Eventually I had a two-foot gap opened, and I was able to slide a leg through.

The MacroStream found my left hand as my right closed back around the Victorinox. Three inches of locking blade were deployed this time in place of the screwdriver. I had decided it was a better option than the mini revolver.

Pushing the shutters open, the musty smell I'd detected before flooded my nostrils. A blast of LED light illuminated a hardwood floor swimming with half an inch of water, likely drainage that had dripped in behind the plywood and penetrated the outdated window frames.

I rotated my boots in and wriggled through the gap. Frank's backpack caught on the window frame, but with effort I made it through and dropped onto the floor beyond. The room I landed in was large and open. A flash of the light revealed some manner of storage closet, with stacks of folding metal chairs and folding round tables leaned against the wall. The floor was scuffed with heavy use. The fluorescent lights overhead dark.

But when I listened, I heard footsteps. They creaked through old joists and floorboards someplace above the ceiling. I thought I heard voices, also. Heavily muffled, but present.

There shouldn't *be* any voices in a boarded-up, evacuated city building. Frank's instincts were spot on.

I found the door and eased my way into a wide, hardwood hallway. My boots left muddy prints on the floor as I turned right, holding the flashlight against my shirt whenever I clicked it on to minimize its power. I only wanted enough light to guide me along. I didn't want to draw any attention.

Thinking back to the glimmer of yellow I'd seen behind the plywood sheathing at the front of the hall, I thought it had come from the building's main floor. Likely, one floor up from where I now walked. That meant I needed stairs.

I located them near the end of the hall. A wooden door blocked the way, with a modern plastic sign indicating what lay beyond. I kept the knife at my side, ready for a thrust or a razor slash, whatever was required. Then I eased the door open.

The stairwell was narrow and dank. It smelled of more mildew as I eased my way up, thumb on the MacroStream's tail switch. A double tap would initiate the strobe function, enough to blind an adversary while I closed for the attack.

I reached the main level and slowed. The voices I'd detected from before had grown louder, and I recognized the accents. Rural and Southern, twanging a lot with impatience and command. It was one voice, not multiple. I thought I recognized the growl of Yellow Teeth, with everyone answering in mere grunts. I still couldn't make out the words because there was music also, playing from a stereo. More classic country titles.

Stopping at the door, I pressed my back against the wall. I twisted the knob slowly, and it rotated on a greased mechanism. The hinges glided silently as I swung it open half an inch.

And then I squinted through.

It was a ballroom—fifty feet wide, twice that long. Gleaming hardwood polished to a shine paved the floor beneath the glow of camping lanterns. In the middle of the room a grand piano stood with its lid propped open, polished white keys reflecting the lantern glow. Windows were covered by shutters and boarded beyond. The ceiling was high and dark.

And clustered on the far side of the piano, gathered around an unfolded tarpaulin, was Randy's gang. I had to lean close to the floor to get a clear look beneath the piano's body, but as soon as I did, I recognized the faces almost immediately—seven in total, with Yellow Teeth calling the shots. Duke, it seemed, hadn't survived his fall down the elevator shaft, but all the others were present and accounted for, dressed in the same stained tank tops they seemed to favor. The tarp was pinned down by boxes and heavy black duffel bags...and dynamite. A *lot* of dynamite.

Although, maybe not as much dynamite as I'd seen in Big Charity. I squinted at the thought, momentarily hung up on it; then I looked quickly to the right, sweeping the wall. Moving past piles of backpacks and stacks of M4 rifles, my gaze reached a recess in the front corner of the room. It consisted of a slightly raised platform encased in a four-foot wall. Hidden by shadow, but I could make out the silhouette of wires running through an opening on one side. There must have been a desk also, because a computer monitor rose above the top edge of the wall.

It was a DJ station, I decided. The modern equivalent of the grand piano across the room, and just outside the station's opening, I detected a small pair of shoes stacked neatly together.

Children's shoes. Autumn's shoes. She always took them off when she slept.

Easing the door open, I glanced left once more toward the army of thugs huddled around the tarp, all muttering and working, stacking sticks of dynamite into an oversized duffel bag. Wiring them up, probably. They were focused, and the grand piano sat between us.

The DJ station was only twenty feet to my right, and the room was inky dark in that direction. By creeping along the wall, I could keep the bulk of the piano between myself and the gang.

It wasn't perfect cover, but it was the best plan I could think of on short notice. I left the stairwell and turned immediately right, keeping myself well outside the dim pools of light cast by the lantern. Moving my feet in easy, rolling motions, my footsteps were nearly silent as I gobbled up yards, knife and MacroStream still held at the ready.

Neither Yellow Teeth nor Randy nor any of their comrades looked up. I reached the DJ station and stepped quickly to the entrance, moving past the shoes and sliding behind the four-foot wall.

Autumn lay huddled beneath the computer desk, the teddy clutched to her chest, her eyes pinched closed. I thought she was sleeping as I took cover behind the low wall and knelt beside her, but I cupped my hand over her mouth all the same before gently squeezing her shoulder.

Autumn's eyes popped open like twin headlights blazing straight to high beams. Her lips parted, and she might have begun to scream, but my heavy hand muffled the sound into silence. Her gaze snapped upward, and I lifted my free hand to hold a finger over my lips.

Autumn's eyes glimmered as fear melted into hope. I relaxed my hand from her mouth, emphasizing my directions with a shake of my index finger. She nodded, lips stretched into a grin as my hand fell away. Then she reached out with both arms and wrapped them around my neck before I could stop her, limp legs dragging the hardwood as her skinny body pressed against my chest.

I staggered, catching myself with one boot as a strange warmth rushed my chest. More than familiarity, more than relief to have found her. It was...not affection. But a sort of connection. An attachment.

My gaze misted over, and I clutched her close. Autumn squeezed hard, and I let her for a moment. Then I patted her shoulder and whispered into her ear, "You ready to go, kid?"

Autumn pulled away, and I was surprised to see tears in her own eyes. She smiled again, but she shook her head. "I can't."

"What?" I squinted. Autumn released me and slumped back into her spot beneath the table. She scrubbed a hand across her face.

"Come on." I kept my voice barely loud enough to be heard. "You'll be safe this time, I promise."

Another shake of her head. "No. You're not listening. There's something you don't know. They have a bomb!"

Her voice rose in an earnest hiss. I tensed, raising a hand and listening for any hint of detection from across the room.

The grunts and redneck muttering continued, as did the music. Meryl Haggard and his "Fightin' Side" were back, and I couldn't help but marvel at the irony of Randy's gang enjoying the song after gunning down a US service member. It was something beyond disgusting.

"I know about the bomb," I whispered. "They're building it now. We'll call the cops as soon as you're safe."

Another shake of her head, more frustrated this time. "No, not *that* bomb. They have another bomb. A really big one."

"What?"

Autumn sighed with the exhaustion of a genius speaking to a complete moron. She grabbed my shirt and tugged me close, bringing my ear only inches from her own.

"The levee, Mason. They've got a big whopper of a bomb on the levee. They're going to blow it wide open before they rob the bank, as a distraction. They're going to *flood the city*."

38

A cold stab of ice penetrated my stomach, the first cold thing I'd felt in nearly a week. It sank into my gut and turned my muscles suddenly hard, as though they were encased in ice themselves.

"What?" I whispered again.

Autumn rolled her head back, mouth dropping open as she sighed dramatically. "The *bank*, Mason. There's a bank next door. The Federal Reserve, it's like a bank for banks—"

"I know," I cut her off. "They're robbing it."

"They're going to try, but first they need a distraction. To get all the cops off Canal Street, right? They're not far away. I heard them talking about it."

"So they're going to blow a *levee*?"

"As a distraction! They have more dynamite. A lot more. Apparently, the floodwaters are still high. If the levee breaks, the city will flood. They say it could be ten or twelve feet of water. Enough to engulf some neighborhood...I don't know which one."

Unbelievable.

Disgust and overwhelming frustration washed through me like the same tidal wave Randy and his thugs wanted to unleash on New Orleans. But more than disgust, I felt a hotter, even less tolerable feeling. I felt foolish. I should have seen this coming. It was right in front of me the entire time. All that extra dynamite. The need for an additional distraction. Blowing a levee and flooding a residential district someplace outside of downtown was a ready-made distraction. The NOPD and the National Guard would swarm the spot—they'd have no choice.

They'd have their backs turned when the bank vault detonated. Randy and his crew would have a clear route of escape. Meanwhile, hundreds or maybe thousands of additional New Orleans homes would be engulfed, many of them already reoccupied by survivors eager to put their lives back together.

No way.

"Come on," I growled, scooping my arms to pick Autumn up. The kid twisted beneath the DJ table, pushing me back.

"*No,*" she hissed. "I can't go!"

"Why?" My voice rose a notch in irritation. I flinched and listened for a disturbance across the room. Still nothing.

Autumn rolled her eyes. "*Listen to me.* If I go missing, they'll blow the bomb. They already said so."

"It's already in place?"

"*Yes.*" More childish impatience. "That's what I'm saying! There's a bomb in the levee *now*. It's remote activated. If I try to sneak off, they'll just blow it. Daddy said so."

The ice in my gut melted into a wash of angry fire. I gritted my teeth and leaned out around the opening of the DJ stand, looking back toward Randy and his pals still busy packing that bag full of dynamite. In a flash of sudden mental clarity, I was able to grasp that this was serious. It was so outlandish, a part of me hadn't wanted to believe it. Maybe hadn't been able to believe it, despite my conviction when I spoke to Frank.

But this was real. These fools were seriously about to set off a massive duffel-bag bomb right in the heart of a major city.

I wanted to take them out. Eight to one, it was a roll of the dice that was likely to land against me. The mini revolver would be no help at all, leaving me to attempt this job with my knife. Maybe I could sneak Autumn away from the ballroom, then lure them out one at a time. Make a noise.

But no. There were too many ways that could go badly wrong. They could come out M4A1s blazing in full auto, spraying lead everywhere. They could mash whatever remote detonation button they had rigged to blast the levee, endangering God only knew how many dozens or hundreds of lives.

And they likely would, too. Because their backs would be against the wall. Desperate men resort to desperate measures, and with a heavy dose of pure insanity added to that cocktail, absolutely anything was possible.

That made *me* the one with his back against the wall. I needed to play this smart, or it would end much worse than it began.

"Mason," Autumn said, "listen to me. You gotta go disable that bomb. Then come back here and get me."

"Are you out of your mind?" I snapped. "You're not in charge here. You're coming with me."

Autumn folded her arms. Her jaw locked. She shook her head.

"Are you kidding me?"

"I'm not going," she said. "There's too much at stake."

"*You're* at stake, kid!"

"No I'm not. Daddy won't hurt me. He won't let anybody hurt me. He wants to control me, not harm me. It's all part of his OCPD."

"What?"

"Obsessive-compulsive personality disorder. It's what's wrong with him. Geez, Mason. Don't you ever read?"

I was too disoriented by the barrage of information to unravel the absurdity of Randy's victim analyzing him with such clinical objectivity. That was a discussion for later. For the moment, I needed to drill down to the heart of the matter.

And the heart of the matter, much as I resisted admitting it, was that Autumn was right. Randy was a moron and a monster for dragging his daughter into a storm, but for all that, she was unlikely to come to any harm directly by his hand. Not in the short term, anyway. Autumn was Randy's prize, after all. His possession. A levee bomb, however, would wreak havoc. Literally hundreds could die—maybe more. It was pure insanity, unleashed.

Heavily armed idiots at work.

"Do you know where the bomb is?"

Autumn's shoulders slumped. "No. They only said something about a neighborhood."

I leaned toward the entrance of the DJ station, listening to the distorted murmur of discussion at the makeshift bomb station. I could pick up words over the continued blare of the boom box, but none of it was useful.

The time for planning and debate had passed. Randy's gang had progressed to the execution stage. Every man knew his job. With barely three hours remaining until sunrise, I had to conclude that *go time* was almost upon us.

And that meant I was on the clock.

I closed my eyes and focused, trying to recount what Frank had said about "the last time". About Katrina, and all the places where the levees had failed. It was a case study for an internet-perusing maniac looking for the ultimate distraction. The ultimate magnet to draw police and National Guard away from downtown and—

Away from downtown.

There it was. It clicked in my mind in the form of a memory. The wind-torn and rain-saturated map from the upturned fake FEMA vehicle returned, and I saw the three marks.

The circle over Big Charity. The X over the Central Business District—what I now knew to be the Federal Reserve Bank. And that one final X in the north of the city, on the western edge of Gentilly. A *big* neighborhood.

I'd asked Frank about the spot. What had he said?

It was along the London Avenue Canal.

"I've got it," I said. "I know where they put the bomb."

Autumn's little face lit up with pride, and that rush of confusing warmth returned to my chest as she squeezed my arm.

"*Go.* Go stop it."

I hesitated a moment longer, re-evaluating Autumn's mental math. As with all her calculations, it was relentlessly accurate. I couldn't bring her with me. Not if these fools had the bomb on remote detonation. Any indicator that the cops were onto them could result in an immediate, impulsive decision to blast the levee and get out of Dodge.

I was better off leaving them to the machinations of their

idiotic bank robbery for a little longer. Randy would keep Autumn safe from the blast. So long as I returned to downtown New Orleans before the gang split, I would still have time to snatch Autumn.

I just couldn't be late.

"I'll be back," I promised, squeezing her little hand. "You stay alert, okay?"

Autumn nodded, no trace of fear in her face. What did she have left to fear, anyway? She'd already faced more trauma in ten short years than many adults faced in a lifetime. She had grown numb to it. She knew how to manage the anxiety.

"Do you know their escape plan?" she asked.

I did know. It was the final piece to the puzzle—and the final mark on the map, that squiggly line traced along the length of the mighty Mississippi, leading ever southward toward the coast. Roads might still be blocked, and an aircraft likely wouldn't be an option, but the swollen river would be wide open. Randy and his gang could race down it easily, make their way to the gulf...maybe board a larger ship that was waiting for them there. Head south toward Central and South America—where countries with low costs of living and no extradition treaties waited.

"Imma be rich, and where we're going, they'll never find us."

"They're gonna take the river," I said. "They'll have a boat. But I'll get you out before then, okay? Be ready."

Another short nod from Autumn. The warmth in my chest constricted into a hot weight. I hesitated, suddenly unsure what to say or do. A lump had formed in my throat.

My gaze fell across the teddy still tucked next to Autumn, and I extended a hand.

"Give me that."

Autumn seemed hesitant, but she handed the toy over. I squished it between my fingers, feeling around its base. It didn't take long to identify a hard lump situated just inside a seam. That seam appeared to have been hastily—and sloppily—re-stitched. I used my knife to cut a slit, and out popped a little white plastic puck, about the size of a quarter. It was branded with a popular electronics company logo. I raised an eyebrow at Autumn.

"Unbelievable." She sighed, something between exhaustion and crushing sadness saturating her voice.

I returned the toy and left the puck on the floor. Tucking the knife into my pocket, I again felt a hesitancy to leave. I knew the right step, I just...wasn't ready to do it.

Autumn broke the tension, reaching her skinny arms around my neck and pulling me close again. She squeezed hard.

"Be safe, Mason."

My eyes stung. I squeezed back.

Then I was sliding to the opening of the DJ station, timing myself to the beat of old country music and the preoccupation of the gang before I advanced to the door. Back to the stairwell. Back through the window and onto the dank streets of hurricane-smashed New Orleans.

And back north, not sneaking this time but sprinting. Headed for Canal Street and the National Guard station.

39

I knew only two things as I broke down Saint Charles Avenue, eventually reaching Canal Street three blocks down from the National Guard station.

One: There was no precise way to predict when the levee bomb would detonate. I could guesstimate that Randy and his crew would trigger it ahead of their breach of the Federal Reserve building, drawing law enforcement away from downtown to respond to a new disaster in the making, but there was no way to know how soon that would be. It could be minutes. It could be an hour.

Two: Regardless of Randy's timeline, I *didn't* have time to explain myself to the cops or the National Guard. They likely wouldn't believe me, for a start. Even if they did believe me, it would take precious time to get the wheels of a response moving. They would want to contact a bomb squad, and a bomb squad might be difficult to find. More than likely, they'd want to run straight to Gallier Hall and kick the doors down, which would leave me with my original problem of

Autumn being caught in the crossfire of what was sure to be an absolute maelstrom.

Put together, those two factors left me with only one obvious solution. Like solving for X in one of Autumn's equations, the result was evident and irrefutable. I had to go to the levee on the London Avenue Canal myself, and I didn't have time to hoof it the way I'd been hoofing everywhere since arriving in New Orleans.

As I neared the National Guard station, I could see the troops wrapping up their meal. Fifty yards farther down the street, the cops were doing the same. There were armored police trucks and patrol cars parked all around the block. Any one of them could provide rapid transportation, but aside from being vulnerable to broken streets and distributed debris, all the police vehicles had one thing in common: they required keys, and cops don't leave their keys in the seat.

I turned instead for the National Guard station, and the three very different sorts of vehicles parked at the edge of it, flat faces pointed toward me with headlights staring like dead eyes. Not cars, not trucks. Some kind of hybrid, born out of the necessity of war, and refined in the fires of combat. The US Army High Mobility Multipurpose Wheeled Vehicle, better known as simply *Humvee*.

There were fifteen or twenty National Guardsmen gathered beneath a tent behind the parked vehicles, sweating in the stickiness of the Louisiana night, clearly killing time until they were called out on patrol. I figured they were most likely a sort of QRF for the NOPD. A quick response force. Muscled backup, held in reserve for emergency use. The Humvees would be fueled and ready to go, impervious to busted roads and scattered debris.

Best of all, Humvees don't have keys.

I turned off Canal Street onto Chartres Street, three blocks southeast of the National Guard station. It was the western edge of the French Quarter, a narrow one-way street with tall, French-colonial-style buildings lining it. Shredded industrial insulation, fragments of glass and roofing metal littered the street. The storm drains still gurgled with overflowing water, and the place stank of mud and rotting vegetable matter. But it didn't take me long to locate what I was looking for. An abandoned vehicle—a bread truck, it looked like, with the windshield smashed in from a flying section of palm tree. It sat catty-cornered across the street, windows blasted with mud, one tire flat.

I circled quickly around the front bumper, activating the tail switch of my MacroStream before clamping it between my teeth. The beam was starting to dim after three days of heavy use. With a complete power failure across the city, I hadn't had an opportunity to recharge the built-in battery, and I didn't know how much juice remained.

No time to worry about that now.

I rolled onto my side beneath the edge of the truck and produced the Victorinox. On the back side of the knife was a curious little tool called a *reamer*—essentially a metal awl, very sharp and extremely sturdy. When deployed, it protruded from the middle of the knife, allowing me to wrap my fingers around the grip and leave the reamer sticking from between my knuckles.

The bread truck's gas tank was built of sheet metal, mounted just beneath the driver's side of the cab. The rusted and flimsy steel was no match for the reamer, and a pungent stream of gasoline exploded through the tiny hole the tool left behind. I punched three more times, opening additional holes and providing additional streams of fuel across the damp New Orleans pavement.

Then I was back on my feet. The flashlight and the knife returned to my pocket. Heart thumping, I stepped back, fishing past my wallet for that sodden book of waterproof matches I had carried since beginning my career as a full-time vagrant and part-time camper. The first match broke. The second sputtered out.

But the third burst to life and arced through the air like a flaming arrow. It landed on the pavement, and for a split second, all was perfectly still.

Then the raw gasoline erupted into a rush of hot flame, blasting against the sides of the bread truck and surging up the streams of gas still flowing from the tank. I watched for only a moment before I ran back around the bumper and sprinted for Canal Street. There was no danger of the fire spreading to the buildings on either side. Everything was still sopping wet from Nadia, the bubbling storm gutters forming a natural barrier to keep the flames from spreading.

But that bread truck would burn. If the flames made it inside the tank, it might even explode, and that was one heck of a distraction. I was taking a page out of Randy Mercer's playbook.

"Fire!" I screamed, swerving onto Canal Street and heading straight for the National Guard station. "Fire on Chartres!"

The guardsmen looked up from the table, temporarily disoriented by the unexpected cry. Confused squints and exhausted frowns broke into temporary shock as the fuel tank of the bread truck ruptured behind me with a pavement-shaking thunderclap. Windows burst. Buildings shook.

And then Louisiana's finest did the thing they stood

before an American flag and swore to do. They grabbed their rifles and ran toward the threat of danger.

I passed them on Canal Street, still sprinting. They rushed by me without question or concern for my identity. I reached the makeshift motor pool and found the trio of Humvees abandoned and unsecured. The first was a standard-duty troop carrier variant with an open bed. It looked a little like an armored pickup truck with four doors, painted desert tan with a rear-bumper-mounted radio antenna secured to the roof. Three speed automatic transmission, six-point-two-liter diesel engine. Four-wheel drive, maximum speed of about fifty-five miles per hour. The workhorse of freedom.

I yanked the driver's door open and threw myself into the hard driver's seat. In place of a keyhole was a simple ignition switch mounted to the left of the steering wheel. I flipped it from ENG STOP to RUN and was rewarded by a yellow WAIT light flicking on just above the switch, signifying that the diesel's glow plugs were warming to life. I slammed the door and put my foot on the brake, counting the seconds.

"Come on...come on..."

Sirens rang behind me. Cops were passing the Humvees and surging toward the scene of the bread truck fire. None of them paid me any attention as I held my breath, waiting for the glow plugs to warm to starting temperatures.

It didn't take long in the tropical heat. The WAIT light cut off, and I twisted the switch to START. A heavy churn of the big motor was followed by a coughing growl. The cabin shuddered. My seat shook.

Then the diesel roared to life, and I released the switch, allowing it to snap back to the RUN marker. The cops who were rushing in beside me made way automatically at the sound of the heavy motor. They still didn't pay any attention to who was sitting behind the wheel of the vehicle. I grabbed the gear selector and pulled it into drive. My left hand found the steering wheel, and my right hand disengaged the parking brake. The big motor roared.

And then I was off, tires spinning, rushing down Canal Street. Turning north beyond the scene of the vehicle fire and blazing through the French Quarter.

Headed for the London Avenue Canal.

40

My selection of the Humvee had a dual purpose. I knew it would survive whatever fields of shattered glass or strewn chunks of nail-infested building timbers I encountered on my five-mile trip northward to the canal. I was also hoping, however, that it would provide me a shield of accepted legitimacy that would prevent another National Guard detachment or an NOPD patrol from apprehending me.

I was right. I passed my first NOPD patrol car barely four blocks into the French Quarter. They blazed the wrong way up a one-way avenue—leading a fire truck toward the scene of the bread truck fire. No hint of brake lights illuminated my rear window as I mashed the gas and resumed my crashing trek toward the Seventh Ward. The Humvee was rigid and relentless as it hurtled through mud puddles and rumbled over debris, shooting every vibration and jarring landing straight into my tailbone and up my spine. It was déjà vu to fleeing the Taliban in Afghanistan. All I was missing was the *chunk-chunk-chunk* of AK-47s barking behind me as blood gathered in the Humvee's floorboards.

When I reached the edge of the French Quarter, I slammed on the brakes and skidded to a halt, ratcheting the backpack off my shoulders and digging out the tattered FEMA map that had now guided me on so many tours of the shattered Big Easy. Street lines and building markings had faded some since Frank had first traced out the bad neighborhoods from the worse. I no longer cared about any of that. I simply traced a path through the tangled streets, up through Marigny and the Seventh Ward, through the Fairgrounds district to the bottom end of the London Avenue Canal, Gentilly on one side, Filmore on the other. Two big neighborhoods packed with hundreds upon hundreds of homes.

All of them would flood if the swelled mass of Lake Pontchartrain was allowed to flow through the canal and into the unprotected lowlands of the city. Those levees had held—so far.

But if there was a breach. If there was a *dynamite*-sized breach...how much water would pass?

The answer was *all of it*. The tidal wave wouldn't stop until hundreds, perhaps thousands of homes were back underwater. Just like Katrina.

Think, Mason. Think.

It was a long canal. Stretching from just south of I-610 all the way to the University of New Orleans. Maybe three miles in total, with levee walls on either side. An impossible stretch of territory to map out on my own, especially with no prior knowledge of where the levee might be most vulnerable. Once I picked a side and journeyed up it, there would be limited options for me to cross to the other bank.

I had to decide now, and the only thing I had to go on was my memory of that map in the fake FEMA truck. That split second before the wind tore it away.

Three marks. One circle, two Xs. I closed my eyes. I focused. I tried to pick out landmarks. I tried to put myself back into that horrific moment right before the full wrath of Nadia descended on New Orleans.

East bank or west? Gentilly or Filmore? And how far north?

I saw the canal. I saw the marking. I adjusted it in my mind, challenging my mental picture.

And then found a bullseye.

"Hey! What are you doing?"

The voice broke through my thoughts, loud and demanding. I saw the National Guardsmen advancing toward me from the face of a hotel-turned-command post. I recognized captain's bars on his shoulders. I noted the suspicion in his voice.

And I simply rammed on the gas. All four tires grabbed and launched me northward. I used Frank's map, pinned against my thigh, tracing with one finger as I hurtled along. A right out of Marigny brought me to Elysium Fields Avenue. I turned left—northward—along that, and gave the Humvee everything it had. The National Guard bulldozers had already done their best to clear the wide avenue. Six lanes, split by a median, served as a highway right through the heart of the old city. I found the Humvee's headlight switch and approached the maximum speed of the low-geared monstrosity. Downed trees and overturned cars lined the streets on either side, collapsed houses and snapped power poles beyond. Water ran in little rivers, sometimes as much as two feet deep in low spots, but nothing compared to what those low spots would look like if the levee breached. Water erupted over the nose of the Humvee, and I hurtled on, blazing through intersections. Driving northward into Gentilly, I passed beneath I-610 and knew that I'd crossed the lowermost extremity of the London Avenue Canal.

I might have already passed the bomb, but I didn't think so. The bullseye on my mental map guided me farther north along Elysium Fields Avenue, through tight clusters of windblasted neighborhoods and right across the intersection of Gentilly Boulevard. I passed a shopping district and a collection of chain restaurants, all smashed and coated in grime. I hurtled back into a neighborhood, the heart of Gentilly, and saw refugees walking amongst collapsed homes. FEMA trucks were scattered about to provide aid, and occasional NOPD cars were stationed to assist.

There were hundreds, maybe thousands of people here who were too far north of downtown to be transported to the Superdome. These were residents. Locals. Longtime New Orleanians who likely remembered Katrina.

And it was all about to happen again.

I turned West on Mirabeau Avenue, slowing the Humvee as I approached the London Avenue Canal. It was so dark without the aid of streetlamps that I actually flipped the Humvee's headlights off, relying instead on moonlight from the clear skies high above. I drove at a growl, approaching the opening of a bridge marked by reflective barricades and a giant sign:

BRIDGE CLOSED.

I stopped the Humvee and threw the door open, jogging to the face of the barricade and squinting across the bridge.

It was the canal all right, and it was swollen to absolute maximum capacity, lapping at the underside of the bridge and sloshing against high steel levee walls on either side. As I turned northward, I looked past a row of homes running along Warrington Drive and noted the moonlight reflecting against a motionless expanse of floodwater. The waterline itself stood five, maybe eight feet over the roofs of most of the homes, pressing against the earth and steel barriers the Army Corps of Engineers had erected, but not breaching. Not yet.

My heart rate quickened as the pressure of the inevitable crushed down on me. It wouldn't take a lot of dynamite to blow a hole in that wall, and even a small breach would quickly enlarge as the weight of all that bottled-up storm surge rushed through, tearing the metal aside and ripping into the earth on its way into Gentilly.

But *where* was the bomb?

I closed my eyes again. Focused on that X as an invisible bullseye. Squinted and couldn't quite picture it. I knew it was on the east bank. I knew it was someplace north of Mirabeau Avenue, but how far?

I looked down the length of the levee as though I were looking down the length of a railroad line, mapping the swell of soggy grass that led up to the wall. Like everywhere else in the city, storm debris littered the embankment in a minefield of shattered dreams and broken lives.

But one piece of debris stuck out of the rest—literally. Rammed into the earth with its face twisted back toward me was a tall black sign. Not a street sign. This was made of thick metal, a hundred yards away, but glimmering gold in the moonlight. I lifted the MacroStream from my pocket and concentrated its dying beam on it, squinting in the darkness.

I somehow felt that I *knew* what I was looking at, but I was still struggling to clarify the recollection.

And then it clicked, just as tires ground on the street behind me. The sign was one of those cast-iron historical markers, placed at the sights of important historical events by nonprofit societies. Black, with gold letters. Battered but indestructible. Impossible to read at this distance, yet I didn't need to. I already knew what it said.

You've got to be kidding me.

"Hey! Hey, you!"

A flood of harsh white light blazed against my face. I twisted, shielding my eyes, and detected an NOPD patrol vehicle parked alongside the Humvee. Not a car, but a pickup truck. Elevated a little on beefy mud tires. A cop dropped out, one hand on his gun as he stepped toward the front bumper.

"Hey! You park this Humvee here?"

I hesitated. He stepped into the spotlight, blocking the heart of the glare for a moment. I saw his face as my eyes adjusted. He saw mine.

And my heart fell. It was Officer Broussard, the guy who had arrested me back at the pastel pink house, and I knew the moment our gazes locked that he recognized me. His body tensed; his hand closed around the pistol strapped to his hip. Then he drew.

"Hands up!"

41

I never gave Broussard the opportunity to draw on me, or his partner for that matter. The second guy was bailing from the police truck as I vaulted over a guardrail and landed on the sloping exterior of the levee. Flashlights blazed over my back, and the shouting resumed. I sprinted, backpack slamming against my spine as I fought to stay upright on the slick grass, headed straight for the bent historic marker planted in the muddy earth. The cops' flashlights illuminated the gold letters as I approached, but I didn't need to read the multi-paragraph account of why the marker was placed in this neighborhood, or what it signified. The headline was enough.

London Avenue Canal Floodwall Breach.

"Stop right there! On the ground!"

I kept running. The MacroStream was out of my pocket, and I was illuminating my own path with rapidly dying light. I detected boot prints in the muck, relatively fresh. They wound amongst storm debris, working northward along the levee wall toward a lonely spot situated behind a vacant lot, sheltered by overgrown vegetation and brush that grew right up to the levee wall. I saw the boot prints mashing through the grass and mud, leading that way. There was a single tire track, also. A wheelbarrow, maybe.

These fools had used a *wheelbarrow* to cart dynamite right to the levee wall. The shamelessness of it all was so absurd I didn't even have time to consider the disgusting implications of planting a bomb on the site of the original London Avenue Canal failure.

It wasn't rocket science. Randy wasn't as smart as his kid. This was brutally simple math. The wall had failed at this point during hurricane Katrina, and the flooding had been catastrophic. So it was the obvious place to plant the bomb.

Broussard and his buddy were fifty yards behind me, but still coming on strong as I skidded to a stop at the base of the slope and looked toward the levee wall. The brush obscured my vision of its base, but the disruption was obvious. The boot prints, the tire marks. I scrambled upward, still clutching the dying MacroStream. It shone at barely twenty percent power, casting a dull LED glow across glimmering wet grass as I reached the top. My boots crashed into the brush as I kicked it away, tearing back vegetation to expose the base of the wall.

And then I stopped. My fingers touched cold sheet metal. I ripped a bush to the side and shone the MacroStream.

It was a metal trash can. No—a pair of them, about fifty gallons in size, capped with galvanized lids. Wires ran out of holes in their sides and joined together at a five-gallon bucket situated in between. I pitched a lid off one of the cans and pointed the light downward.

It was dynamite. Filled right to the brim, stick after stick of it, all wired together.

"Stop right there! Hands up!"

Broussard was almost on top of me as the MacroStream finally died. I rammed it into my pocket and looked over one shoulder, snapping my fingers.

"Light!"

Broussard raced in, service pistol drawn, face beet red with outrage. He was likely still angry about my Houdini escape in the Seventh Ward. I really couldn't care less. His duty light rode in his off hand, still blazing at me. I needed it.

"Hands up, jackass!" Broussard's voice barked with Cajun outrage as his partner orbited right, gun also drawn. The partner saw the bomb as he stepped behind me.

"What the—"

The whispered curse fell flat. I snapped my fingers again.

"*Light,* Broussard!"

The muzzle of Broussard's pistol dropped an inch as he stepped forward. His partner was already barking into his radio, calling for backup. Calling for the bomb squad. Calling for anything and everything that could be sent to the London Avenue Canal.

It was all much too late. It could be five seconds or five minutes before the bomb went off, but it wouldn't be fifty. It wouldn't be an hour. The sun would rise soon. Randy and his thugs wanted to be far, far away from New Orleans by then.

"What are you—"

"It's a bomb," I cut Broussard off. "I don't have time to explain. Point your light on it. I'm going to attempt to disarm it."

"Are you kidding me? Did you plant that?"

"Would I be here if I did?" I shouted, my patience finally failing. "Point the light!"

Whether by an overdose of confusion or the commanding tone in my voice, Broussard complied. The pistol lowered, and the light leveled on the center of the bomb mechanism—that five-gallon bucket. Broussard stepped forward. I stiff-armed him in the gut, shoving him back.

"Don't move!"

I bent toward the mucky grass and swept it gently with my fingers, searching out pressure pads or auxiliary triggers as I inched slowly forward. It was a lesson the Taliban had taught me—one of their many evil little methods for blowing kids from Kansas into bloody chunks. I didn't think that Randy was that smart, but I could already tell by the organization of the wiring running out of the trash cans that somebody in his crew had experience with explosives. Maybe not military, maybe demolition or mining. Something commercial. It was likely the job where they had sourced the dynamite in the first place.

Whatever the case, I couldn't afford to underestimate them any further.

"Don't move!" Broussard snapped again. "Don't budge another inch!"

"You ever been to Afghanistan, Broussard?"

No answer.

"You know what an IED looks like? You know how to disarm one?"

No answer.

"I didn't think so. So shut up."

I inched forward again. This time Broussard didn't object. His breath came in ragged, panicked little bursts as his partner finally finished with his radio and rushed back to the scene of the bomb.

"What's he doing?" the partner gasped.

"He...he says he can disarm it."

"Hey! Hey, you!"

I tuned them both out. I reached the five-gallon bucket and peeked inside. It was dark, but it wasn't difficult to detect the basic shape of a detonation box—a little black plastic container that might once have been a lunch box. It didn't matter. Just like the Taliban, Randy's crew had improvised. And just like the Taliban, they favored remote detonation. There was a cell phone in the bucket. A burner-type phone, taped to the outside of the detonation box. Its screen was black, wires connecting it to the box.

My chest tightened. For the umpteenth time that week, I was back in a war zone. Louisiana vanished around me. Time slowed. My fingers stiffened.

"You were military?" the partner demanded.

"Light," I said simply.

Nobody moved. I gritted my teeth. "Either grow a pair or hand it off!"

Broussard grew a pair. He closed in next to me and pointed the light into the bucket. A curse escaped his lips as the LED glow illuminated the detonation box and cell phone. I assumed there was a battery inside the box—something to generate the detonation spark. I'm not well versed in the use of dynamite. It's not something I used as a Ranger, but the basics of explosive demolition aren't that complex. The problem lay in the duality of the trash cans, each fed by a cluster of wires. Had there been only one trash can, I would have already slashed the wires, disconnecting the detonation device from the explosive. Done deal.

But with two cans, there was always the possibility, however unlikely, that one can was rigged to automatically detonate if the other was disconnected. It was an anti-bomb squad boobytrap. Another trick of the Taliban.

"Bomb squad's on the way," the partner said.

"How long?" My voice was perfectly flat, betraying none of the stress I felt.

"Thirty minutes," he breathed. "They're outside the city."

Of course.

"We don't have thirty minutes," I said, reaching into my pocket. The three-inch blade of my Victorinox deployed with a *snap*. The knife still smelled like gasoline. The sharpened edge glimmered beneath Broussard's light.

"Don't!" Broussard's voice cracked with sudden panic. "Lower that knife."

There was urgency in his voice, but no command. I looked up.

"You got a family, Officer?"

Broussard swallowed. Sweat dripped from his nose. The service pistol still clutched in his right hand twitched as the muzzle drooped toward the ground.

He nodded. I tilted my head toward the flood zone behind us.

"So do they."

Then I grasped a handful of the wires running to the right-hand trash can and looped them over my knife blade.

42

The question of my next two seconds—and potentially my final two seconds—all hinged on how smart I thought Randy and his crew were. Smarter, or at least as smart, as the average Taliban bomb doctor?

Maybe the real question was how vicious they were. If they were cold-blooded enough to rig a bomb that would blow a cop into lunch meat if it were found.

Perhaps neither of those were the true questions. Perhaps the true question was simply whether I could afford to roll the dice and wait thirty minutes for the bomb squad to arrive. I knew in my gut that was a question I had already answered.

So I cut the wires. One harsh, jerking pull of the knife brought the razor-sharp blade ripping through rubber and thin copper. My heart thundered. Sweat dripped from my busted nose. The fog in my brain left by the hydrocodone wavered for a moment, and a flash of pain burned from my rib cage.

But the bomb did not explode. I immediately grasped the second bunch of wires routed to the left-hand trash can and cut again, tearing and jerking until the last was severed. The knife burst free. I rocked back on my heels, thrown off balance. I caught myself in the mud, gasping for air.

And then the cell phone in the five-gallon bucket illuminated through the thin plastic as a default ringtone chimed like an orchestra of doom.

But nothing happened. I sat down with a heave and dropped the knife, scrubbing sweat off my face. My chest was so tight it hurt to breathe despite the heavy painkillers. My head buzzed. My breathing came in snapping bursts. Every time I blinked, I was on a dusty mountain road in Afghanistan, sitting beside an IED that had almost blown my Humvee in half. I blinked again and saw New Orleans. Then Afghanistan. It was a mirage, a distortion. My head went light, and I shook it hard, fighting to clear my vision.

Officer Broussard stood over me, handgun pointed to the ground, his own face chalk white as the cell phone continued to ring. Then he looked at me, and I knew what was coming next. Whenever the shock faded and mental clarity returned. It was happening now, right before my eyes. His jaw was locking. He was reaching for his handcuffs.

"On your feet," he growled.

Yeah. No thanks.

I folded the knife closed and dropped it into my pocket. Broussard jabbed his weapon toward me. In the distance, police sirens rang, and Humvee engines surged. The QRF, maybe. One Humvee short. They were responding to the scene until the bomb squad could be assembled.

Not that it mattered now.

"You're coming with *me*," Broussard said.

I stood, head still spinning a little. Broussard's handgun followed me. His partner stood back, his own gun lifted, but his gaze locked on the bomb. Still disoriented.

"You gonna shoot me?" I asked.

Broussard didn't answer. I could see the shock in his eyes. The reality of his near brush with death. He was no doubt thinking about his family—a beautiful young wife and beautiful small children. He was still stunned.

"I didn't think so," I said.

Then I shoved past him and broke into a run. Broussard shouted after me, but he was too overwhelmed. It didn't make him a bad cop. Just a green one. I found the Humvee waiting right where I'd left it, the engine still churning. By the time I had it pointed eastward toward Elysian Fields Avenue, fresh squad cars and National Guard Humvees were roaring in. None of them moved to stop me as I mashed the gas pedal to the floor and raced amongst the smashed houses and tangled power lines.

My heart thumped as I checked my watch. It was five thirty a.m. Only about an hour until sunrise, and Randy had dialed for the levee bomb. That meant that even now, he and his crew were beginning their bank robbery. The generators would be sabotaged. The little bomb would blow a hole in an exterior door. The big bomb—the one in the duffel bag—would be carted in toward that giant vault.

It might not work. Or it might bring the building down. They were dumber than the average Taliban fighter—they wouldn't know either way. But either way, Autumn was far too close to ground zero.

I reached Elysian and powered south, diesel thundering in my ears as the nonexistent suspension sent shock waves crashing up my spine. More cops rushed by. A firetruck howled along with them, lights flashing. A loudspeaker mounted to the roof of a National Guard deuce-and-a-half truck called for people to take cover and brace for flash flooding.

Whatever that meant.

I ran the Humvee all the way through Gentilly. Back beneath I-615, headlights bucking as I crashed over the twisted remnants of a swing set that had been left in the highway. I entered the Seventh Ward. I was headed for Marigny.

I had just crossed beneath I-10, only a mile from the Central Business District, when Randy's vault-busting bomb went off. An earth-shaking blast. A thunderous roar. And an instant cloud of debris illuminated by the moonlight as it erupted into the air over downtown New Orleans.

I had been right about Randy and his crew. They weren't smart. They'd used too much.

Way too much.

43

The Humvee's engine thundered as my boot rammed all the way to the floor, yanking the wheel right toward the heart of downtown. All I could think about was Autumn, her fragile body hurled across the street to land in broken pieces as that load of dynamite went off like too much gasoline on a backyard bonfire.

Fools!

Not just Randy. Not just his pals. Myself, as well. I'd been a fool to leave Autumn there with them. I should have taken her. I should have lunged out of the shadows and rolled the dice with the mini revolver. I should have clawed Randy Mercer's eyeballs from his stupid fat face.

My arms shook as I yanked the Humvee onto Rampart Street and thundered through the outskirts of the French Quarter. It was all too familiar territory by now. The front bumper of the Humvee slammed into the back corner of an abandoned minivan and hurled it onto the sidewalk, glass shattering and steel crunching. Water erupted across my already muddied windshield, and the diesel surged. I blasted past a screaming cop car with lights flashing and smelled concrete dust on the air.

A lot of it. The kind that is pulverized and shot skyward by an ordnance blast. It smelled of chaos and impending carnage. It smelled like *war*.

Canal Street loomed ahead, snapped palm trees and bent light poles marking the intersection. The temporary police outpost stood to my right. The National Guard station to my left. Directly ahead, the dull glow of the generator-powered Superdome was obscured by a haze of foggy gray. All that concrete and building dust hurled into the sky like so much confetti.

And then I heard another sound, much softer than the blast, but still audible through the storm-torn streets. Automatic gunfire.

I yanked the Humvee's wheel left and screamed through the intersection, leaping a fallen power pole and hurtling straight across the median when the blocky tires failed to deliver the turn radius I had expected. To my left were additional Humvees, a trio of them racing in from the lower half of the French Quarter. National Guardsmen huddled behind the muddy windshields, M4 rifles visible like toothpicks sticking out of a soufflé. There were NOPD squad cars, also, and an armored truck. They were all surging south down Carondelet Street, Saint Charles Avenue, and Camp Street. All headed for Poydras and the Federal Reserve building beyond.

Running toward the sound of the guns. Literally.

I gunned the motor and joined them. Battered hotels and boarded-up restaurants blazed past on every side as I surged along at maximum speed, still thinking about Autumn in the heart of that gathering storm of gunfire. Her little ears ringing. Her legs helpless to carry her to safety. Maybe crying into her teddy, her battered and abused psyche finally breaking.

I struck Poydras Street just west of the Superdome. There were cops everywhere, metal barricades erected to contain the refugees, and now blocking my path. I rammed straight through, yanking the wheel left as the barricade panels buckled over the Humvee's hood and twisted beneath its tires. Nothing would stop the heavy war machine. It grabbed wet pavement and ground onward, east toward the smoke rising from only blocks away. I recognized the face of the office building that stood directly across from the Federal Reserve Bank—only, all the glass was blown out now. Dust clouded the air, and shards of oak tree limbs lay strewn about Poydras Street. The bomb had shaken the entire block, but clearly it hadn't killed its originators. At least not all of them. Several of Randy's gang members must have dug in behind the broken walls and blown-out windows of the bank, because gunfire rained from their position in a storm. I recognized the familiar star-shaped muzzle flash of M4A1s dumping green-tipped 5.56mm ammunition into the block as police car windshields shattered and armored Humvees pinged.

Things had not gone as planned. The cops and the National Guard were responding more quickly than Randy and his chums had anticipated. Now the chaos would begin.

I slammed on the brakes at the outer perimeter of the armored vehicles, about a hundred yards from the five-foot metal fence that surrounded the Federal Reserve, and threw the door open. There were four National Guardsmen huddled behind a matching Humvee only yards away, three armed with rifles and one with a sidearm. I sprinted to them, scrambling over a mass of tangled power lines, heedless of the bullets skipping off the pavement and whistling past my head. Just as I reached the Humvee and slid into shelter behind its armored mass, one of the guardsmen was leaning out around the front bumper and returning fire with his M4.

The weapon snarled, and I gasped for breath as hot brass rained over my muddied T-shirt. Scraping the casings away, I clawed my way upright and instinctively looked to the guy with the sidearm.

His arms bore first lieutenant patches. His name tape read *Landry*.

"You in charge?" I shouted.

A fresh blast of gunfire slammed into the Humvee, and everybody ducked. Everybody but me, anyway. I already knew I was sufficiently covered, an instinct born out of a few dozen such brutal situations. These guys, I decided, were brand new at this. They'd never been deployed.

Welcome to Afghanistan.

"Hey!" I shook the lieutenant by the shoulder. "You in charge?"

His breath rushed through a sagging mouth. Then he seemed to collect himself, and he shook his head.

"Captain's in charge!"

"Where is he?"

Another blast of gunfire, crazed and wild, slammed like hail against the Humvee and whizzed overhead. It was worse than most gunfights in Afghanistan. Far crazier, more desperate.

What were they *thinking*?

"Where is he?" I repeated, ears ringing.

"I...I don't know!"

I looked over my shoulder, back toward the line of Humvees, patrol cars, and one armored police truck pulled up to face the reserve building. The absence of their levee bomb had cost Randy's gang. Instead of generating a distraction, they'd generated a mini Waco.

And everybody knew how that story ended.

"Listen to me!" I shook the lieutenant by the arm again. "There's a kid in that bank! You hear me? Ten years old, paralyzed from the waist down. Blonde hair, blue eyes. You gotta tell your people to stop shooting!"

Another confused frown. "What?"

"*Stop shooting!*"

As if interpreting my pleas as a challenge, the storm of gunfire erupting from the bank redoubled. Bullets ricocheted off the Humvee and skipped against the pavement. One of them scraped off the lieutenant's helmet, and the next hit a guardsman in the boot. She screamed and crumpled, blood spurting over the blacktop.

"They're shooting at *us!*" the lieutenant screamed.

I released his arm and shoved him away, rushing to the side of the wounded soldier. She was young, likely still a teenager. Strawberry hair and agonized green eyes. Blood stained her DOD-issued boots as she clutched at her foot, rocking against the front wheel of the Humvee.

"Give me your leg!" I called.

Nobody answered. I grabbed the guardsman's foot anyway and went to work on her laces. They were double-knotted, and I went for my Victorinox. Despite the dulling of slicing through copper wire, the blade tore through the paracord laces, allowing me to loosen the boot.

"Hold her!"

The two other enlisted guardsmen finally followed orders, pinning their wounded comrade against the front tire of the Humvee as I removed the boot with a smooth tug. She screamed, helmet slamming against an armored fender. Her sock was already soaked in crimson, and half a toe fell out of the boot. I discarded the footwear and snatched the med kit off the spine of the nearest guardsman. There were a lot of things packed inside—a tourniquet, bleed stop, and various other hemostatic equipment. The only thing I wanted was gauze. I found a wad of it and ripped it out of the packaging, then pressed it against her busted foot. She screamed and jerked. I maintained pressure and read her name tape.

Guidry. Another classic Louisiana name.

"You a Saints fan, Private Guidry?"

The girl blinked hard, breathing through her teeth. She managed a nod.

"Who Dat."

"Go Falcons."

Guidry flushed crimson and lifted a trembling middle finger. I patted her arm. "You're gonna be fine. You're a hero."

Turning to her nearest companion, I grabbed his sleeve and tugged him close, placing his hand over her foot.

"Maintain pressure. She can't lose blood. You understand?"

He nodded. I squeezed his arm. "Backup is on the way. Stay low."

Then I scooped Guidry's fallen M4 off the ground. It was the standard model, not the A1 model. That meant it only fired in semiautomatic or three-round-burst mode, but I was fine with that. I'd never been big on spray and pray, anyway. I liked to place my shots where they'd hurt most.

"Wait!" It was the lieutenant. I looked over my shoulder.

"Where are you going?" He allowed more fear into his voice than any officer should. I gave him a pass.

It was his first firefight.

"To finish this," I said. Then I sprinted from behind the Humvee.

44

C oncrete dust still hung in the air as I departed the cover of the Humvee, already locked in on my next point of concealment. It lay behind a muddied and storm-blasted Honda Accord, parked on Poydras Street since before the storm. It was an altogether inferior form of protection as compared to the armored Humvee, but the Humvee stood in direct line of fire from the bombed-out bank building. The Accord stood at an angle.

I needed an angle to get in a good shot beneath the raking cover fire of Randy's gang. They would run out of ammo eventually, but by then, Guidry's foot might not be the only casualty.

I made the rear bumper of the Accord just as a burst of 5.56 hellfire raked toward me. It pinged off the Accord's back bumper and shattered a taillight. I slid behind the rear wheel like a baseball player sliding into home base, grinding my jeans against the pavement. My body was so alive with adrenaline and so numbed by hydrocodone that I didn't feel it. I couldn't feel anything.

I simply rolled my back against the side of the car. Pressed the M4's stock against my shoulder and flipped the selector switch to semiauto mode. Measured my breaths until I fell into the natural tempo of combat.

And then I pivoted outward, swinging around the rear of the car and raising the rifle all at once. There was no optic, just iron sights. The ghost ring of the rear encircled the front post. The world faded around me, nothing mattering except that front post as it fell over my target, sixty yards distant. A shadow behind a blown-out bank window. A hint of movement as a rifle barrel pivoted toward me.

But I fired first. Three quick squeezes of the trigger—not the same as a three-round burst. More controlled. All three bullets zipped through the window and struck home. I heard the scream and saw the shadow fall. Then I was sliding back into cover as the return fire blasted toward me in a storm of revenge. The Accord's rear glass exploded into ten thousand little cubes, raining over my head and sliding down my shirt. Body panels popped and pinged as steel-core ammunition tore through them. The air was thick with gun smoke. My ears rang with the melee.

But my heart rate was perfectly even, my body calm. In a strange way, this was so much less stressful than disarming the bomb or braving Nadia's wrath. Open combat was a brutally simple thing, and I'd had a lot of practice with it.

Scrambling to the front of the Accord, I gained a new line of sight through a broken rear window and the shattered rear glass. I could see most of Saint Charles Avenue. The Reserve building smoldered as small fires clogged the air with gray smoke. A good chunk of the roof was missing, and one corner of the outer wall was caved in. From blown-out windows on the first floor, half a dozen points of muzzle flash engaged the cops and guardsmen even as additional Humvees screamed onto the scene, soldiers bailing out in full combat gear.

I focused on one target at a time, measuring my breaths and squeezing off careful shots. One gunman went down, his face split open by my own steel-core messenger of death. The next guy was smarter, swinging irregularly in and out of cover to unleash short bursts of gunfire against the line of law enforcement vehicles. There was no way to predict his pattern, and if I rushed a shot that missed, that bullet would zip through the window and land someplace inside the bank building.

Was Autumn in there? Maybe Randy had left her in Gallier Hall. There was no way to be sure.

I gritted my teeth and focused, daring the gunman to appear again, already taking the slack out of my trigger and pressing it right to the breaking point. Only a twitch away from firing. Front sight post resting over that black spot in the Reserve wall, the world faded, my breaths timed...

And then something caught my eye. Not from the bank, but to my left, along Saint Charles Avenue. A moment of hesitation forced my body to automatically relax off the trigger, preventing an accidental shot. The gunman appeared in the window for just a flash, and I missed him.

But I was no longer worried about him. I was leaning left now, craning my head to get a better look down the street. The movement I detected spoke to my battle-trained mind. It sent up alert flags of a covert maneuver happening at the edge of my peripheral—perhaps an attempt by the enemy to flank me or even circle behind. It was the kind of thing war would teach you to be paranoid of, but this wasn't a flanking maneuver. It was an escape attempt.

I saw three men leaving the Reserve building together, each heavily laden down. The first I recognized as Yellow Teeth. The second was one of his nameless associates. Both men wielded M4 rifles, and both men were laden down with bulky duffel bags packed to the brim with some unidentifiable contents.

Then came the third man, and when I recognized him, my blood went cold. It was Randy Mercer, and in place of a duffel bag, he carried Autumn slung on his back the same way I'd carried her out of Big Charity. She clung on with skinny little arms, wide and terror-filled eyes darting around the street in obvious desperation. As I watched, the three men reached the edge of the park that faced the Reserve building, and turned east. An instant before I lost them in the inky black predawn darkness, Autumn's head twisted around. She saw me through the busted rear windows of the Accord. Her wide eyes streamed with tears, and her lips parted. She managed a desperate scream.

"Mason!"

Then she was gone.

45

Muzzle flash blinked to my right, and from someplace behind me, a guardsman shouted a command to his troops. All of it was ambient and meaningless noise to my zeroed-in mind. I wasn't even thinking about my target from five seconds prior.

I was only thinking about Autumn slipping straight away into the darkness. Randy and his ringleader chums had abandoned whoever remained of their gang to die in the bank, and they were hauling straight out of town, bringing Autumn with them.

I scrambled out of cover behind the Accord and dashed left instead of right, away from the sound of the guns and east along Poydras Street. I would never make it down Saint Charles Avenue without being ventilated by gunfire from the bank—at least two gunmen still survived inside and were still dumping fire at random. But if I circled the block, I might have a shot at catching Randy and his crew.

Somebody called to me from the line of police cars, ordering me to stop. I ignored them and kept sprinting, reaching the corner of Poydras and Camp Street and sliding around it just as the cops turned their fire on me, already confusing me for one of the enemy amid the fog of war. Handgun rounds pinged off the concrete, and one of them sliced through the top of Frank's backpack, but I kept going. Up the narrow street, sloshing through mud puddles and breathing hard. The rifle rode in the low ready position, stock planted against my shoulder, finger held against the receiver. Ahead, the eastern side of the park loomed as a tangle of hardwood limbs framed against a sky that was just starting to turn gray instead of black. Four figures exploded from the park. They were two hundred yards away, already turning south again and still hustling. I raised the rifle.

"*Stop!*"

They saw me. The third man raised a handgun and popped off a crazed, useless shot. But they didn't stop, and even as I dropped the front sight post over the cluster of moving bodies, I knew I couldn't shoot. There was too much danger of hitting Autumn.

I lowered the rifle and ran again, stretching my legs this time. Forcing additional speed out of my exhausted and battered body, not settling for anything less than maximum effort. There was no marching cadence echoing in my skull, no poetic drive ripped from memories of bootcamp or Afghanistan to fuel me on. There was only the thought of Autumn and her horrified, tearstained face. Her child soul, finally shattered by the culmination of violence and abuse unleashed over her. Screaming my name. Pleading for me to make good on my promise, to not allow Randy to whisk her away.

If he made it to the coast, reaching whatever method of permanent escape waited there, she would likely be gone

forever. Lost in the mire of third-world countries with no
extradition treaties, raised by an abusive old man who lived
to crush her under his thumb.

No. Not a chance. This ended *now*.

I reached the park just as the four figures vanished
around the next corner. The rifle felt like a toy in my sweaty
hands as I hurtled onward, stretching out, gobbling up the
gap between us and knowing that I was making good time. I
would overtake them. I would draw within headshot range
and drop three bodies in a lake of blood.

I would recover Autumn.

But then another sound rose above the fading gunshots
behind me. A low cough, a rough growl. A churn. It was a car
engine, just around the next corner. I reached the edge of the
block and turned left, raising my rifle again.

I was met by a storm of close-quarter handgun fire,
forcing me to scramble back behind the edge of a brick wall
as the motor surged. I stole a glimpse and saw the taillights
of a small SUV flashing red as the transmission dropped into
drive. Then the vehicle was racing away from me. The back
glass was cracked open, two faces and a handgun visible.

Randy Mercer and Autumn Mercer. The girl was
clutched close to his chest, preventing any chance of a
rushed shot. The gun jammed out the back window, pointed
toward me, and dumped bullets at random.

Then the SUV slid around the next corner, turning
south. It was gone as fast as I'd first seen it, and I was
sprinting again. Losing ground now even as my head
pounded and the breath burned in my lungs. I reached the
intersection and looked south to see the SUV weaving amid
storm debris and parked cars, moving a little slower than
before but still much faster than I could ever hope to run. It

was already half a mile distant and fading quickly. Going where?

To the river.

I remembered the squiggly line on the map. Randy and his crew had clearly staged the SUV as part of their getaway scheme. They must have a boat staged, also, down by the river. The two duffel bags I saw them carrying would be loaded with cash stolen from a busted reserve bank vault.

The final phase of their plan was now in play—the getaway phase. It was my last chance to stop them.

Ignoring the path the SUV had taken, I hurtled eastward, again demanding more of my worn body than it wanted to give. Pushing ever harder. Not counting the paces or even the blocks, but only focused on a giant blue sign visible at the end of a row of apartments and felled sidewalk trees:

RIVERWALK.

I reached the edge of downtown New Orleans just as the fatigue began to set in. I was breathing hard. My heart thundered. It wasn't overwork or injury or a lack of sleep. It was all three burning into a cocktail of impending defeat, but I wouldn't acknowledge it. I turned south and ran again, rushing past an outlet mall to my left and searching beyond the buildings for any indicator of a port. The Crescent City Connector bridges rose against a graying sky, my eyes adjusting easily to the growing light. I skipped over tangled power lines and circled around a trio of cars rammed into the curb like forgotten toys.

I knew I was near to the river without needing to see it— I could smell the muddy water. As I focused every muscle on my next stride, I saw brake lights burst out of an alley a mile

ahead. A small SUV, moving fast. Turning right and blazing
south in front of the convention center. Passing beneath the
Connector bridges. Screaming around debris and burning
rubber at every acceleration. Driven as though a madman
sat behind the wheel.

I leaned ahead and gave chase even as the SUV pivoted
left, toward the river, and disappeared behind the far corner
of the convention center. It was still so far ahead, and my
strength was leaving me rapidly.

But I dug deep. I reached someplace into the darkness at
the back of a shell-shocked and war-scarred soul and
demanded *more*.

I thought of Autumn and those terrified eyes, and I
found it.

The convention center felt as though it were ten miles
long as I raced past, still dodging debris and jumping over
tangled power lines. Limbs and lawn furniture lay strewn
across the street, joined at times by the rotting carcasses of
small animals. I didn't even notice the stench anymore. I
crossed beneath the bridges and finally reached the end of
the street where it dead-ended against a smashed chain-link
fence tangled with broken bushes.

I wheeled left, gasping for breath. I couldn't hear the
SUV anymore, and I didn't see it. It was now far ahead. The
street I turned onto was shorter than the last. Felled palm
trees lay all over it. Directly in front of me sat another
massive steel building stretching to either side, blocking my
view of the river.

It looked like a dead end, but it wasn't. I saw the horizon
above the gravel parking lot to the right of the building,
catching the first glowing kiss of a sun only minutes away

from rising. Some vehicle had passed that way, disturbing the dirt. Dust still hung in the air.

I reached the next intersection and turned right. I saw the parking lot at the end of the steel building. It was surrounded by another smashed fence and more debris. An overturned sedan and a motorcycle tangled amid the brush. But there was one vehicle that rested upright, slid into the far corner of the lot with three doors slung open and the engine still running. As I reached the parking lot and raised the rifle, I was already following the muddy boot prints running from the nose of the SUV and across the lot. Beyond the building. Down a path toward the river. The smell of muddy water was much stronger now. I could taste it on the sticky stale breeze.

I accelerated, ignoring the SUV.

And then I heard a new sound, sharper and much angrier than the gentle rumble of a car. It surged, screaming over the Louisiana morning.

It was a boat engine.

46

I made it to the dockside just as the flat-bottomed metal boat carrying Randy, his chums, his stolen money, and his kidnapped daughter raced southward along the Mississippi. The vessel was twenty feet long and printed with the logo of the Louisiana Department of Wildlife and Fisheries—no doubt stolen from a fleet of rescue vessels trailered to the city after the storm.

And now carrying Autumn Mercer away, into permanent doom.

I slid to a stop along the dockside, heaving for air as the boat roared downstream. A syrupy field of mucky water lapped right up to the edges of the wooden planks, and in the dim light, the flat-bottomed boat was already growing hazy at a hundred yards. But it was still in range.

I raised the M4 and focused not on the human occupants of the boat, but on the outboard engine. It was large and black, covered in a plastic shroud, shrieking as it shoved the boat ahead at thirty or forty miles per hour. The front sight post fell over it. The world faded out. The trigger reached the breaking point under gradual pressure.

I squeezed. The rifle cracked, spitting a single bullet across the churning water and smacking into the engine shroud. I knew I hit it because a section of plastic exploded into the air, but the boat churned onward, and when I pressed the trigger again, nothing happened.

I rotated the weapon and checked the chamber. It was locked back over an empty magazine, bone-dry. I hadn't brought a spare from Guidry's chest rig. I hadn't even seen any.

My heart pounded, and I slung the rifle down, my gaze snapping quickly to either extremity of the dock. A giant paddle wheeler was tied off just upstream, its porches and railings smashed by Nadia's wrath, two fins missing from the paddle. There was a little tugboat farther on, chained to a pylon, much too slow to be useful.

Then I saw the fishing boat. Or maybe it was a dockside utility craft. Whatever it was, it was only about fourteen feet in length, and it was tied up at the very end of the pier. Muddy and heavily worn, with a sun-bleached plastic housing encasing an exhausted two-stroke motor. Another survivor of the storm, I couldn't imagine that it had weathered Nadia tied to this dock, but it had clearly been abandoned here for a lack of utility. It looked ready to sink. Ready to just fade beneath the muddy surface, there to become a home for six-foot catfish.

But it was my only option.

I sprinted to the end of the pier and jumped directly behind the boat's console, already digging for my Victorinox. The abused blade slashed through the bowline, freeing the craft.

Two inches of water sloshed over the floor as I hurried to the console, unconcerned about whether it was runoff water from the pier or whether the boat was actively leaking. I didn't have time to wonder. As the little craft was dragged by the current away from shore, I dropped to my knees beneath the console and stared up at a mass of tangled control wires. The boat was old—much older than I was. It had been rigged and repaired a dozen times by a dozen different mechanics, probably none of them certified for the work. I located the wires running out of the back side of the ignition switch and used the knife to cut them free. Then I was biting off insulation, tearing it free with my teeth. Twisting wires together and muttering to myself.

"Come on, baby...come on..."

The motor turned over. A rough, angry sound, like a bear roused too early from hibernation. I broke the wires and pressed them again, providing a surge of electricity to the objecting starter. It whined again, and the motor turned over. I grabbed the throttle handle and rocked it backwards and forwards, adding fuel to the carb. I hit the wires again.

The motor surged to life with a blast of putrid smoke. I abandoned the wires and pulled myself up by the steering wheel, rocking the throttle handle back to neutral, locking it into gear, and ramming it forward. The propeller caught. The two-stroke howled. Then the bow of the little boat rose lazily out of the water, and I spun the wheel southward. Water washed over my boots and ran into the stern as the motor gained momentum, RPMs rising.

I raced back beneath the Crescent City Connector bridges as the first hint of orange light highlighted the sky over my right shoulder. I could see—not well, but well enough. The dark water was easy to follow as I pushed the boat to maximum power and ascended to plane.

I thought about the Louisiana coastline, miles south of New Orleans. It was a long, long ways along the Mighty Mississippi. Thirty miles, maybe? Forty? I really didn't know. I'd only ever seen it on a map. What I did know was that Randy and his crew were prepared, and I was not. They had staged the Wildlife and Fisheries boat and clearly had an escape route planned all the way to South America. I had no idea how much fuel was left in the tanks of my aged craft. I had no idea if it would make it around the next bend, or if they could move faster.

I could only hope that the added weight of four bodies instead of one, plus the bulk of all that stolen cash, made a difference.

I reached the first turn of the river and pulled the wheel hard right, crossing as close to the washed-out bank as I dared. I passed commercial container ships lined up along either shore, left there to weather the storm. I swerved around floating debris, and I pointed eastward. I could see for nearly two miles.

And I saw my quarry. Randy's boat raced ahead, engine planted deep in the water, bow stabbing toward the sky. It wasn't a very fast craft—it was designed to be stable, not quick, with plenty of room in the wide hull for what should have been a team of eight sweaty rednecks. Even with only three rednecks and a kid, however, the boat made a little less speed than my own craft. I could tell that the distance between us was shrinking—very slowly. Only by inches at a time.

But it was shrinking. Three hundred yards was collapsing steadily toward two-fifty. A tinge of hope rushed through my chest.

Then they saw me. I knew it, because one man pointed.

It might have been Randy. I couldn't be sure in the dimness. I squinted, then plummeted to the floor as muzzle flash lit the horizon. It was another M4A1, and it spat bullets in a crazed spray upstream. One skipped across the bow of my boat; another shattered the mucky windshield mounted over the console. I managed the wheel from the bottom, rising cautiously every few seconds to check my heading.

I continued to close on them. I thought I saw Autumn resting in the back of the boat, marked by the snap of her blonde hair against the morning wind. I leaned low for shelter next to the console and braced myself, willing for my boat to gain another yard. Another foot. I could risk the bullets and deal with three idiots if I could just close the gap.

But I wasn't closing the gap, and now I thought I was actually losing ground. As we approached the next gentle bend in the Mississippi, I could tell that the distance between us was starting to extend again. Behind me, my engine choked and struggled, pushing the craft as hard it as it could downriver, but as I looked to my feet, I noted that more of that murky water was lapping closer to my ankles, confirming my fears about the old boat. It was leaking rapidly. Three inches was growing closer to four, and with those four came additional weight that slowed the vessel, dragging it inevitably toward that catfish city far beneath my boots.

I struggled with the wheel, fighting to keep myself on course. Shots from Randy's boat had ceased as their lead developed. I pushed the throttle against its lock, hoping for a little extra power. We rounded the next corner in the river, and the last of New Orleans faded behind us. It was nothing but trees on either side now, with occasional glimpses of metal-roofed riverside homes reflecting the first rays of the sun. There were no other boats. No help from the coast guard or the NOPD. No Parish police.

In the blink of an eye, I felt as though we had transitioned into a swampy dystopia, surrounded by water and vegetation, with nothing but the endless twists of the Mighty Mississippi leading ahead forever.

I wasn't going to last forever. I might not last more than another five minutes. The water had reached my ankles, and my boat was struggling to maintain plane. The river bent slowly to the right, orbiting a giant finger of land that was consumed by flooded-out trees. I thought I saw another metal roof, but I saw no piers. No place to land the boat unless I ran it right into the forest.

I was approaching the need to make a decision, and it wasn't a decision I wanted to make. I could push my vessel until it sank right beneath me, or I could run it up on shore and watch Autumn disappear...likely forever.

I looked downriver. With Randy's lead once again extended to three hundred yards, I had to squint to make out Autumn's face. She sat against the stern, huddled down next to the engine. Wide eyes looking back at me. Windswept blonde hair lashed her face. I couldn't see the fear, but I imagined it anyway. The defeat. The hopelessness. It cut me straight to my core, and I knew I would run my boat straight to the bottom of the Mississippi before I would give up the chase, even if it was pointless.

But I wouldn't have to, because even as Autumn gazed back at me as a distant speck, I saw her moving. Her hands disappeared beneath the stern of the boat. She bent, and her shoulders twitched as she yanked something. A black line appeared next to her face, rising over the side of the boat.

She plunged it into the river. For a long moment nothing happened, and I squinted in confusion.

Then the outboard on Randy's boat coughed. The pitch of the howling engine shifted to a gurgling growl. Power bled away, and then I understood.

The fuel line.

Autumn had yanked it right out of the fuel tank and plunged it over the side. Even now the engine was sucking river water into the combustion cylinders—and Mississippi River water doesn't combust.

"You go, kid!" I shouted into the wind as Randy and his goons fought with the controls. The boat had plummeted off plane, and the engine had already died. With five inches of water washing against my shins, I had also fallen off plane and was making only chugging progress toward them, but the gap was starting to shrink again. They saw me coming, and panic ensued. Randy snatched up the M4 his buddy had wielded only moments before, and opened fire.

He managed only three crazed, inaccurate shots before the weapon went silent, either jammed or empty. Whatever the case, Randy didn't wait to fix it. He slung the rifle down and clawed for a handgun. We were three hundred yards apart now. My boat ran like a swimming pig, propelled as much by the current as the engine. I crouched behind the console and braced myself for the unknown.

I had a mini revolver with five rounds of .22 Magnum in my pocket. A three-inch locking blade. And my bare hands.

It had to be enough.

But as the gap between us closed to two hundred yards, I saw a trolling motor swing off the boat's bow and plunge into the water. Yellow Teeth was working it, his hands moving in a panicked blur. The bow of his vessel snaked sideways as

Yellow Teeth added power. The third man was busy gathering up heavy duffel bags, and Randy snatched Autumn up, cuffing her violently right across the face. Autumn's head snapped back, and she screamed. He pulled her close.

The bow of their boat had turned a full ninety degrees. The overworked trolling motor churned at full power, dragging them along at a crawl.

But a crawl was enough. I already understood their strategy, and I steered my sinking craft to counter it. We were both headed inland, toward that bulge of swampy trees and muck that the river bent around. They would reach the shore only a hundred yards ahead of me. I would reach it just before my boat was swallowed by the Mississippi.

We were carrying the fight into the swamps.

47

Randy's boat slid between flooded trees and vanished into the forest just as the overworked motor of my vessel coughed on an emptying fuel tank. I kept the throttle pressed to full speed, pointed my bow into the same slot of water Randy had chosen, and abandoned the controls. I advanced to the bow, snapping my Victorinox open in my right hand and clutching the mini revolver in my left. Once again, the knife felt like the first-choice weapon.

Darkness closed over my head even as the rising sun spilled over my shoulders. The canopy of trees that interlaced their aged limbs above the swollen banks of the Mississippi was impossibly thick, the water choked with vegetation. I saw Randy's boat run up on the muddy bank, the trolling motor grinding as the four-man party vanished into the swamp. My own motor died with fifty feet to go, and I leapt off the bow.

Murky water closed up to my stomach. I thrashed ahead, gaze darting from tree to tree as I searched out a path. I could hear the three men thrashing through the brush, cursing and dragging the sodden duffel bags behind them. Autumn called my name and then screamed. My blood ran hot as I exploded out of the water and onto the bank. I looked briefly into the boat for the fallen M4, but it was empty, not jammed, the bolt locked back over the exhausted magazine. I saw no other weapon. Nothing more useful than my own knife and peashooter.

I turned back to the swamp and passed into the trees. Mud sucked up to my ankles with each step, underbrush tearing at my legs. My heart thumped a steady drumbeat as the noise of my targets grew suddenly quiet amid the swamp. I couldn't hear Autumn. I couldn't hear footfalls or grunts. Only the chirp of insects and the song of morning birds broke through the trees.

Randy and his crew had stopped. They had likely split. They were laying an ambush for me.

I lowered the knife and hunched myself down, bunching muscles in preparation to spring in any direction at the first hint of trouble. Looking between the brush at my feet, I noted the tracks splitting in three directions. Every step was a heavy one, large boots tearing through the mud. Two men carried money bags, and Randy carried Autumn. It was impossible to guess who was who. I selected the path to my right and slipped into the brush, slowing my own steps. Falling into the stance of a hunter.

I'd done this before. Not in Afghanistan, but in Ranger School, during the Florida phase. Outside Eglin Air Force Base, in the panhandle, fighting through swamps to achieve complex objectives. Always on the alert for the enemy. Exhausted and starving, underequipped and ready to drop. But forced to press on.

That training was years old, but it was alive in my muscle memory. I slipped from tree to bush with near perfect silence, choosing solid ground by instinct and keeping every sense in play to hunt my enemy. Not only sight and sound, but smell. Searching for body odor, cologne, or even shampoo to contrast the stench of mud and rotting animal carcasses.

I was like an animal myself. A stalker at the top of the food chain, and I sensed my target only yards away. To my left—no. To my front left. Northeast on the compass face. I could feel his presence. I thought I heard his breathing, whistling between rotten teeth, just around the next tree.

He sprang out, and I sprang right at the same moment. It wasn't Randy, and it wasn't Yellow Teeth. It was the third man. He led with a handgun, rocketing out from behind the tree, the black muzzle racing toward me. A gunshot cracked, and a bullet whizzed to the left of my ear. I faked right, as though I were headed around the tree. He withdrew to pivot the gun in that direction, ready to confront me.

But I had already swerved left again, back into the line of fire from only a moment before. I was launching myself out of the mud. The mini revolver was cocked, my left hand dropping. He saw me coming in his peripheral and twisted back. Our bodies closed to within two feet. His gun swept toward me, panicked shots slicing through empty air as he pivoted. Brass rained over the mud. I pressed the button trigger of the mini revolver, and it bucked in my hand. A .22 slug spat from the muzzle and rocketed into his gut. He choked and stumbled.

Then my knife hand fell. A sweeping blow that came down from left to right, leading with the knife edge. Stainless steel tore into his throat and ripped through his windpipe, shredding and dragging. He went down in a spray of blood, gun slipping from his fingers. It plummeted into a mud puddle, and he fell next to it, ghastly eyes staring up at me as he fought for a final breath.

It never came, but bullets did. A hail of gunfire from the storm-torn trees only yards to my left. I slung myself right, plummeting to the mud as bullets zipped over my head and ripped through tangled foliage. There was no time to fish for the third guy's fallen handgun. No time to think about angling for a shot against the man hunting me through the trees. The gunshots were loud and incessant, not far away. My instincts kicked in and commanded me to take cover—any cover.

Mud coated my arms, and grimy floodwater splashed over my face as I wiggled beneath a toppled cypress, bullets slicing the air only inches over my head, and limbs dragging across Frank's backpack. I didn't think my aggressor actually saw me. He was just popping off shots, hoping to get lucky. He nearly did as a slug broke through the cypress bark and whistled past my busted nose, humming like a giant bumblebee.

I crouched in my newfound shelter and wiped grit from my face, listening to the sounds of a suddenly still forest. A grunt from twenty yards through the swampy carnage was followed by the familiar *thunk* of a handgun slide closing over a fresh magazine.

He'd run dry. But he'd also reloaded.

I calmed my breathing and rolled into a crouch, on the move again. I couldn't afford to remain still. There were still two armed men scattered someplace amid the swamp, and I had to assume they were both moving, trying to encircle me.

Not that these were tactical geniuses, but they were armed idiots.

Maybe just as dangerous.

I returned to my feet ten yards behind the cypress, now tangled in a mass of vines and contorted foliage, floodwater running nearly to my knees. Head down, mini revolver and knife at the ready, I wove through the swamp as though it were an obstacle course. Sweat streamed down my back. My eyes burned; my head pounded. Minutes dragged by, and I buried myself in the swamp, now fully detached from my bullet-spraying aggressor. Still moving in circles, still searching for my next target.

And then I heard the scream. It was shrill and young. Female and desperate. A man grunted, and then Autumn called my name.

"*Mason!*"

The shout came from my left, maybe fifty yards away. Sunlight beat down from the east, but I couldn't see a thing. Mist, glare, and broken trees blocked my view. Autumn screamed again; then somebody crashed into the water like a falling log.

"Get back here!"

It was Randy. I pivoted toward his voice and clawed my way over another fallen tree, still sweeping my gaze left and right for any sign of Yellow Teeth. Landing in the muck beyond, I looked through a tangle of vines and finally saw her.

A toppled oak tree had left a tangle of thick limbs, smashed and pressed together like a maze of wooden fangs. Randy clambered near the top of it, a handgun clasped in one fist, his filthy wifebeater tank top catching on the limbs as he fought to climb through.

Autumn lay beneath him, resting on her stomach on my side of the tree, face and body encased in mud as she used both arms to drag herself through the filth, legs trailing behind her. She'd fallen—or maybe dragged herself—through the tree limbs, providing a momentary gap between herself and Randy.

But her father was coming, only yards behind. He was too big to fit through the same gaps she could, but he was plenty strong enough to climb straight over. Autumn's progress was little better than a slithering crawl.

Crystal blue eyes met mine, wide with panic and plea. Randy reached the top of the busted oak and scrambled to catch himself as one boot slipped. His gun hand was fouled up among the limbs. He hadn't even seen me yet.

I raised the mini revolver and cocked the hammer. It made a little snap in the stillness, like a stick breaking. An inconsequential sound in that environment, yet Randy's primal instincts alerted him to the danger. His gaze locked with mine. My finger descended over the button trigger.

Then Autumn screamed.

"No! Don't shoot my daddy!"

My brain stalled. Randy shouted. Indecision dragged the moment out into slow motion.

Then Randy broke the status quo. His foot slipped again, and this time he lost his balance, and then he lost his grip on the tree. He plummeted head-first between the limbs, crashing through that maze of razor oak shards like an animal falling into a trap. He shrieked as wood shredded flesh and clothing, and I lowered the gun. The hammer came down with an easy flex of my thumb. I tore through the vines, looking over both shoulders for any sign of Yellow Teeth.

I couldn't see him. I could only hear Randy screaming. I reached Autumn and scooped her up. Tears streamed down her face as she choked and shook.

"Don't kill him, Mason. Please don't kill him."

"I'm not gonna kill him," I promised. "Come on!"

I turned back into the vines, leaning low and enveloping her skinny little body in my arms as best I could, just in case Yellow Teeth reappeared. We made it sixty or seventy yards through the swamp carnage before the hair stood up on the back of my neck. I could feel it in my spine. It had been far too long since I'd last seen Yellow Teeth. The gang leader had gone quiet, and I knew that could mean only one of two things.

Either he had split, taking the money bags and crashing his way to freedom. Or else he was stalking me, biding his time, waiting for a kill shot as I fought to bring Autumn to safety.

I couldn't bet on the first option. I had to plan for the second. Reaching a small clearing, floodwater rose to my knees as I sloshed toward a cypress tree that had survived Nadia's wrath. It was bent, battered by the abuse of the wind, its limbs trailing close to the water. But it was still standing, offering refuge from the morass of vines, debris, and mud.

I reached the tree and lifted Autumn up.

"Grab a branch," I hissed.

She obliged, and I helped to heave her onto a thick tree limb about five feet off the water. Autumn didn't stop there, heaving her body up with those skinny little arms, strengthened by years of pushing herself around in that wheelchair. She grunted and stretched, eventually reaching a sheltered spot six or eight feet above my head, where she could straddle another limb without fear of toppling off.

She clutched the mucky teddy close to her chest, eyes still streaming with tears. I lifted a finger to my lips, and Autumn nodded once.

Then I turned back to the trees. The hair on my neck was standing up again. I could feel the danger like electricity in the air.

Yellow Teeth hadn't fled the swamp. He was still out there, and he was hunting me.

48

I crept away from Autumn's tree, leaning low to the water with my weapons held just above the surface. The ground rose a little beneath my flooded boots, the floodwater dropping as low as my ankles at times, but rarely disappearing completely. Instead of fighting the tangle of vines and toppled trees, I embraced them, seeking out the new pattern of natural concealment that Nadia had left for me.

Moving slowly. Breathing easily. Making almost no sound. Leveraging every trick Uncle Sam had paid so many tax dollars to teach me. Only, I wasn't hunting an enemy of the state. I was hunting an enemy of humanity.

From one hundred, then two hundred yards away, Randy continued to scream and curse, his voice filled with pain as he fought to extricate himself from the tree. I ignored him, moving in concentric circles, widening my path and mapping out the terrain.

I found my first kill lying on the ground with his wide eyes frozen skyward in a death grimace. Blood stained the shallow water around him, but when I dipped my hand into the muck, I couldn't find his fallen pistol. There were fresh boot prints in a high spot of mud a few yards away, too large to be my own.

Yellow Teeth had been here. I bent under the concealment of a tangled bush and traced his trail as it vanished back into a pool of water.

The trailed curved. He was moving in circles also, the depth of his boot prints significantly deeper near the toes as opposed to the heels. He was walking on the balls of his feet. Gliding along.

Yellow Teeth knew something about stalking, also.

I found the money bags next, hidden beneath the brush. Two giant duffels, bulging with invisible contents. Instead of approaching, I merely inspected from twenty yards away, then moved on.

The bags might be the bait in a trap. I didn't want the money.

Water rose to my waist as I proceeded through the swamp, ducking beneath a toppled tree and keeping my gaze always moving. I thought I was circling pretty near to the busted oak where Randy lay. His screams had subsided into agonized groans, carrying through the undergrowth like the misery of a wounded pig.

But still, I hadn't found Yellow Teeth. I'd lost his trail in the last expanse of floodwater. I couldn't smell anything but mud and my own sweat. Sunlight bearing down from the east cut through the tangled vines and limbs, blinding me as I looked eastward. I squinted and tensed, sensing that another life form was close to hand. In the stomach-deep water, I felt a tremor. The hint of a ripple.

And then I saw it. Two reptilian eyes gleamed just above

the waterline, hardened green-black skin breaking the surface as bright white teeth flashed, and the mouth lunged at me.

A maddened dump of adrenaline engulfed my system, overwhelming my brain and galvanizing my muscles. I threw myself sideways as the gator burst through the water, mouth snapping closed only inches beyond my arm. He was huge—eight or ten feet in length, rising out of the mire with a lunge. His body landed with an explosion of mucky water that rained over my head. Tail snapping, body twisting, he vanished beneath the surface.

I ran, boots digging into the mud, mind blinded with sudden panic. It was a fear I'd never experienced. Worse than being hunted through desolate mountains by blood-thirsty Taliban. Worse than kidnap or near drowning or being jumped by thugs with baseball bats.

This was an animal. It was primal. It was man against his longest and most hated enemy—nature itself. Muck closed around my legs, and I hurtled toward a patch of high ground ten feet away, marked by another battered cypress tree and a field of broken limbs. Somewhere beneath the surface, the alligator's tail brushed my leg as he turned. He was pivoting beneath the surface, flexing through the water. Starved by Nadia's displacement of marine life and small animals. Eager for red meat. Even now clawing toward me, maybe only an instant from tearing my leg off.

I hurtled toward an island of high ground, water dropping from stomach level to shin level in mere feet. On raw instinct, I abandoned my slogging run and launched myself ahead, bunching my leg muscles and hurling myself forward.

It was the right move. Only inches behind my boots, the

gator once more erupted from the water, jaws snapping like a rifle crack as I tumbled into the mud. I lost the Victorinox. I lost the mini revolver. A spray of slimy water exploded over my head, and I thrashed, landing hard on Frank's backpack with my head spinning.

And then Yellow Teeth appeared out of the trees like a wraith, lips spread into a wolfish grimace that exposed his hallmark rotten smile. Even as the gator crashed back into the water, Yellow Teeth was orbiting toward me. A handgun rose, caked in mud, the muzzle clogged with it. Sights leveled against my chest. Evil black eyes gleamed with victory lust. His finger dropped over the trigger.

My fingers dropped over the mud. I slung myself left as I clawed a hand full of muck from the swamp floor. My body twisted, and I flung the gunk. The gun cracked. Hot lead broke through a curtain of Louisiana humidity and ripped beneath my right arm, tearing through flesh and scraping my rib cage only inches above my existing knife wound. I screamed, and Yellow Teeth shouted. The mud I'd slung hit him in the face like a black snowball, and he stumbled backward, clamping on the trigger again.

It was no use. The gun had failed to return to battery, choked by muck. I trembled on the ground, burning pain ripping through my side despite the strength of the fading hydrocodone. My head spun, days of exhaustion and dehydration building into a mind-numbing cloud as I planted my fists into the ground and powered myself upright.

Blood ran down my side. My eyes blurred with sweat, teeth crunching on grit. I stumbled on my feet and twisted toward Yellow Teeth just in time to catch the handgun right in my chest. He'd slung it like a baseball, and it landed with a thud. Air whistled between my teeth, and I choked.

Then he was on me, launching his way out of the mud, eyes wide and teeth bared.

"Come on!" he howled.

I was vaguely aware of the water surrounding us, torn by ripples, with half a dozen gleaming orange eyes visible just above the surface. I was vaguely aware of Autumn shrieking my name from across the swamp. I was vaguely aware of the pain, the disorientation, the hunger, the shredded muscles, and my own pounding head.

Vaguely aware. But paying attention to none of it, because only one thing now mattered. I met Yellow Teeth at the halfway mark of the muddy island, throwing myself forward to match his charge. Colliding in a mass of swinging arms and snapping teeth.

It wasn't martial arts. It wasn't even a street fight. This was pure animal carnage, the basest of all mortal combat. A no-holds-barred contest for survival. We both hit the ground, and pain erupted through my arm as he bit me like a dog, rotten teeth sinking in deep and ripping with harsh jerks of his heavy head. I thrashed, driving my right fist into his rib cage again and again. Kneeing him in the stomach. Rolling on top and jerking my arm loose of his head, conscious of the tearing of skin and flesh. His face appeared as a sickened, bloody bullseye. Mouth spread into a grin, eyes alight with hatred. I got in a hit hard enough to shatter teeth, then his back arched, and he threw me off.

I landed at the edge of the island, my head smacking a rock and sending stars bursting across my brain. The trees overhead swirled. The brightening Louisiana sky faded into a dark tunnel. Autumn screamed my name again, crying to me for help.

I gasped for breath, suddenly unable to move. Numb. Dazed. Blood streaming from a gunshot side and a torn arm. Yellow Teeth hauled himself upright, howling like an animal. He turned toward me, bending to scoop something off the ground. It was red and shiny metal, coated in mud but reflecting a little of the sunrise.

It was my Victorinox.

Yellow Teeth flipped the knife point downward and spat blood. He stalked toward me, boots slogging. Stumbling a little. But coming.

"You been a thorn in my side, boy," he growled. "Now imma gut you like I shoulda done the first day we met."

I gasped for air. I struggled to get up, driving one elbow into the mud. Yellow Teeth reached me and planted a boot into my sternum, driving me back into the swamp. The Victorinox glimmered over my head.

But something else glimmered to my left. I saw it only inches from my fingers. Sticking out of the mud, a baby rosewood grip. A tiny hammer.

Yellow Teeth's weight crushed down through his leg, and the air left my lungs. I choked. He bent down, grinning at me. Blood dropping from his lips and splashing on my neck. He grabbed my chin and yanked my face around, fingers digging into my flesh. He aimed the Victorinox for my exposed windpipe.

And then I reached the revolver. Fingers closed around that baby grip. My thumb drew back the hammer with the snap of a metallic twig. Yellow Teeth heard it, and his gaze darted right.

I swung the gun in. I pivoted the muzzle toward his gut. I snatched the button trigger.

Flame and mud erupted from the muzzle at the behest of

a .22 Magnum slug. It zipped through his wifebeater tank top and raced into his intestines, so fast and sudden he didn't even react.

But I didn't stop shooting. The hammer snapped back. The button trigger broke. Again, and again. The last three rounds of Frank Miller's backup piece shredded Yellow Teeth's stomach like individual pellets of buckshot. He choked, and the knife slipped from his hand. It landed point first in the mud next to me. He toppled sideways.

I dropped the pistol and took the knife, twisting to follow him. He landed in the mud. I landed next to him.

And the knife landed in his heart, all the way up to the hilt.

Yellow Teeth gasped once, and his mouth fell open. Then he was simply gone. I pulled the knife free and slouched over him, still gasping to regain my breath. From the swampy waters all around me, those orange eyes stared unblinking, fixated on the carcass.

Then Autumn screamed again. I looked through the trees toward the sound, back toward the cypress where I'd left her. As I blinked away the sweat, I thought I saw the busted oak tree where I'd last seen Randy. He wasn't there any longer, but I heard him shout.

"Get down from there, girl!"

I heaved myself upright, still clinging to the knife. Dizziness overwhelmed my skull as I staggered away from Yellow Teeth's body, abandoning it without a second look. I kept to the high ground and used the passing vines to steady myself, fighting through a tangle of uprooted trees, listening as heavy tails dragged through the mud. Reptilian feet propelled thorny bodies onto the high ground.

And then razor-sharp teeth sank into lifeless flesh.

"I'm coming!" My voice was hoarse and barely audible. I sloshed through ankle-deep water and nearly fell over a rotting log. Autumn called again.

But she wasn't calling to me. She was calling to Randy, her panicked voice cutting through the swamp.

"No, Daddy! Don't! There's a ga—"

Autumn's voice was overpowered by a sudden, inhuman scream. I burst through the trees to the edge of the flood-water where I'd left Autumn. She was still up in the tree, still straddling that limb where I'd left her.

But the inhuman scream wasn't hers, it was Randy's. He'd made it halfway to the tree before the gator struck. It got him by the leg, and even now the two of them were thrashing through the muck. Randy appeared for an instant in a pool of blackish crimson water, eyes wide and panicked, one hand reaching for the tree.

Then the second gator appeared, and the third. He disappeared beneath the surface, and I lunged ahead. The Victorinox slid into my pocket, and I crashed through the water to the base of Autumn's tree. I grabbed the lowest limb and hauled myself up, pulling my legs free of the water just as more razor teeth snapped at my heels.

I dragged myself upward, slouching against the trunk and reaching Autumn. She fell into my arms and buried her face into my chest, sobbing uncontrollably. I wrapped both arms around her skinny little body and clutched her tight.

"Don't look," I whispered. "Just don't look."

49

I passed out in the cypress tree as the sun beat down, Autumn still clutched tight in my arms. It wasn't sleep, and it wasn't unconsciousness. My body simply shut off, overwhelmed by stress and physical torment to the point where the only possible answer was to descend into blackness.

Except it wasn't perfect blackness. It was more like a dreamscape. I saw myself in the tree from third person, clinging to Autumn. I saw myself driving the knife into Yellow Teeth's chest, chasing the gang up the river, and disarming the bomb. I saw Nadia make landfall, and the floodwaters rise.

I saw other places, too. The campground in Tampa. The bank in Jacksonville. The sheriff's station in Alabama. A basketball court in Atlanta. A lonely seaside town in North Carolina.

Mia, resting against my chest in the back of a pickup truck beneath the desert stars.

It all swirled together so quickly that it felt like one

image, and I was outside of it all, not actually inhabiting my own body, but still experiencing all of its mental torment. I was hungry. I was worn. My head pounded. Every part of me hurt.

But it was the confusion that rang most clearly through it all. The inability to connect with anyone, no matter how hard I tried. I reached out for Mia. I grasped at her hand. My fingers went right through her as though her body was made of mist. She smiled, but she didn't seem to see me.

Then it all faded away into pure, absolute blackness. I couldn't see a thing. I was lost in a swirl that bore no dimension, no mass. It was emptiness. It was meaninglessness. It was death, beckoning me onward.

Until I saw the light. Not the bright, warm glow that people describe when they envision a soul's departure to heaven. This was a lightning bolt, ripping through my mind like a bullet, blazing instant, intense light across a narrow path that wound out of a swamp. The bolt spread across a midnight sky in a spiderweb of brilliant blue, bathing the whole world in total illumination, brighter than midday.

Then it was gone, just as quickly as it came. But I could still remember the path. I took a step, faltering at first. Almost falling. I reached out and saw nothing. I couldn't find my way.

The lightning struck once more. Just as sudden, and just as quickly gone.

I saw the path again. I fought onward.

"You alive, Sharpe?"

The voice was wearied and raspy, but it broke through

the fog. I blinked, my vision wavering, fading, and then returning.

I lay on my back, something dark green stretched high over my face. A tent roof, I realized, and that confused me. Sweat trickled down my neck, and I was yet again transported to Afghanistan.

But no, the voice wasn't that of any of my comrades in arms. It was familiar, but more recent. I blinked again.

Then I saw him. Frank Miller leaned over my cot, pressing one hand to my wrist to measure my pulse. My vision clarified, and I recognized the hum of background noise throughout the tent. Low voices murmuring. Medical devices beeping. An IV pole stood next to my elbow, with a long tube feeding into my arm.

I was back in the FEMA aid station. Or *a* FEMA aid station, anyway. A medical tent, surrounded by aid workers and medical staff.

Sudden fear clutched my stomach. I tried to sit up.

"The girl—"

"Easy." Frank pushed me back down. "She's right next to you."

He shifted, and I looked right. Sure enough, Autumn lay on the cot alongside mine, her little body covered by a thin blanket, blonde hair brushed free of the mud, eyes closed as she slept. A bloody teddy still clutched to her chest.

I let out a sigh I didn't know I was holding and collapsed into the pillow. I fought through the metal fog to identify my last memory, and traced it to the swamp alongside the Mississippi River. The animal fight for survival. Yellow Teeth, Randy.

The gators.

"How did you find us?" I whispered.

Franked grunted, smiling a little. He bent next to the bed and lifted a small black object from the floor. It was a police radio, a crack running through its screen, dirt clogging the holes of the microphone.

"Forget about this?" he asked.

I had forgotten about it, completely, but then I remembered my original plan to radio Frank after snatching Autumn from Gallier Hall. It felt like a lifetime ago.

"The girl found it in the backpack after you crapped out," Frank said. "I guess she figured out how to use it. Smart cookie."

That brought the dimmest smile to my lips. I looked to Autumn again, and the smile softened. I nodded once. "Yeah...smart cookie."

Then I thought of the swamp again, and the three bodies I'd left there. My stomach tensed, and I swept my gaze around the tent. I didn't see any cops. There were no hand-cuffs binding me to the bed.

"What else did they find?" I asked.

Frank cocked an eyebrow. "They didn't find the gun I lent you, if that's what you're asking. I don't suppose you've got it hidden somewhere."

I shook my head. "Don't think you want it back, honestly."

"Figured as much. They did find a body."

"A body?" I tried not to emphasize the singularity of my question.

"Yep. One body, torn to shreds. I guess the gators were hungry. They didn't eat the money, though. Nearly four million dollars, all in cash." A small shake of his head. "Heck of a thing."

I could see in Frank's eyes that he didn't believe the

simplicity of the scene for a second. As a veteran cop with years of investigation under his belt, why should he? He knew how to read between the lines.

But as a veteran cop with years of investigation under his belt...he also knew when not to.

"Thank you, Frank."

The old man patted my arm and stood with a tired sigh. "I'll find you something to eat. Don't go nowhere."

He laughed at his own joke as he departed, leaving Autumn and me alone in the steamy hospital tent. Reaching across the gap between our beds, I stuck my thick, dirty fingers through her small, skinny ones. Her hand was warm. Autumn's eyes blinked open, blurry blue locking on me. The vaguest hint of a smile—albeit a very sad one—crossed her lips. She squeezed my hand.

Then we both closed our eyes and faded back into the black, hands still clasped together.

50

F rank Miller might have been content to leave questions unanswered, but the distinguished Officer Broussard of the New Orleans PD was not so gracious. He had all kinds of questions, most of them of an indignant flavor, and even went so far as to have a detective join him for a four-way interview that included Autumn. We sat at a metal table in one of the FEMA camps, shoveling down mediocre food while Broussard drilled us with questions, and the detective just tried to stay awake.

I knew from the start that the investigation would never lead anywhere. I'd wrecked two gangbangers in the Seventh Ward and scared off two more, but the old lady those thugs were harassing had already testified on my behalf, confirming a justifiable act of violence. There were two other eyewitnesses from a house across the street who corroborated her story. The guys I'd pounded were known New Orleans gang members with rap sheets a yard long. It was a simple story.

Broussard pivoted next to the bomb. He was most

curious about how I knew about it, and why I hadn't called the police. Both were stupid questions. There was no way to call the police with all the phone towers knocked out, and I knew about the bomb for the same reason I'd come to New Orleans in the first place. I was here to recover my niece, Autumn, who had been kidnapped. There were cops in Mobile and Mississippi who could back up that story. I hadn't planted that bomb, but I had disabled it, so what was the problem?

Lastly came the issue of the gunfight outside the Reserve Bank, where eyewitnesses only testified to my assistance of local law enforcement and the National Guard, and the final confrontation with Randy and his gang on the banks of the Mississippi.

But by the time Broussard reached that subject, he'd already lost his colleague. The detective breathed a curse and shoved his chair back.

"Good grief, Broussard. There's nothing here. I've got actual work to do."

The detective stomped off, but Broussard remained seated. He narrowed his eyes and focused on Autumn. She was picking at a pudding snack pack. Her eyes were still bloodshot, her head hunched. The bloody teddy held beneath one arm.

"He's your uncle?" Broussard demanded.

Autumn simply nodded.

"Can you prove that?"

Autumn wrinkled her nose. "Do you want a genetic test?"

That brought a flush to Broussard's cheeks. He stood, draining his coffee and crumpling the paper cup. He gave me a long stare, then leaned over the table.

"One final question."

I waited.

"How did you escape that day in the Seventh Ward? I cuffed you myself."

I indulged in the hint of a smile, unable to deny myself the enjoyment of watching the frustration boiling beneath his taut face. I shrugged.

"Guess I'm just slippery like that."

The flush darkened, and Broussard stomped off, leaving us to our meal.

Autumn set her pudding cup down and licked her lips. She watched the cop disappear into the crowd of sweaty survivors, then turned to me.

"Slippery like that?" There was a knowing tone in her voice.

"Some enigmas defy computation."

That brought her own hint of a smile. She shook her head. "Not for me they don't."

She looked back to her plate, poking the last of her mac and cheese with a spoon, but not really seeing it. Her eyes watered. She blinked hard.

I wrapped an arm around her shoulders and squeezed.

"Come on, kid," I whispered. "Let's get you out of here."

51

Getting back to Hattiesburg was easier said than done, but we managed it eventually. Traveling as a muddy duo, we secured passage aboard a fuel truck headed north to Birmingham. The independent trucker was making a small fortune transporting diesel fuel for FEMA's generators, but he was an old salt with an easy-going mentality. The truck was a day cab, forcing Autumn to ride on the floor behind the giant gear shifter. She didn't complain, and even participated in helping the trucker to shift as hot Louisiana wind buffeted us through the open windows.

It was a hundred miles to Hattiesburg, and the entire route was backlogged by relief traffic. I didn't complain about the delays, an uneasiness in my stomach building the closer we drew to the hospital where I had left Jessica. I'd been unable to call ahead—apparently Nadia had done a number on the cell network for a few hundred miles in every direction, and none of the self-important aid workers would loan me a satellite phone. I still didn't know if Jessica was even alive, and Autumn hadn't asked.

I didn't want to contemplate the possibility of arriving on scene with a fatherless, traumatized child only to learn that her mother had also passed into the great unknown. It was easier not to think about. To just take the next step, and hope for the best.

The trucker was kind enough to take us off the highway and right up to the hospital, squealing to a stop near the main entrance. He tipped his dirty ball cap to me, wishing me good luck. Then he extended a hand to Autumn, thanking her for a job well done.

"You gotta future on the open road, missy! Ain't no doubt."

Autumn ignored the proffered handshake, extending both arms to wrap his stomach in a hug instead. The guy stiffened, caught off guard. Then he patted her back, eyes misting over.

"All right, all right now. Truckers don't hug!"

Autumn giggled and gave him another squeeze. Then she turned her arms to me, and I carried her out of the truck on my back. As we entered the hospital, I turned toward the lineup of wheelchairs waiting just inside, but Autumn clung on to my shoulders.

"Can you...can you carry me?"

I nodded, and we headed through the doors to the main nurses' station, where I inquired about Jessica. I had planned to leave Autumn in her wheelchair while I made the request. I wanted to know ahead of time if the worst had happened, so that I could break the news to her softly. But I knew that wasn't what I would have wanted if I were in her shoes.

Autumn had certainly earned a little adult respect.

"Jessica Waverly?" the nurse questioned.

"That's right."

"And you are?"

"Mason Sharpe and Autumn Mercer. Autumn is her daughter."

The woman swept her gaze over our filthy and disheveled appearance, then went to work on her computer. She squinted, face contorting in focus. My stomach tightened, and Autumn's arms tightened around my chest along with it. We both held our breath.

Then the woman looked up. "Wait...are you the missing girl?"

Autumn nodded. "That's right."

A beaming grin bright as the morning sun stretched across the woman's face. She bolted upright.

"Don't go anywhere!"

She disappeared through a doorway, leaving us standing awkwardly in the lobby for a few minutes. I shifted my weight from one leg to the other, trying to ignore the throbbing in my rib cage or the pounding in my head. I was still taking the middle-weight painkillers that FEMA medical staff had issued me, but I'd cut the dose in half of my own accord. I didn't want to risk addiction.

The door burst open again, and the desk nurse returned. This time, however, she was accompanied by another nurse in wrinkled green scrubs, big cheeks stretched into a high-wattage grin.

"Autumn?"

My companion tensed around my shoulders.

"Yes..."

"Oh lawd, child! Praise Jesus!"

The nurse exploded from behind the desk and wrapped us both in a suffocating hug. Autumn choked, and the woman released a little pressure.

"Who are you?"

The big nurse stepped back, still beaming. "I'm your momma's nurse, child."

"Momma?" Autumn's voice wavered.

The nurse nodded. "You wanna see her?"

JESSICA WAVERLY LAY in a hospital bed on the third floor, head half shaved, stitches running across her scalp and down her neck, skin still purple and black with bruises. Her left leg wore a cast up to her thigh, and her right wrist wore a brace.

But for all that, I'd never seen her look better. Her face erupted into an ear-to-ear smile as I carried Autumn into the room. Outside in the hallway a commotion of cheering nurses were lost as I deposited Autumn onto the bed. Both mother and child were sobbing, wrapping each other in tight hugs, clinging on for dear life. Jessica rocked back in the bed, jerking her IV stand as tubes and wires tugged against the machines. She laughed. She cried. I stood awkwardly by and faded toward the wall, content to observe the happiness and bask in its glow. I'd been overheated for all of the past week, but I'd never felt quite this warm. Not from the inside.

"I was so worried about you!" Jessica choked, still clutching her child. "Why do you stress me so?"

"Me?" Autumn laughed. "Momma, I was worried about *you!*"

Another impassioned hug, then Jessica finally released Autumn long enough to look at her. She wet a thumb with her tongue and scrubbed dirt from beneath the girl's eyes. She smiled and shook her head, tears still dripping from her cheeks. She pulled Autumn in for a hug again and at last turned to me.

Her eyes were so full of tears I could barely see the color of them, but I could see the deep gratitude.

"Thank you," Jessica mouthed.

I simply nodded, hands in my pockets. Then I turned for the door.

Autumn must have heard my footsteps. Her head popped up, and she turned quickly.

"Wait! Where are you going?"

I looked over my shoulder and grinned. "Where do you think? I need a Baby Ruth."

52

I ended up spending a week in Hattiesburg. The first item on my long agenda was to take a bus to Mobile to retrieve my truck and the lock box of cash that I kept hidden beneath the seat. Even though I'd been gone for multiple days without officially checking out, the greasy clerk at the desk hadn't towed my truck. It rested right where I'd left it, strewn with storm debris, but generally unharmed.

I thanked the man. I noted that much of his face had turned purple. He seemed eager to see me leave.

Back in Hattiesburg, I checked into what should have been a cheap hotel—but of course, I had to pay the hurricane rate. Then I returned to the hospital to check on Jessica, check on Autumn, and finally, to check up on myself. The emergency room doctor had a few salty remarks about Frank's stitching work on my rib cage, but the FEMA medical staff had done a good job on the bullet graze across my rib cage and the bite marks in my arm. He was impressed. He prescribed antibiotics, which I accepted, and opioid painkillers, which I refused. I asked him about my busted nose, and he simply laughed.

"Not the first time, is it?"

In truth, it was only the second time I'd ever broken my nose, but after the first time, I had denied surgery in favor of saving a few grand, and simply had my nose reset. The second bust was worse than the first, and it had been days since it occurred. The pain was so constant I'd simply tuned it out.

"You need surgery," the doctor pronounced. "The sooner, the better, if you'd like to smell any roses."

"Can't you just reset it?"

Another laugh. "What's left to reset?"

I took the antibiotics and left the snarky physician to his rounds, resolving to make my own decisions about surgery. For the next several days, I just wanted to not think about anything. I wanted to sleep. I wanted to enjoy lots of good air-conditioning and lots of hot food.

I wanted to make sure that Jessica and Autumn were well taken care of. That required a lot of hospital visits, a lot of late afternoons watching movies with Jessica and playing cards with Autumn. She was a cheat, of course. That wicked little mind of hers could count cards like nobody's business. We played for candy bars, and I lost them all.

Seven days after Nadia's landfall, the storm finally dissipated over Detroit, only a few hundred miles north of where Katrina had dissipated so many years earlier. Law and order had been restored to New Orleans—at least, as much as it ever was. News stories about the brazen robbery attempt had blended into an endless stream of media noise about the state of the Big Easy and the tragedy of the Lower Ninth Ward yet again succumbing to floodwaters.

No mention was made of trash cans full of dynamite found on the London Avenue Canal levee wall, but I did get to see Frank again. He appeared on Claiborne Avenue, dressed in boots and jeans with big leather work gloves. In the backdrop, his home was visible, a dirty brown waterline encircling the roof where the floodwaters had settled before eventually being drained away.

The reporter asked him what his plan was. Frank stared into the camera a long time, looking very tired.

Then he simply shrugged. "Rebuild."

I watched him trudge off toward his house, a trash bag in one hand as he collected debris, and a part of me wanted to head back south and help him. Maybe pick up a hammer and drive a few nails. I figured the extra muscle couldn't hurt.

And yet, in a deeper way, I knew I couldn't. Not because I was afraid of the work or had any better place to be, but simply because I knew what it was like to lose everything. To watch your life disintegrate right before your eyes, leaving you with nothing but a trash bag and a heap of rubble.

You appreciate the help. You respect the good intentions. But more than anything...you just want to be left alone.

Or maybe that was just me.

Across the hospital lobby a bell dinged, and I looked up to see stainless-steel elevator doors rolling open. Jessica appeared, walking with the aid of a crutch, trailing Autumn in her wheelchair. It wasn't a hospital wheelchair, it was a brand-new folding model dressed out in deep purple with white wheels. I'd found it at a big box store while shopping for groceries, and it seemed like something Autumn would appreciate.

I hadn't been wrong. The kid beamed as she rumbled

along, propelled by a nurse, a freshly steam-cleaned teddy clutched close to her skinny little body. The teddy still bore some dull bloodstains if you looked closely. Likely, it always would.

But it was so good to see Autumn smile, who would notice?

Outside, Jessica's beat-up old station wagon waited, loaded down with all her things. I'd filled the tank and messed around with the carburetor until it ran a little more smoothly. I wasn't sure if it would get them all the way to San Francisco, but if there was one thing I knew anything about Jessica and Autumn, I knew they were women who would find a way.

Autumn gave me a huge hug while Jessica helped the nurse load the wheelchair into the back of the car. Skinny arms encircled my neck and pulled me tight, failing to let go even as the moments stacked. I felt a quake in her spine and heard a sniff. When I pushed her away, I found tears draining down her cheeks, eyes laced with red. She sat in the passenger seat of the station wagon, legs hanging out, shoulders slumped. Never looking more pitiful.

"Hey," I said. "What's this? This doesn't compute!"

It was a weak joke, and it didn't earn a smile. Autumn's gaze simply dropped.

"Scared of California?" I asked.

A little shrug. Extending one finger, I propped her chin up until our eyes met again. Her nose trembled. I smiled.

"You're going to do great things, Autumn. I'm gonna see your name in the newspaper one day."

That brought a sarcastic smile. "Nobody reads newspapers."

"I do. Sometimes."

"You would."

"Hey!"

A little giggle. Her face dropped again. I knew what she was thinking, but I couldn't bring myself to voice it. The hot weight in my own stomach was too heavy. Too dominant.

"Will...will I see you again?" Autumn whispered.

My own eyes stung. My throat constricted. I pulled her into another hug and squeezed harder than I had before, clenching my eyes shut before anything slipped out.

"Bet on it," I whispered.

Then I let her go, and the brave face of the kid who had endured kidnap, a hurricane, and near death returned. She smiled, and I flipped a candy bar out of my pocket.

"One for the road, computer brain."

Behind the car, I found Jessica leaning on her crutch, struggling with a lighter, a cigarette dangling from her lips. She couldn't get a flame, so I dug into my pocket for the camp matches and obliged. As smoke clouded around her head, a security guard called for her to move to the smoking zone. She waved him off, and we both proceeded a few paces from the door—me moving a little stiffly, and Jessica working the crutch like a seasoned pro.

I wondered if it was the first time Randy Weaver had broken her leg. Likely not. But it would be the last.

Jessica's hand trembled as she smoked. Her eyes looked a little haunted, her hair swept over to conceal the shaved part of her scalp where all the stitches were. She wouldn't face me.

"You should really quit that, you know," I said, just to say something.

Jessica snorted and tugged on the smoke, gazing off

across the parking lot. Then she nodded slowly and dropped the cigarette, stamping it out with her good leg.

"Maybe I'll try," she said.

Then she faced me, lips pursed. Looking like she might cry, or she might curse, or she might just turn around and crutch walk her way back to the car without another word.

She did none of the above. She simply spoke calmly, voice wavering just a little.

"Look, I know it's forward, but I spent too much of my life biting my tongue and regretting it. So I'm just gonna say it."

I pocketed my hands, waiting. I had a pretty good idea what she was about to say. I had no idea what to say in return.

"You should come with us."

I looked away, inhaling slowly, and measuring my thoughts. Out of the corner of my eye, I saw Jessica flush.

"I just mean...you know. As a friend. You should come with us."

I looked back. Jessica was staring at me. Her lip trembled. "Or...not as a friend. If you want."

I wasn't sure what to say. I expected her to express an insecurity about being alone. Not because she couldn't handle it, but because humans are made to associate. That's how we find our security. I even suspected that she might want me to tag along for a while.

I never suspected a proposal of a deeper relationship. I wasn't sure what to do with it.

"Jessica—" I started.

She cut me off, holding up a hand. "Forget the not-a-friend thing. I just think you're good for Autumn. Okay? She needs a good man in her life. And I mean, we get along, you and I. You ain't got a place to stay. I got a free place to stay..."

Now it was her turn to trail off, and the flush returned to her cheeks. Her hands began to tremble again, and she looked quickly away, reaching for her cigarette pack.

"Confound it."

I put a hand on her arm, squeezing gently. Jessica wouldn't look up. I kept my voice low.

"You know something?"

Jessica's lips twitched. She mumbled: "What?"

"You're a good mom."

Heavy blinking preceded an accepting nod. She fidgeted with the cigarette pack.

"Thank you for saying that."

"It's true. Autumn's lucky to have you. And you're right, she does need a good man in her life. Somebody to be what Randy always should have been, but..."

"It ain't you." Jessica sighed.

At last she looked up. There was sadness in her gaze, but no more tears. I shook my head gently.

"No. It isn't me. And it's not because I don't care about her or because I don't like you. It's because...I've got my own stuff to figure out. My own demons to wrestle. And no kid deserves to be put through that. No woman does. Not right now."

Jessica thought about that a moment. A hot Mississippi breeze tugged at her hair, and she pressed it behind one ear. Then she leaned up on her tiptoes, put an arm around my neck, and kissed me.

It was a sweet kiss, not a sensual one. She tasted of cigarettes and smelled like a hospital. But I still appreciated it. I gave her a squeeze; then Jessica turned for the car, crutch walking with ease. On her way, she deposited the half-empty pack of cigarettes into a trash can.

I called after her, "There's an envelope under your seat. Don't open it until you hit the highway."

Jessica looked back. She shot me a sarcastic grin. "Is it stolen?"

I laughed. "What do you take me for?"

She laughed back. Then she got into the car and fired up the engine. I was pleased to hear a smoother rumble than before. She shifted into gear, and the suspension sagged as the overloaded car turned slowly out of the hospital lot and toward the highway.

Autumn waved as they went. I waved back.

And then I turned for my truck, walking slowly in the summer sun. I fired up the engine and thought I should render myself the same service I had rendered Jessica, and give the carb a clean.

Then I turned east, back toward Alabama. Back toward Mobile.

Because I had one more question to answer.

53

The Cathedral-Basilica of Immaculate Conception had weathered Nadia well. The columns outside the front entrance had sustained a little wind abrasion and would likely need to be repainted, but the structure was undamaged, and the square out front seemed oddly quiet, as all the FEMA tents and storm evacuees had already moved out.

I stepped through the towering doors and into the cavernous sanctuary, walking slowly to avoid any heavy footfalls. When I sat on a pew, I eased my way down, avoiding the gunshot-like cracks of flexing, century-old planks.

I saw the pastor—or priest or father—I had seen before, on my last visit. He was busy lighting candles at the altar, and we made eye contact, but he made no acknowledgment of my presence.

That was okay with me. We were the only two people in the room, and the stillness was very calming. I bent my head and looked down at the small, leather-bound book in my hands. It was smoother than I remembered, and a few of the stains left by use and age had been polished out of the leather. When I opened the cover, I found the pages clean and mostly wrinkle free, if a little stiff.

The specialist who had originally brought me to Mobile had done a stellar job on Mia's Bible. You could still tell that it had sustained water damage, if you looked carefully, but it was very readable. Just holding it brought comfort to my mind that was nearly strong enough to block out the ache of sore muscles, the sting of rib cage stitches, and the incessant burn of my busted nose.

Almost.

The priest left me for twenty minutes, taking his time with an impressive display of candles before he at last journeyed down the aisle to sit next to me. Neither of us spoke for a while, just admiring the glow of all the little lights, reflected off that high mural ceiling.

It was serene in a way almost nothing man-made ever was. It felt...spiritual.

"I thank our Lord that you survived the storm, my son," the priest said at last.

I nodded, unsure how to respond. He turned slowly toward me.

"Is your heart still burdened with our conversation from before?"

I remembered his gentle speech about talking donkeys. About trusting God. About waiting for a word.

And I frowned.

"I..." I trailed off. Closed my mouth.

He waited, once again undisturbed by the passage of time, like a boulder in a meadow. The grass bent around him beneath the wind, but he just remained.

It was a welcoming presence. It made me feel like he wanted to hear me out.

I faced him. "I experienced something I can't explain."

A soft nod. But no comment.

I rewound my mind back to the prior week. Just before Nadia made landfall. That dark moment of absolute desperation, searching for Autumn.

And then...

"I needed to find someone," I said. "It was dark. I didn't know where to look. I was lost. The storm was coming."

He cocked his head. Still no comment.

"And then there was lightning," I said. "The brightest, longest lightning I've ever seen. And I saw what I needed to see."

I remembered the sudden, prolonged flash of blue. Illuminating the overturned, fake FEMA truck where I found the map marked with Xs.

The key that had opened the door. Exactly what I needed, exactly when I needed it.

The priest squinted. I wasn't sure if I'd been too vague, or if he simply didn't understand the implications. I decided to clarify.

"I'm told...well, I heard that hurricanes don't produce lightning. Something about the lack of vertical winds. But there was lightning, illuminating right what I needed to see..."

I trailed off. The priest's face stretched into a small smile. He leaned forward and put a hand on my arm, giving me a gentle squeeze.

"Hurricanes don't produce lightning?" he asked.

I wasn't sure if it was a rhetorical question. I said nothing, and he nodded once. "And donkeys don't talk."

He gave my arm a pat, and then he stood, turning for the aisle. I stood with him, still confused. Still somehow dissatisfied with his explanation. It wasn't as clean as I wanted. It wasn't as clear.

"Wait."

The priest stopped. His aged hands traced the back of the next pew. He waited for my question.

"What...what does He want?" I asked.

Again, the old man smiled, as strong and steady as that boulder in the meadow.

"He wants you to take the next step, my son. Just take the next step."

ABOUT THE AUTHOR

Logan Ryles was born in small town USA and knew from an early age he wanted to be a writer. After working as a pizza delivery driver, sawmill operator, and banker, he finally embraced the dream and has been writing ever since. With a passion for action-packed and mystery-laced stories, Logan's work has ranged from global-scale political thrillers to small town vigilante hero fiction.

Beyond writing, Logan enjoys saltwater fishing, road trips, sports, and fast cars. He lives with his wife and three fun-loving dogs in Alabama.

Did you enjoy *Storm Surge*? Please consider leaving a review on Amazon to help other readers discover the book.

www.loganryles.com

ALSO BY LOGAN RYLES

Made in the USA
Monee, IL
30 April 2024

b3bfc613-7dcb-4686-bfda-74b4222b206bR01